Cold Case

A Madge Franklin Travel Mystery

By
Kate McLaughlin

Strategic Book Publishing and Rights Co.

Strategic Book Publishing and Rights Co., LLC
USA | Singapore

For information about special discounts for bulk purchases, please contact Strategic Book Publishing and Rights Co. Special Sales, at bookorder@sbpra.net.

ISBN: 978-1-946539-59-5

Book Design: Suzanne Kelly

DEDICATION

*This book is dedicated to all those, past and present,
who, through their wisdom and foresight, have
guaranteed from development and exploitation
areas of natural beauty and wonder.*

ACKNOWLEDGEMENTS

My sincere thank you goes to you, my readers. Your enthusiastic support for *Fast Food Kills* and your constant inquiry as to "When will the next one be out?" not only kept me engaged with my characters but also kept me writing and rewriting. You are the reason I do what I do!

Additionally, this book would never have become a reality without the love, encouragement, and support of friends and family.

Thank you to Kelly and Jill for your continued guidance on law enforcement protocol.

To the Monteagudo family, endless thanks! Marlene, your willingness to plow through that raw first draft giving me insight and encouragement. Marco, your thoughtful observations helped me pull the pieces together. Shilo, this would still be wasting away on my laptop without your patient tutelage in pushing the right buttons.

To awesome Anette, you were only supposed to check for readability, but your eagle eye caught many little boo-boos the rest of us missed.

To daughter Stacey, thank you for finding time in your already overscheduled life to edit, critique, support, and encourage.

To my husband, partner, supporter, and friend, my undying love and gratitude for giving me the time and space to indulge my goofy imagination.

To the real Annie and Gerard, I extend my deep gratitude, not only for your friendship, but also for your willingness to be the travelers who allowed Madge and Paul to tell the touristy part of the story.

Regarding the story, dear reader, please understand, except for the occasional poetic license, representations of towns, parks, and museums are as accurate as I could make them without turning them into travel brochures. Beyond that, the events in this story are strictly the product of my overactive imagination.

Happy reading!

ACRONYMS

JMU—James Madison University

LE—Law Enforcement

VC—Visitor Center

FLETC—Federal Law Enforcement Training Center

BOLO—Be on the Lookout

SAR—Search and Rescue

CCC—Civilian Conservation Corps

AT—Appalachian Trail

UMCOR—United Methodist Committee on Relief

Carry-out—the term used by park rangers when referring to retrieving a sick or injured hiker from the wilderness.

PROLOGUE

September 2010, Appalachian Trail, Virginia

Hidden deep within the forest, he waited. He had simply been told to go, hide, wait, and when the time came, he would know. Day passed into night. Night passed into day and still he waited. He had provisions for three days and wondered if that would be enough. He could only assume it would be.

As the sun broke through the clouds in the early hours of day three, he heard the voice. Soft, gentle, quiet as a whisper it spoke. "Soon. Be prepared."

He smiled and nodded. Knowing he would be leaving this spot, he surveyed the ground. He'd been careful not to let any trash fall as he ate his meager meals. He'd stepped ten paces away in different directions each time he needed to relieve himself. The rocks and roots of his hiding place would tell no tale of his having been there. All was good. And so he waited.

They were laughing quietly as they came around the bend. She in front. He behind. She was small. He stood head and shoulders above her. Both wore daypacks—not the large backpacks carried by serious through-hikers.

As the couple passed his hiding place they slowed, then stopped to look at the view. The man heard the voice whisper, "Now."

The male hiker dropped like a rock when the tire iron connected with the back of his head. Using a booted foot, the man kicked the hiker over the edge of the mountain and watched as his body bounced off the rocks and out of sight.

Too shocked to scream, the woman offered only token resistance when the man picked her up, threw her over his shoulder, and carried her into the woods.

June 2020, above Naked Creek, Virginia, just inside Shenandoah National Park

"Tell me again why we are doing this," Angie grumbled aloud to herself as she scrambled over leaf-covered wet rocks trying to catch up with her friends. The other three girls had already crossed the stream and were impatiently calling to her from the other side.

"Angie, for goodness sake, hurry up! You hike like an old woman, girl. Put a wiggle in it!"

"I'm hurryinggggggg," Angie called back as her feet flew out from under her and she landed in a heap in a hole filled with wet leaves.

Sitting jackknifed between a tangle of rocks, Angie shouted, "Thanks a bunch, guys! Now my bottom's stuck in this stupid hole." Spreading her knees as best she could, Angie began throwing leaves, sticks, and rocks from out between her legs when she suddenly got a strange look on her face.

"Guys, I think I've found something odd," was all she said as she pulled a human skull from the detritus.

CHAPTER 1

As Madge Franklin stepped out of her motor home to begin her afternoon walk through the campground, four college-age women ran breathlessly toward her.

"Ranger! Ranger! Wait! Help! We need to talk to you!"

"Hey. Take a breath," Madge replied with a smile. Then noticing the near panic on the girls' faces, she became serious and asked, "What's the problem?"

They looked from one to the other as though they were not sure who should speak or what they should say, so Madge took control.

"Is anyone hurt or lost?" she asked.

The girls shook their heads no, so Madge continued. "Okay, sit down at the picnic table, drink some water, catch your breath, and then, one at a time, tell me what's going on."

While the girls followed her directions, Madge used the time to look them over. They were roughly the same age, early to mid-twenties. Their clothes looked new and more high-end than usually worn by serious campers and heavy-duty hikers. Two wore small daypacks, while the other two used fanny packs. Each had two water bottles, and they all carried hiking poles. None wore headwear of any kind.

Finally calmed, one girl spoke up.

"I'm Angie Brown. We're graduate students. We're here for a summer program at JMU. None of us is local, and we heard we should experience camping and hiking in Shenandoah. We came here a couple of days ago and set up our tents. It's our first time camping," she said somewhat sheepishly.

Taking a deep breath, she continued. "We hiked some of the waterfall trails, then someone told us about this hike to a waterfall that isn't listed in the trail guides. You have to bushwhack to

1

it, and we were working our way down when I fell into a hole. As I was trying to dig through the leaves and sticks to get out I found a skull. A human skull. Even though it looks like it's been there a long time, it scared us and we knew we should report it as soon as possible."

As the other girls nodded in assent, Madge reached for the radio hooked to her belt. "Any 210 unit, 235."

"235, this is 211. Go ahead."

"We have a non-emergency situation at Site I 218 that still needs your attention ASAP."

"Copy that, 235. It will be drive time from Skyland Lodge."

"Copy."

Clipping the radio back to her belt, Madge continued to study the young women. They did not strike her as the type to be pulling a joke. However, who knew anymore? Besides, it would not be her problem. Since she and husband, Paul, were campground hosts, not rangers, she would have nothing to do with the follow-up on this. Finally, she said with a sigh, "I just called for a law enforcement unit to come here as soon as possible. As you heard, since this is not an emergency, it will be at least fifteen minutes before anyone arrives. I would prefer you wait here until an LE unit gets here. Is there anything anyone else has to add to what Angie has told me?"

Gloria, a narrow-shouldered, dark-haired girl with short-cropped hair, spoke up. "We put the skull back in the hole and didn't poke around to see if there were any other bones. We've seen enough TV police shows to know that if it's a crime scene, even a very old one, we should be careful not to destroy evidence."

"Yes, but we took pictures and GPS coordinates, and we tied a red bandana on a bush next to the hole so it could be located without us having to go back down there," said Sheila, a seriously academic-looking young woman.

"You're right, of course," Madge replied. "But this may be a case of too late for that. We'll just have to wait and see. In the meantime, I'm going to go inside for paper and pens. I'd like for each of you to write out your memory of the event and then finish with your contact information. So, make yourselves comfortable, and I'll be right back."

When she was about to enter the RV, Madge turned and added, "Also, at this point, please don't talk to each other. It would be best if your memories were just yours. I'm sure you went over this several times on the way here, so let's just give it a rest until you write it out."

CHAPTER 2

It was closer to thirty minutes before the white and green SUV with the light bar on top crunched to a stop on last fall's acorns and oak leaves in front of the Franklin's RV. As the two rangers exited the vehicle, they each reached in, retrieved their hats and placed the familiar flat Smokey Bear hats on their heads. Ranger Miranda Jones and Ranger Pablo Garza wore their serious police officer faces as they walked over to the picnic table. They nodded to Madge, who nodded back and began making introductions.

"Angie, Patti, Gloria, and Sheila need to tell you about an experience they had today. I've asked each of them to write up the experience to the best of their memory. And they've each provided their contact information. Angie, since this was your discovery, you tell the tale."

As Angie related the day's events, the two rangers remained expressionless. When Angie finished, Miranda asked for the papers they'd completed. After glancing at them, she turned to Pablo and said, "I'll go call this in and be right back."

Walking back to the SUV, Miranda took several deep breaths before sitting down in the driver's seat. How best to report this was uppermost in her mind. Since cell phone service was sketchy, Miranda rejected that option. Using an open radio channel would cause too much excitement, since anyone in the park with a radio could hear the transmission. Using an encrypted channel to contact her direct supervisor seemed the appropriate option. Knowing District Ranger Jason Banneker was in the office, she informed him that some hikers, while bushwhacking down to Naked Creek, found a human skull, and she asked how she should proceed.

Dead silence followed for some seconds before Jason radioed back, "What's your location?"

"I'm at the Franklin's RV with the hikers," Miranda replied.

"Stay there. I'm on my way."

Banneker tapped his desk with the eraser end of a pencil as he thought through his next move. Shaking his head from side to side, he picked up the phone and placed a call to his supervisor, Chief Ranger Julie Thorn.

"Julie, Jason here. Look, we may have a situation, or it could be nothing. However, if it turns out to be real, it'll land in your lap. So, I thought it best to give you a heads up. Got a call from Miranda about some hikers finding a human skull while bushwhacking to a waterfall. They're at the Franklin's now, so I'm heading over to check this out. You gonna be around for a while?"

"I will be now," came the resigned response.

"Good. I'll get back to you as soon as I check this out."

Locking the door on his way out of the office, Jason wondered if this could possibly be for real. He'd been a ranger here for almost eight years, and, as best as he could remember, everyone who had gone missing had been located—no, wait. There had been that case he'd heard about. Maybe ten years ago a couple had disappeared off the Appalachian Trail. No trace of them had ever been found, and the case, after so many years, simply went cold. With his heart rate quickening, Jason climbed in his cruiser and calmly drove the short distance from the maintenance/law enforcement area to the campground.

CHAPTER 3

Madge and Paul Franklin occupied the camp host site in the older section of the Big Meadows Campground. More heavily wooded than the newer section, the upper area of this older section provided large, pull-through sites for RVs while a lower section, closer to the view and the Appalachian Trail, catered more to tenters. The campground host site sat between the two areas directly above the rustic log cabin-style building that housed flush toilets, lavatories with hot and cold running water and, in cold weather, heaters.

As campground hosts, Madge and Paul shared their duties with another host couple, Don and Barb Commer. Neither couple paid for their full hookup site. The Franklins worked as a team for two full and three half days a week, but were available at any time they were on-site to help campers or hikers visiting the park. Wearing uniforms of brown pants and tan shirts, which bore the National Park Service insignia, most visitors did not notice the 'volunteer' stitched into the patch on their sleeve. Consequently, they were accustomed to being hailed as 'ranger' and didn't usually bother to argue the point.

Having worked with the Franklins several times over the past couple of years, Jason felt sure Madge would not have called if she had any inkling it was a prank. By the time he arrived at Site I 218, he'd given up trying to control his heart rate and was working strictly on maintaining a professional demeanor. The four women were at the picnic table chatting with Pablo and Miranda.

As Jason drove up, Madge emerged from the RV carrying a tray with paper cups, a pitcher of lemonade, a bucket of ice cubes, and a bowl of peanut butter filled pretzels.

"Hey, Jason," Madge said. "I thought you guys might use a snack. If you don't need me right now, I'm going to track Paul down and we'll take a run around the campground."

"Sure. That'll be fine. Thanks," was Jason's clipped response.

After setting the tray on the table, she walked toward the road and pulled a walkie-talkie from her pocket. Keying the mic, she asked, "Hey, Mountain Man, what's your twenty?"

"Hey there, Thursday. I'm down on Hippie Hill. What's up?"

"Heading your way. Tell you in a minute," was all she said as she broke into a gentle jog.

Madge's chestnut curls bounced out from under her ball cap as she jogged down the narrow asphalt trail leading from the upper, older campground to the walk-in tenting area known affectionately as Hippie Hill. Petite and perky at fifty-nine, Madge Franklin easily passed for ten years younger. Although she and Paul had been married for over thirty years, to see them together you might think they were newlyweds. Spotting Paul coming up one of the trails from deep in the woods, Madge broke into an all-out sprint across the parking lot and began hopping from one foot to the other until Paul joined her on the asphalt.

Paul grinned as he looked down at his wife. "Wipe the feathers off your face, Kitty Cat," he said as he guided Madge down another path to an empty campsite. Putting his hands around her waist, Paul lifted Madge onto the picnic table, stepped back and said, "Okay, now tell all."

"Oh, my gosh! You'll never believe this!" Madge gushed. "It nearly killed me to stay calm and nauseatingly professional, at least till I was out of sight," she added with a little giggle.

"Okay, so do tell. What's so exciting?" Paul asked as he looked steadily at the quirky little wife he adored.

"Welllll . . . ," Madge began before launching into a detailed account of the past couple of hours.

When she finally stopped talking, Paul shook his head from side to side. A little smile crept into the corners of his mouth as he finally said, "Now, Madge, we're out of here in a couple of weeks. How difficult is it going to be for you to walk away from this one?"

"Not difficult at all," Madge snapped. "Not my problem," Madge continued with that determined jut of her chin Paul knew so well. As she looked around, carefully avoiding eye contact with Paul, Madge added softly, "If they find anything, they'll call in the local coroner, determine all kinds of stuff, like when, who, and maybe how. Then notify the FBI, who will look at the evidence and decide if they want to bother with it or let park service handle it. I won't even get to go to the scene or be consulted or anything. So why would walking away from it be an issue? It's not my problem."

"Uh-huh. It never is. But somehow you always manage to poke that cute little nose of yours in. It'll be interesting to see how you get there this time."

Continuing to avoid eye contact, Madge answered, "Well, this time I'm not getting involved, but I do hope Jason won't be so tight-lipped that we can't at least know how things are going."

"And you'll be inviting him over for dinner, when?"

"Oh, soon. But first I want to check back with the girls," Madge said matter-of-factly. "Make sure they were treated okay. See if there's anything they need. Stuff like that." Another pause. Then, Madge's eyes lit up and she snapped her fingers, and looking at Paul she continued, "We're off tonight. We should see if they'd like to join us in the Tap Room for dinner and drinks. I'm sure they are way too traumatized to cook."

Chuckling, Paul lifted his wife off the picnic table and set her on the ground. Before letting her go he lifted her chin, looked into her large, dark brown eyes and hugged her to him.

CHAPTER 4

Later that day, as Madge, Paul, and the four women hiked up the short trail from the campground to Big Meadows Lodge, Paul pointed out that when using the trail, especially after dark, hikers should be extra alert for bear.

"There's a female that has called this area home for as many years as we've been coming here. We've never known her to be aggressive, but you wouldn't want to bump into her in the dark. All you really have to do is talk as you walk. Just a little bit of noise lets the local critters know where you are and, trust me, they'll do everything in their power to avoid an encounter."

Madge chuckled as the four women drew closer together and, rather than talking, became very quiet. "Really," she said. "While there are a good number of bear here in Shenandoah, they won't bother you unless you bother them, or have coated yourself in peanut butter or bacon grease. They don't see people as a food source unless they've become habituated to human food. Then it's only the human food that interests the bear. That's why we are so fierce about food storage here. As they say, 'A fed bear is a dead bear,' and we don't want to be forced into killing any of our bears because of human stupidity."

"Wow," Angie said, "you sound serious."

"I am," Madge replied. "I get frustrated when people sign the food storage agreement and then blatantly ignore it. I have trouble believing they don't understand and even more trouble believing they simply don't care. With food storage issues, it's hard for me to maintain a calm, informative demeanor when what I really want to do is read them the royal riot act. I'll leave one written warning, and then, if they don't comply with the rules, I just let law enforcement or animal control deal with it. Let's talk about something else. That subject makes me grumpy."

By then the group had reached the top of the hill and were heading toward the 1930s-era lodge.

"Oh, how lovely," remarked Sheila. "I didn't know what to expect but somehow didn't expect anything quite so—rustic."

Madge and Paul both laughed. "Rustic is a good description. The lodge was built in 1933 by the CCC and is on the National Historic Register, which means any renovations have to be in keeping with the original concept," Paul said. "To accommodate more visitors, they built detached additions that can be maintained in a more modern manner."

"Some prefer the more modern lodge about ten miles north of here called Skyland. It was a local resort before this became a national park. Because Skyland Lodge is on Skyline Drive, people sometimes confuse the names. Don't misunderstand me, Skyland is very nice, but Big Meadows is it for us. We have so many memories tied up here. The only thing that makes me really sad is that my all-time favorite band that I loved coming to hear is no longer together. It was a trio of rangers from here in the park. Awesome musicians who played my kind of music. Oh well. The only thing whining about change does is make me sound old," Madge mused.

"Perhaps we could continue this conversation inside, at a table, with food in front of us," came Paul's suggestion.

Everyone laughed as they entered the flagstone-floored lobby, turned left and headed down the narrow staircase to the hallway leading to the Tap Room.

CHAPTER 5

Nightly live entertainment, rather than food, served as the draw for the Tap Room. Because it was still early, Madge, Paul, and the girls had their pick of tables. With a stone fireplace and sofas and comfortable chairs on the left, a bar across the back, and tables scattered around the rest of the room, the group decided to pull together two small four-seater tables in front of what would later become the entertainment area.

Sporting a huge smile, the manager greeted Madge with a hug, saying, "It's good to see you. You two don't show up here as much as you used to."

"I know, Debbie. It's getting harder and harder to get away in the evenings, but we do miss listening to your Patsy Cline impersonation. Will you be able to give us a rendition tonight?"

"More than likely. Mike Charles is playing, and he usually invites me to take the mic if I'm not too busy. What can I get you folks?"

"Fix me something fruity with white lightning," was Paul's immediate request.

"White lightning?" asked Gloria with raised eyebrows.

"You know—moonshine. The legal kind made locally," Paul answered.

"How about giving us a few minutes while you fix Paul up," Madge suggested. "Our friends have never been here before, so they probably could use some time with the menu. I'll just stick to my usual glass of house red."

"You got it." And with that, Debbie was off at a trot to the bar.

"Well, let's see," Paul mused as he pretended to study the menu.

"You know what you're getting, so it's silly for you to be so interested in a menu you know by heart," Madge chided with a twinkle in her eye.

"You never can tell. They might have changed it, or I might decide to be adventurous," Paul responded sagely.

Looking at the girls, Madge explained, "Paul's addicted to the burgers, and it's not likely he'll deviate, but we play this silly little game every time we come. It's become something of a ritual. The burgers are excellent, but so is the pizza, and you can't beat the sweet potato fries. The fruit and cheese tray has potential but is somewhat boring if they are down to only one kind of cheese. And sometime before you leave the area, you'll have to be sure to have the blackberry cobbler, blackberry ice cream, and something with the blackberry syrup."

"Okay then," said Sheila. "Madge, what are you having?"

"I think this is a pizza night for me."

After some hemming and hawing, the girls settled on their drinks but continued to debate what they would eat. After placing their drink orders with Debbie, Madge asked the question that had been burning in her brain.

"So, how did things go with you and Jason?"

"Well, okay, I guess," Angie answered. "I told him what happened. We showed him the pictures we'd taken, and he had us text them to his phone. We gave him the papers we'd written up with our contact information, and we gave him the GPS coordinates."

Patti chimed in with, "He told us we wouldn't need to go back down. In fact, he told us *not* to go back down but told us to make ourselves available to, let's see, the local police, park service law enforcement, the FBI, and the local coroner."

"He said it was too early to know who would be handling the case, and we should just wait patiently to hear from someone," Gloria added.

"From what he said, he and some of his people were going down as soon as he finished talking to us to secure the scene, but I don't know what that means exactly," was Angie's observation. "I don't know how much securing they can do in the dark."

"You'd be surprised," Madge offered with a chuckle. "Although they seem pretty low-key, they are a hundred percent well-trained, professional cops who are used to a lot of night work. They'll probably tape off a good sized area and maybe even leave someone down there overnight to make sure no one wanders in."

"How come you and Paul aren't involved?" asked Gloria.

"We're not rangers," answered Paul. "We're volunteers working as campground hosts."

"Really? That's cool. I guess. Ah, how does that work? How do you get that kind of job and, when you're not here, where do you live?" Angie asked.

Madge and Paul exchanged glances, then Paul smiled and nodded to Madge. "Go for it, girl."

Taking a deep breath, Madge began. "To begin with, we live in the RV full-time. In other words, we have no other home, and we've been on the road, working as volunteers with several different organizations, for about six years. Sometimes we work as campground hosts, sometimes we work on service projects, and sometimes we work as resource interpreters and front desk greeters. It just depends on what the organization needs. Mostly we've worked with the National Park Service, like now. We've also worked with US Fish and Wildlife and with an organization called NOMADS, which is a branch of the United Methodist Church. NOMADS is for people with self-contained RVs and allows us to go around the country doing service projects and disaster rebuilds."

"Why?" asked Gloria. "I mean you're retired, right?"

"Uh-huh," Madge nodded.

"Well, there's golf and sitting by the pool and just relaxing. Stuff I thought people looked forward to doing when they retired," Gloria observed.

Chuckling, Madge said, "We get that a lot. I guess, to be honest, we love to travel, and all my life I've wanted to see what was around the next bend or on the other side of the mountain. I've always wanted to understand how other people live. I'm more comfortable with structure in my life, and volunteering not only provides that structure but it also forces me to continue learning. Working in different parts of the country allows me to check out all the different cultures and subcultures that make up this great country of ours. Besides," she added with a shrug, "for me, golf moves too slow, and sitting by the pool bores me to tears. So this has been the perfect answer."

As Madge finished speaking, Debbie stepped in with a tray of drinks. Placing them in front of each person, she asked if they were ready to order. Everyone said yes and waited for Debbie to take out an order pad.

"Okay, let's hear it," she said.

Looking from one to the other, the girls seemed unsure as to what they should do when Debbie saved the moment by adding, "I don't use an order pad. Mind hasn't gone just yet, so shout out what you want so I can tell the kitchen."

Orders placed, they sat quietly for a minute until Paul picked up his glass and announced, "A toast. To new friends, new experiences, and new adventures." As they clinked their glasses together, a man entered with a guitar case and began setting up some sound equipment that had been sitting off to one side of the room.

CHAPTER 6

The next day, as Madge slipped out of the RV to take her early morning turn around the campground, squirrels scampered through last year's leaves and the occasional doe nibbled on tender new grass shoots. The world felt fresh and clean.

Spring comes late at three thousand feet above sea level, and the soft morning sun intensified the chartreuse of the young leaves bursting from the surrounding trees and bushes. Early morning mist, rising from the lakes, rivers, and streams in the valley below, obscured any potential valley views. A few groggy tenters warmed their hands in front of cheerily crackling fires.

Being in no hurry, Madge ambled around each campground loop, waving to folks who were up. While she walked, she also made mental notes of any coolers that had been left out overnight. It wasn't long before the fragrance of bacon, sizzling over open fires, reminded Madge that Paul was more than likely waiting for her so they could jog over to the Wayside for breakfast. Jogging the two-mile round trip to the Wayside helped them justify the extra calories when breakfasting there instead of at home.

Returning to the RV, Madge paused to chat with Mike, from maintenance, who was servicing the restroom closest to the host site. "Hey, Mike, how's it going?" Madge asked.

"Can't complain," came the answer. "Other than a bunch of kids on D loop goofing off in the men's room, things have been pretty good. Nothing unusual."

"That's what I like to hear. Let's keep it that way."

"'Bout time you got back, Ladybug. This here boy's about to starve to death!" Paul teased as he emerged from the RV.

"Oh, poor baby. Let's change that jog to a dead out run and get you to food even faster," Madge quipped with a big grin.

"No, that's okay. I like to hang onto my reserve. You know, in case of emergency," Paul replied as he and Madge began gently jogging up the road to the asphalt path that paralleled the road leading back to the Skyline Drive and the Wayside.

"Wait," Madge called out as they reached the top of the hill. "I want to stop by—briefly—and tell Don and Barb about the two sites that left their coolers out. No one was up when I went by, and I didn't have any paperwork with me anyway. Still, they either need a written warning, or, better still, they need to be spoken to about leaving those coolers out."

Fifteen minutes later Madge and Paul sat sipping their coffee while Paul shuffled a deck of cards and complained, as usual, that it always seemed to be his turn to deal. Fiercely competitive, they liked to play gin rummy while waiting for their meals.

"Do you want to see the score sheet?" Madge asked sweetly.

"No, I know what it says—it's my deal," Paul said with resignation. Then brightening, he added, "But it also says I'm ahead!"

"Yes—for now," Madge continued in her sweetest voice.

As Paul dealt the cards, the folks at the next table asked, "What are you playing?"

"Gin rummy," Paul replied.

"That's such a good idea!" the woman observed. "My husband and I have trouble talking in restaurants because he's hearing impaired, so we usually sit looking as though we're bored. We're not. But playing cards would be a much more fun way to pass the time. What a good idea!" she repeated.

Chuckling, Madge and Paul simply nodded and continued to play. About halfway through their second hand, breakfast arrived. Putting the cards away, Paul attacked his pancakes, eggs, and grits while Madge carefully made a sandwich of her dry wheat toast and country ham.

Breakfast over, the two began the trek back to the campground. Instead of jogging, they opted for a brisk walk until they spotted the crowd of hikers stopped up ahead. In addition to the hikers, several cars were stopped in both directions.

"Um, looks like we have a bear jam," Paul observed, and he and Madge broke into a full sprint.

16

Sure enough, a short way up the hill, a sow and two small cubs were rooting through the leaves and turning over rocks and dead logs.

"Hey folks," Madge said, spreading her arms out to the sides as she stepped in front of the leading edge of the crowd. "I need you to step back and give mamma bear plenty of room. It's exciting to see the bear, but we need to remember this is their home and it's up to us to be good guests. That means not crowding the locals, so, please, step off the hillside and back onto the asphalt path."

While Madge tended to the pedestrians, Paul gave the drivers the option of either carefully pulling onto the shoulder or proceeding on their way. Bear jams could last for hours and had the potential to create nightmare traffic problems. If this bear decided to hang around for any time at all, Madge or Paul would call it in and let law enforcement take over. Fortunately, mamma bear evidently didn't find many grubs to munch on so she and her cubs headed up the hill and were soon out of sight.

As folks returned to their cars and the hikers proceeded on their way, Madge and Paul just smiled at each other and nodded. Each knew what the other was thinking: *Love seeing the bear. Glad we can protect them from over-curious tourists!*

Finally, Paul observed, "You know, we don't have our slingshots with us. Maybe we should start carrying them when we're out."

"That wouldn't be a bad idea," Madge said thoughtfully. "After all, we did take the class and the slingshots were issued to us. It only makes sense to carry them. However, we've never had to use them. Clapping and shouting 'shoo bear' has always been enough."

"Hmm—so far. But I really think we've just been lucky. And since it's spring and the cubs are so young, sows can be pretty unpredictable. You can do what you want, but I'll be carrying mine from now on," Paul added with unusual conviction.

Looking askance at her husband, Madge mimicked a kowtow and said, "As you wish, oh great wise one!"

17

CHAPTER 7

As they neared the log cabin housing the campground office, Madge suggested stopping in to catch up on anything they might need to know about when they went on duty at one. Using his key to open the side door, Paul stood back to let Madge go in ahead of him. As the two entered the tiny cabin, Ranger Brian Sauders hung up the phone and greeted the two with, "Hey, you are just in time."

"Uh, just in time for what?" Madge asked.

"To lend a hand with a BOLO. That is, if you don't mind putting in a little extra time. LE just asked me to contact you. Seems we may have a missing person. Section hiker was supposed to hook up with friends at Loft Mountain last night but never showed, and they haven't been able to contact her on her cell. It would be good if one of you could stake out a spot on the trail just south of here and talk to hikers coming north. We could use the other one to drive up to Skyland, hit the trail there, and catch any northbound hikers from that point."

Madge immediately offered to take the trail out of the campground while Paul opened the key box and removed the keys for the government-issued hybrid parked beside the building. "Who are we looking for?" Paul asked.

"Her name is Lilly Roberts. She's twenty-four years old, five feet six inches, and a hundred and twenty pounds. She has dark brown, almost black hair, brown eyes, and, according to her friends, she's gorgeous. She's been section hiking for several years now. Working her way north. Friends say she's been out about ten days and planned to hike only as far as Thornton Gap this time. They've met her on the trail before, and she's always been at the campground waiting for them, so they are really concerned. You do understand this is second- and third-hand info. I've not talked directly to any-one other than LEs."

"Of course. Any chance you got her trail name?"

"Nope."

Madge chuckled and shook her head. "Oh well. Guess 'Have you seen a gorgeous, northbound twenty-four-year-old brunette hiking alone' will have to do."

Looking around the cramped space, Madge wondered—as she always did—how on earth the first ranger assigned here back in the thirties raised a family in the roughly twelve-by-twenty foot, one-story log cabin. *That was real dedication,* she thought for the hundredth time as she checked to make sure she had her notepad and a working pen. "I'll grab the radio from the RV on my way," she said as she exited the building right behind Paul. "Do you want your backpack?" she called as Paul folded himself into the car and began adjusting the seat and the steering wheel.

"I'll be fine. Should be back by noon," Paul called as he closed the door to the white, stripped-down hybrid.

Madge blew him a kiss as she continued along the road at an easy jog. The RV sat no more than 200 yards from the ranger station, and the spur leading to the Appalachian Trail began across the street directly behind the RV.

Once inside the RV, Madge thought water and a protein bar would be good additions to the Jr. Ranger backpack everybody teased her about. She didn't care what people thought. The pack was just the right size for her and, besides, it was another way she showed her support for the National Park Service and its programs. After hooking the radio to her belt, slinging the backpack over her shoulder, and locking the RV, she was finally on her way.

***

Still covered with last year's oak leaves, the spur leading to the Appalachian Trail skirted the edge of the hill directly behind the RV. Angling steeply uphill, the trail turned out to be both

19

rocky and leaf covered. Madge began berating herself for not picking up her hiking poles. She knew she wouldn't need them on the short section of the actual trail she would be on, but this little spur could be an ankle breaker. She slowed down and carefully watched each foot placement.

When the concrete post bearing metal trail markers came into view, she exhaled a little sigh of relief and, heading south on the Appalachian Trail, picked up the pace.

CHAPTER 8

Her favorite spot was not more than half a mile down the trail. She decided this would be the perfect place to catch northbound hikers. While walking at a steady pace, she felt no need to hurry. Now that she was on the trail, she'd be able to talk to anybody she met. She decided to use the time to truly enjoy the walk in the woods. The only sounds were of chipmunks and squirrels scampering among the leaves and the rat-a-tat-tat of a woodpecker busily searching for breakfast grubs. There were just enough new leaves on the trees for the ground to be dappled with the early morning sun. A few jack-in-the-pulpits were trying to peek their heads up from the heavy covering of fallen leaves. Breathing deeply of the clean, fresh air, Madge smiled, thinking how lucky she was to be able to spend time in this little piece of heaven on earth that President Hoover had been wise enough to protect by creating Shenandoah National Park.

As she crested the hill and rounded the bend to her spot, she brushed aside her thoughts of President Hoover and focused on settling in to await any northbound hikers. Her space consisted of a bare, level area to the right of the trail. Several large boulders protected it from the 3,000-foot drop to the valley below. Sitting on the ground with her back against a boulder, she enjoyed the view of the famed Shenandoah Valley and understood why the Irish and Scottish who settled the area felt so much at home here.

Madge chuckled as she remembered the time she, Paul, and another couple had hiked to this spot. She and the other woman decided to sit on the boulders and let their legs dangle over the edge. They were enjoying watching two red-tailed hawks circle above when suddenly the hawks extended their talons and dove straight at the two women. There was no place to go. They couldn't go forward—it was 3,000 feet straight down. Getting back off the boulders was tricky. All they could do was watch as the two hawks headed straight for them with razor-sharp talons in the lead. Their husbands were engaged in deep conversation and oblivious to the impending tragedy. As Madge and her friend shrank as far back as they could on the boulder, the hawks suddenly changed their minds, pulled in their talons, and flew away. It probably wasn't nearly as close a call as it seemed, but that was the last time Madge sat on the boulders. However, she still chuckled each time she came here to enjoy the serenity, even if she did enjoy it now from the safety of the ground instead of from the top of the boulders.

Removing the backpack, Madge lowered herself to the ground. As she leaned her back against the boulder, she wiggled around until she found a spot where her back rested comfortably against the cold rock. Sighing happily, she pulled her pack next to her, removed her water bottle, took a big drink, and, making sure she could see the trail and that northbound hikers could see her, she began to reflect on the events of the past year.

It seemed inconceivable that just last fall she and Paul had been recruited to work as agents for a semi-government black-ops outfit. They spent several weeks in training at a place called The Retreat, which was just a few miles from where she now sat. Then they spent a good part of the end of last year RVing around the Southwest with a suspected serial killer. They couldn't tell anyone about what they were actually doing when they were on assignment with this top-secret organization.

They'd never had to use their cover story of working for a travel service scoping out cool and interesting places for bus companies to offer tours. But, then, maybe they'd never be called on again. Maybe that was a one-time event and they could just continue with their life as full-time RVers, happily volunteering with different organizations whenever they were moved to do so.

The sounds of laughter and scuffling feet interrupted Madge's reminiscing as a young family rounded the curve in the trail and came into view. A boy about eight and a girl about six walked in front of their parents. The sticks the children carried looked to have been picked up on the trail. Since no one wore backpacks, Madge thought they were probably staying at the lodge, but, just in case, she hopped up and greeted them with a friendly, "Hi folks."

"Hey Ranger. Were we making too much noise?" asked the mom.

"No. Not at all," Madge replied. "You folks staying at the lodge?"

"That's right," said the boy.

"And we're hiking on the Appalachian Trail," his sister chimed in with great enthusiasm.

"I hope we get to see some bears," her brother added.

"Well," Madge laughed. "You probably could if you were very quiet. Our bears are pretty shy, and when they hear you coming, they slip away and hide. If you hike over to the campground, you can walk all around there and see lots and lots of deer. They're more used to having people around and aren't bothered by hearing you laugh and talk. Just don't get too close."

"Thanks," the kids said in unison as they tugged on their parents' hands in an obvious hurry to be on their way.

Madge was about to settle back down when she heard another hiker coming from the south.

Striding purposefully along the trail, a lone hiker came into view. He propelled himself along with a pair of serious-looking metal hiking poles, and nothing in his demeanor suggested he wanted to stop to chat. Nevertheless, Madge stepped onto the trail and hailed him with, "Excuse me, I need to ask you a couple of questions."

Stopping directly in front of her, the man appeared to consider the question. "Okay," he said with a chuckle, "ask away."

"You look like you've been on the trail for a few days. Perhaps you've run into a young woman we're trying to track down. Unfortunately, we don't know her trail name, but she's a twenty-four-year-old section hiker. She's five feet six, weighs about a hundred and twenty pounds, and has dark brown hair and brown eyes. I understand she planned to do the section between Roanoke and Thornton Gap. Any chance you've run into anyone meeting that description?"

"Well, maybe. Couple days ago I passed a really good-looking gal who could be the one you're looking for. Went by the name of Sunshine. Planned to stay Thursday night at Blackrock Shelter, then meet friends on Friday at Loft Campground."

"You must have done more than just pass her on the trail."

The hiker chuckled again. "We lunched together. I have to admit, I tried to hit on her, but, while she was friendly, she was strictly business, and I'm moving along a lot faster than she was. She's not in any trouble, is she?"

"We certainly hope not. When did you say you lunched with her?"

"Um, that would have been Thursday, about five miles south of Blackrock Shelter."

"Thanks. So, I get the feeling you're on something of a mission. Mind giving me your contact information, or at least your trail name and destination for tonight?"

"Don't mind at all. I'm Joe Stennett, but on the trail I'm just plain Hiker. And you're right. I am on something of a mission. I actually have a reservation for the next two nights at Skyland. I tried to talk Sunshine into joining me in a nice room, complete with all the comforts, but I guess my charm couldn't cut through the last two weeks without a shower."

Now it was Madge's turn to laugh. "Actually, you look pretty good for two weeks on the trail without benefit of indoor plumbing. I won't keep you any longer, but you've been very helpful. Could you use an apple to keep you company?" Madge asked as she bent to pick up her pack.

"Apples are always welcome company. Thanks," Hiker said. "Hope Sunshine's okay," he said over his shoulder as he proceeded along the trail.

Madge unclipped her radio and reported her conversation with Hiker to Brian, who suggested she stay there a little longer to see if anyone came along who had seen Sunshine on Friday. So once again she settled herself on the ground, with her back to the now-warm rock, and continued to relive the events of the past few months.

She couldn't suppress the smile when she thought of Donny and Troy.

Right from the start, Donny Banks and Troy Sheldon stole Madge's heart. The two men functioned as the Franklins' train-ers, mentors, handlers, and, when necessary, backup.

However, while Donny coached them in martial arts, and Troy managed their weapons training, Madge thought of them more as her kids.

Because of his three years as an Army paratrooper, Paul's ability with weapons and at hand-to-hand combat surprised no one. Chuckling quietly, Madge remembered how 'the boys' reacted when they learned she had a black belt in mixed martial arts and was a crack shot with an assortment of pistols, rifles, and shotguns.

The peaceful quiet of the forest and the warmth of her memories coupled with the warmth of the sun made for sleepy eyelids. When Madge realized she might drift happily off to a midmorning nap, she shook her head a couple of times, rolled her shoulders and got to her feet. After taking a long drink from her water bottle, she turned to face the boulder she had been sitting against. Placing her hands on the warm rock, she let her upper body bend to her shoulders while, one after the other, she stretched her calf muscles.

While deciding whether to hike or continue to hang out, three hikers rounded the curve just south of Madge's loca-tion. This group looked to be serious through-hikers in the middle years of life. They moved along at a no-nonsense pace until they spotted Madge standing in the middle of the narrow trail.

"Excuse me. I won't take but a minute of your time, but I need to ask about a hiker you may have seen," Madge said in her most professional manner.

After briefly glancing at each other, they relaxed, reached for their water bottles, and the one in front said, "Sure, go ahead."

"Thank you. We are looking for information on a woman about twenty-four years old. We believe her trail name is Sunshine—"

Before Madge could finish, the second man put his water bottle aside and said, "Yes, we passed her yesterday around noon at the Doyles River parking area. She was just settling in for lunch. Said she was in no hurry because she was only going as far as Loft Mountain Campground."

"Noon yesterday. Was she alone?"

"As far as I know. We didn't see anyone else around."

Sighing deeply, Madge said, "Thank you, but please give me your contact information in case law enforcement needs to talk with you."

"Sunshine's a beauty and as sweet as they come," observed the man in front. "There's obviously a problem, or you wouldn't be out here asking questions. Can you tell us what the problem is?"

"She never showed up at Loft Mountain."

At that point, the man in the back handed Madge a business card and said, "We work together. Anyone needing us can call the number on this card. We can be reached as long as we have cell service. Now, if you'll excuse us, we'd like to be on our way."

"Certainly. And thank you," Madge replied. Looking down at the card, Madge read: George G. Jordan, Clergy.

CHAPTER 9

As Madge watched the men disappear down the trail, she radioed that she was returning to the office.

Clergy, she thought. *Guess that lets them off the hook! But it doesn't look good for Sunshine.* Hiking now with determination, Madge continued to think through the various possibilities. *Our people are probably hiking the trail between Doyles River Parking and Loft Mountain right now. Best case, Sunshine just tripped and twisted an ankle and is sitting quietly waiting to be found. Not so good—she fell down the mountain but is conscious so will hear people on the trail and will be able to call out to them. That would be great! Really not so good—she fell and is unconscious and—really, really bad is, well, I don't even want to go there! I wonder if we're using dogs.*

Ten minutes later, Madge entered the campground office. "Any news?" she asked.

"Not yet," Brian replied, shaking his head. "And it's been crazy busy around here. How 'bout you? Did you have any luck?"

"Actually, I did. We need to contact LE and let them know three clergy talked to her yesterday around noon at the Doyles River Parking area. Do you know if we are already into a full-blown SAR?"

"Haven't heard that we are, but you can be sure once we report what you've just told me, search and rescue will go into full swing. Jason's in his office. I think you should be the one to call this in," Brian said as he turned to the open half of the Dutch door to greet a camper.

Walking around behind the partition that separated the already small space into two even smaller areas, Madge sat down at the green metal, government-issued desk and reached

27

for the phone. Jason answered on the second ring, thanked Madge for the information and told her he would talk to the South District ranger responsible for dealing with the incident.

"Okay," Madge said. "Just remember, Paul and I are both available to help in any way we can. We've completed SAR training, and I've also worked radio relay. So—if you need us, don't hesitate to call."

"Thanks, Madge. We'll be in touch."

Madge sat for a few moments lost in thought. It always troubled her when people got lost or went missing in the park. When problems arose, her basic nature demanded action. She found it frustrating not to be directly, or even indirectly, involved in finding solutions. She empathized with anyone being out overnight in these mountains if they were either injured or unprepared. Even in June, the nights could get quite cold. Then there was always the issue of food and water, not to mention God's creatures, both large and small. Putting herself in that situation she shivered and reaffirmed the need for all the survival gear Paul teased her about keeping in her backpack.

Sighing heavily, she got up and went back around the partition to check the board. A registration card tucked into a numbered slot enabled the rangers and camp host to keep track of the occupancy status of the 231 campsites. Scanning the board, it looked to Madge like it was going to be a busy night. Less than half a dozen campers were expected to check out by noon, and less than a dozen additional sites were open for folks with no reservation. Chances looked good that Paul would be heading down about four o'clock to put up the Campground Full sign. Madge smiled. It pleased her to see so many people willing to forgo their cell phones and electronic gizmos and immerse themselves in nature.

"Brian, I heard you radio Paul to come back in. I'm going to head back to the RV and fix lunch. When he shows up, send him home. That is if he wants to eat before we start our shift."

"Not a problem. What's for lunch?"

"Nothing exciting. Just meat and cheese sandwiches. I'm putting on a pot of green chili stew for supper, and there'll be enough to share, if you're interested."

Brian looking quizzically at Madge. "I've never heard of green chili stew. What is it?"

"Meat, onions, potatoes, and roasted New Mexico green chilies. In other words, awesome!" Madge replied with a grin. "And it comes with warm corn bread or tortillas."

"Spicy?" Brian asked.

"Maybe a little, but not what you'd call hot. Just enough kick to let you know you're still kickin'."

"Ha-ha. You're a hoot, but, if you're sure you have enough, I'll try it. I was going to call the Wayside for takeout, but your cooking is better."

"Now, you're a man who knows how to talk to a lady. Flattery will definitely keep you fed! Paul and I will be back by one. See you then," Madge said as she scooted out the door.

Before heading to the RV, she wanted to look in the checkout drop box. As she prepared to cross the road to the box, Paul drove over the speed bump and tooted the horn at her. She grinned, checked the box, and then trotted over to the car as Paul closed the door.

"Heard you found some guys who talked to our missing hiker," he said.

"Yeah, but I'm not feeling too good about this since she still hasn't turned up," Madge answered while avoiding eye contact.

"Agreed," Paul said as he carefully studied his wife. "And I know that look. What's going on?"

"Nothing. That's what's going on. Absolutely nothing. You know how that drives me up a wall."

"You mean you not being involved drives you up a wall," Paul answered with a twinkle as he draped his arm over his wife's shoulder. "Let me return the key and we can commiserate on the way home. You'll feel better if you unload, and I still have good, broad shoulders."

CHAPTER 10

Madge said nothing as she and Paul walked to the RV. Once inside, he got out napkins, paper plates, potato chips, and cookies. Madge, still not talking, spread mayo and spicy brown mustard on two slices of rye bread. Adding ham and Swiss cheese, Madge finally broke the silence with, "You want lettuce and tomato?"

Peering over her shoulder, Paul said, "Uh-huh. Looks kinda naked the way it is."

That made Madge laugh. "Okay," she said as she looked up at her husband of thirty-odd years.

"How are you always able to make me laugh when I need it most?"

"Just thought that was part of the job description."

Still laughing, Madge said, "Okay. You get the raise."

She added the lettuce and tomato, cut the sandwich in two, and placed a half on each of the plates Paul had ready with chips and cookies.

Pouring soda into two ice-filled red plastic cups, Paul drawled, "It's mighty pretty outside, ma'am."

"Okay, but if the gnats or flies start biting, I'm heading back in," Madge replied in her best matter-of-fact manner.

Dappled shade over the picnic table created a pleasantly peaceful feeling. The gentle breeze that wafted through the woods kept both gnats and flies away. While they ate in silence, Madge began to relax. At last, between bites of cookie, Madge said, "I should hate it when you're right, but actually I find it kind of endearing."

Looking innocently at Madge, Paul asked, "What endearing thing have I done this time?"

"You know. About me not being involved."

"Oh. That."

"Yeah, that. Would you call it a character flaw?" she asked.

Chuckling, Paul responded, "No. Not a character flaw but definitely a character trait. That and your legs—and smile, and eyes, and so much more—is what I found, and still find, so attractive. I'll admit that 'little terrier with a bone' characteristic can be challenging at times, but you can think outside the box—as the saying goes—and you are usually right. While I understand your frustration, I really can't offer any help other than be a sounding board."

"Wow! Wow!" Madge said softly as she gazed at her husband. "That was amazing!"

"Just tellin' it like it is, ma'am," Paul quipped. "Feelin' better?"

"Yeah. Actually I am. And I have an idea."

"Uh-oh. Here it comes," Paul said with mock fear.

"No. It's nothing drastic. I just thought since we are so close to The Retreat I'd give the place a call and see if anybody we know happens to be around. I know it's a long shot, but who cares? Doesn't cost anything to call, and the worst case would be no one would answer."

Paul gave her a look that said, 'Who do you think you're kidding?' but he actually said, "That's a great idea." Nodding, he added, "I can't believe we've been here all this time without trying to get in touch."

"Well, so many different teams use the place, there's probably a constant turnover. And, after all, we have no idea where Charles is based when he's not at The Retreat. Then heaven knows Donny and Troy could be anywhere on the planet doing their cloak-and-dagger thing. Still, I'll call the Brookville Travel number and see what happens. Hmm, that means going up to the lodge to get cell service, or I guess I could try over by the amphitheater. But first, I need to get supper in the crock pot."

Collecting the plates, cups, and napkins, Paul said, "I'll do the dishes."

"Don't strain yourself," Madge laughed as she entered the RV.

CHAPTER 11

Instead of walking to the office to begin their one o'clock shift, the Franklins hopped into the golf cart the park provided, which enabled them to respond to problems faster than trotting around on foot. The only drawback was the inability to cut across country. All the campground loops were one-way, and everyone, even law enforcement, obeyed the rules of the road. After all, they needed to set a good example for the campers.

As Paul backed the golf cart onto the gravel area between the office and the picnic table, Don and Barb stepped out of the office door.

"What took you so long?" Barb asked. "We've been waiting for the last forty-five seconds!"

"Guess you'll need to dock our pay," Paul responded in mock seriousness.

"That's a great idea! I'll run it by Brian and see what he thinks."

"So," Paul said, "give us a hint about all the fun we're going to have."

"Well, let's see," Barb responded. "D65 needs another hour. Hopefully the reservation coming in on that site will be late. You may need LE to help you out with A32 and 33. That's a bachelor party—twelve guys—and beer pong seems to be their preferred activity. Other than that, looks like we're going to have a full house. Good luck. Have fun. Let us know if you need any help."

Laughing, Paul said, "Thanks a lot! How'd last night go?"

"Actually, it was reasonably quiet, considering we were almost full. Momma bear and her two cubs made their usual stroll through the backside of the walk-ins. We'd warned folks to expect the visit, so there were no problems. People kept their distance and so did momma. But she brought the cubs close enough for a Kodak moment, which thrilled everyone."

"It's pretty amazing that seeing the wildlife never gets old," Paul replied.

"Okay, gotta go," Barb said. "We're running down to Stanley to the Food Lion. Need anything?"

"Nope. We're good. But thanks," Madge said. "Be safe."

As Madge and Paul entered the office, the Commers walked off to their RV, which sat directly behind the office.

"Hey guys," Brian greeted them. "Did you see the Commers?"

"Yep, and got what we think was a full report," Paul said. "Have you heard any more about the missing hiker?"

"No. Sorry. But on another note, I do have a couple of things I'd like you guys to take care of. Seems someone over in your area is running their generator, and we've had a complaint about a barking dog on Loop B. I don't have a site number for either one, but the folks that complained about the dog said it's a 'yappy' dog that's locked in a hard-sided pop-up. Both of these just came in as the folks walked past the office on their way to afternoon hikes."

"Hey, that's what we get the big bucks for, right?" quipped Paul. "According to Barb, you should dock our pay. Seems we were forty-five seconds late."

"That Barb! She's a trip!" Brian laughed. "You guys actually work really well together."

"Yeah, we like them a lot," Paul replied. "They're good people."

Madge jumped in with, "Once we get these checked out, I'd like to run over to the amphitheater to make a phone call. Shouldn't take but a minute and we can check the picnic area while we're over there."

"Sounds good. I'm fine here. The afternoon rush hasn't started yet so take your time. I'll radio you if anything comes up."

With that, the Franklins headed out the door. Looking at each other, Paul asked, "You driving or riding?"

"I'll ride," Madge answered. "Where to first?"

"Umm. Let's check on the dog. It's closer," Paul said has he drove the golf cart onto the road, turned right and headed for Loop B.

As they headed down the hill, they could hear the sound of an unhappy little dog. Hoping the pooch wasn't in any distress other than being left alone, Paul turned onto the parking pad in front of the pop-up. Without saying anything, he and Madge just looked at each other as the barking became even more frantic.

"Well ding rats and fudge buckets!" Madge snapped. "What are we supposed to do now? I don't think even LE can open the door. The poor little thing must have heard us drive in 'cause it's gone into hyper drive. Think we should try to talk him down?"

"I don't know that it will do any good, but I'll give it a try," Paul said as he exited the golf cart. The barking became more frantic the closer Paul got to the camper. By the time he stood by the door the dog was not only barking but also jumping against the door and whining. "Hey, little guy," Paul began in a soft, calming voice. "Are you all alone in there?"

Rewarded with a combination of barks, whines, and door scratches, Paul looked at Madge. Then, shrugging his shoulders, he began walking back to the golf cart. "This is way over our pay grade," he said as he climbed back in. "I'm heading back to the office and turning this over to Brian."

"I hope there isn't someone in there passed out!"

"Madge! For goodness sake, don't go there!" Paul admonished in exasperation.

"Well, you never know."

Once back at the office, Madge waited in the golf cart while Paul ran in to make his report. Shaking his head as he got back into the cart, he said, "Would you believe it! There's nothing anyone can do. LE can't go in without probable cause, and a barking dog doesn't constitute that."

"You're such a softy. But I feel the same way. That's a perfect example of having a problem right in front of you and having your hands tied so that you can't fix it. If I continue to think about it, it will just make me crazy. So—let's see if we can fix the generator issue," Madge said with firm resolve.

"Sounds like a plan," Paul said.

They heard the generator as soon as they entered the older section of the campground. Looking at each other, they just smiled and shook their heads.

"Sounds like it's coming from down at the end of F," Paul observed as he steered the cart to the right turn into Loop F.

Sure enough, the generator in the large RV at the end of the loop was running. Madge smiled as Paul gave her the 'guess I'll go talk to them' look.

"Feel like a little bet?" Madge asked.

"About what?"

"Well. How much you want to bet that's a brand-new RV, and this is their first time out in it. Also, this is their first time in any kind of campground, let alone one without hookups."

Laughing, Paul answered, "No way would I bet against that. But I'll go see if you're right."

Paul knocked gently on the door, which was opened by a woman about his age. They talked briefly, she smiled an embarrassed smile, the generator shut off, and Paul returned to the golf cart.

"You were right on," he said. "They got in late last night and slept in today. Her husband went up to check-in just before noon and they hadn't read the rules yet, so they didn't know about the generator hours. She was very embarrassed, apologetic, etcetera, etcetera. I told her we'd be happy to give them a crash course in camping and RVing if they were interested. They're on the first day of a month-long adventure. Remember the excitement of our first time out?"

"In what? The pup tent? The pop-up? The first, second, third, or fourth RV? Which did you have in mind?" asked Madge with that innocently questioning face.

"All of the above, Miss Smarty Pants."

Laughing, Madge said, "Yeah, I remember them all with great fondness." Then with a sigh of pleasure she added, "Actually, each time we hit the road feels new because it's always a new adventure."

"Two more weeks, baby. Just two more weeks and new adventures await."

CHAPTER 12

They decided to run the campground before checking on the picnic area and attempting to call Brookville Travel. As they expected, very few folks could be seen in the campground. The great majority of campers spent the day hiking to various waterfalls and other scenic locations. Very few stayed in camp to read, relax, and nap. At one site they found a smoldering campfire, which they extinguished with water they carried in the cart. They also left a written warning, or WW, as it was known, about the danger of leaving fires unattended. At another site, a bowl of puppy chow sat out beside the dog's water bowl. They left a WW as a reminder about food storage because, yes, dog and cat food counted as an attraction to the local wildlife.

"All's quiet on the Western Front. Ready for the picnic area?" Paul asked with a smile.

Madge just nodded as she looked around. She couldn't decide which she liked better: the quiet of an almost-empty campground, or the people sounds and cooking smells of an almost-full campground. Sighing, she asked Paul, "Which do you like better? The campground like it is now, or later today when everyone gets back?"

"Well," Paul pondered as he pulled over and turned off the motor. "Listen. When it's like this, you can hear the little birds chirping to one another. You can hear the chipmunks rooting around in the leaves and you can hear that crazy pileated wood-pecker. He sounds like a jackhammer and I can't hear him or any of the other critters when everyone's here. But when we do late afternoon rounds and see people playing and working together and smell steaks, burgers, kabobs, and whatever being cooked over open fires, I get the feeling there's hope for this mixed-up world. I really believe the best place to get your head on straight and get your priorities in order is by going back to nature. So, I guess I want it both ways."

"Goodness! I'm glad I asked. Had no idea you'd turned into such a philosopher. But I can't say I mind," she said as she leaned over to kiss his cheek. "Besides, I probably couldn't have said it better myself. Maybe we could arrange for *Leaves of Grass* and *Last Child in the Woods* to be required reading before you can get your 'adult certification card.'"

"In your dreams!" Paul said with a laugh. "Let's get going. Park Service isn't paying us to sit here enjoying life."

"I don't know. Think of it as setting the example. You know, when campers see us taking the time to 'smell the flowers' as it were," Madge said rather primly.

"All right, Miss Example. We are now heading for the picnic area. Weather's clear, so you should get a pretty good cell signal."

"We can only hope," Madge said with resignation. "I'd sure like to know where we're calling when we call 'The Brookville Travel Service.'"

"Why don't you just ask? That's more your style than just wondering."

"Hmm—now that you mention it—you're right. Asking is more my style. If we actually contact anyone, maybe I will!"

"Now that's my girl! You're beginning to sound like the old Madge I know and love so much," Paul quipped as he made the turn into the picnic area on the hill above the bathhouse.

A small herd of deer—mostly moms with young fawns—nibbled the tender grasses and flowers growing thickly among the huge oak trees sprinkled within the picnic ground. A one-way road circled the area in a counterclockwise fashion with several areas of parallel, perpendicular, and angle parking available. Halfway around the circle, Paul arrived at the amphitheater area and, just beyond that, the dumpsters.

The lunch crowd had evidently moved on, but what looked to be a church youth group busily unloaded lawn chairs and coolers from one of the two vans parked close to the restrooms. While Madge dialed her cell phone, Paul got out of the golf cart and began walking up to the picnic area. He wanted to check the fire rings to be sure none contained live coals, and he knew Madge would be more comfortable making her call without an audience.

Her phone showed just two bars, but Madge took a deep breath and punched in the numbers that she hoped would get her to Charles Benson and her 'boys.' On the third ring, a pleasant woman answered with, "Brookville Travel Service. How may I direct your call?"

"Charles Benson, please," Madge replied professionally.

"Thank you. Hold please."

Madge took a deep breath, tapped her foot several times and nearly fainted when she heard, "Madge, how are you?"

"Charles?"

"Yes. Of course. To what do we owe the honor of this call?"

"Ah, well, we're doing our campground host thing at Shenandoah, and, since The Retreat is so close, I thought I'd see if anyone was around. We kind of miss you guys."

Chuckling, Charles said, "We miss you too. And you could not have timed this better. We have just finished six weeks of intensive training and could use some downtime. If you can get some time off, the boys can run over, pick you up, and you could spend a few days with us while we decompress."

"Charles, are you for real?" Madge asked incredulously.

Laughing now, Charles responded, "Of course I am! I would not joke about something like this. Everyone is here. Ben and Bev, Eric, and, of course, your boys."

"This is awesome and unbelievable and incredible and fantastic." The words spilled out almost faster than Madge could speak them. "Monday and Tuesday are our days off, but I think we can pull a switch with the other hosts for tomorrow too. Can I let you know in about an hour?"

"Certainly. Unless you have changed in the last few months, I have no doubt we will be seeing you tomorrow," Charles said with such warmth Madge could actually hear the smile in his voice.

Madge fairly squealed as she disconnected. Climbing out of the golf cart, she hopped from one foot to the other, then simply jumped up and down while doing what appeared to be a shimmy. Paul watched as he hurried back to the cart, and, when he was within speaking distance, said, "Either you got hold of someone and have great news, or you are having some kind of bizarre seizure and need immediate medical attention."

"Oh, funny man, funny man! *We are going to The Retreat!*" Madge shouted with pure joy.

CHAPTER 13

"I love the Commers!" Madge stated with conviction as she slipped her toothbrush into her overnight bag. "We'll have to do something really special for them for letting us off for a full three days in a row. Knowing them, they won't let us do a schedule switch. What do you think about a gift certificate to the lodge for dinner?" Madge continued as she zipped around the RV straightening this and that. "Well, maybe that's not such a good idea. They don't usually go up there. A gift basket! That's it. A gift basket with good local wine, blackberry syrup, maybe some pottery or fancy soap or candles . . ."

"Madge, are you nervous, excited, or what?" Paul asked from his comfy chair in the living area. "You're babbling like a crazy person and hopping around in here like the proverbial cat on a hot tin roof."

"I know," Madge sighed as she leaned her elbows on the kitchen counter and rubbed her hands over her face. "I hate to admit it, but I'm nervous and excited. I know it's only been about, what, six or seven months since we've seen the team? But we were so close. And, you know, people change. And, for me, it's like going home. They became family, and, like Thomas Wolfe says, you can't go home again."

"Well, looks like you won't have long to stew about it, since the boys just pulled up," Paul said with a chuckle as he headed for the door with his overnight bag in his hand.

"Oh, my gosh," Madge said, gazing out the kitchen window at the big silver Hummer parked in front of her RV. The tinted windows didn't allow her to see who was driving, but that didn't matter since the driver's door opened and Troy Sheldon unfolded his six-foot, four-inch frame from the driver's seat. The big man, in his early thirties, grinned when he saw Paul emerge from the RV. The two men greeted each other with manly hugs and slaps on the back as Donny Banks came around the front of the Hummer.

"Dang, but it's good to see you two," Paul said as he turned to Donny and repeated the hug and backslaps. "You look pretty good for having just finished six weeks of intensive training," Paul added with a laugh.

Both men laughed, and Troy said, "Charles likes to stretch a point to make a point. We put some youngsters through enough challenges to end up with less than half the class we started with, but they were the ones feeling the 'intensive' part. Donny and I just did what we usually do, right?" he asked, turning to Donny.

Before Donny could answer, the RV door slammed and, looking up, they saw Madge standing by the steps with her hands on her hips and a smirk on her face. Paul stepped back, leaned against the Hummer and waited for the reunion of Madge and her boys.

Donny and Troy looked at Madge, then at each other. Neither man spoke nor smiled as they marched slowly and purposely up the small hill toward Madge.

"Oh, it's gonna be like that, is it?" Madge challenged as she changed into a fighting stance.

Both men stopped side by side roughly four feet in front of Madge, and Troy asked Donny, "Me first?"

Not taking his eyes off Madge, Donny replied, "I don't know. She looks like she could take you, and Charles would not like that. Better let me handle this."

"Uh-huh," Madge said as she broke into a grin. "You just come on and try. I've been trained by the very best, and I'd hate to hurt you on such a beautiful morning!"

By now everyone was grinning from ear to ear and Donny replied with open arms, "Come here, you! I'm so glad you haven't changed!"

Falling into Donny's arms first, then being passed to Troy then back to Donny, Madge felt the last six or seven months fade away. Paul simply shook his head as the three friends walked toward him. "Feeling better, little girl?" he asked Madge.

"Feeling fine, thank you. Feeling fine," she replied happily as she looked up at one then the other of her boys. "Guess we should lock up, or do you two want to come in and hang out for a while?"

"No," Troy said, "we need to get going. Eric's beside himself about having you to cook for again, so we'd best not be late for lunch. Getting on the bad side of the chef borders on seriously stupid."

Paul collected Madge's overnight bag, locked the RV, and climbed into the Hummer behind Troy. Arm and arm with Donny, Madge walked around to the other side and climbed into the front seat beside Troy.

"How long did it take to get here?" she asked. "We have a key to the gate at Tanners Ridge, if that would make the drive any shorter."

"Don't need it. There's a little-used shortcut that practically puts us on top of The Retreat. The gate there is seldom locked, but, if it should be, we have a key."

"I'm not going to ask," said Madge. "Park Service is kind of fussy about civilians using their roads without permission. If any of my LE friends take exception to you using their road, I'm just going to sit here and scream that I'm being kidnapped."

"Let me know how that works for you," Donny quipped as he gave her seat a good shake.

"Hey! What is this? Are you turning on me?"

"Nope. Your reputation precedes you. But we're pretty tight with the LEs here. We're all federal officers, remember. After you called, we did a little checking. Seems you created quite a stir with that human head thing."

"It wasn't me!" Madge protested. "I just happened to be the messenger. Anyway," she groused, "I'm not involved, so they needn't worry about me interfering. We're leaving in about two weeks, so I'll be out of their hair for an undetermined amount of time. Besides, now they have a missing hiker to deal with. Guess that spreads them pretty thin. Wonder if they could use some help," Madge said thoughtfully.

"Now Madge, you promised," Paul admonished.

"Just kidding. Just kidding," Madge responded, shaking her head and rolling her eyes as Troy turned off the Skyline Drive onto a fire road.

CHAPTER 14

After surviving twists, turns, ruts, rocks, and gullies, the Hummer finally turned onto what Madge considered to be a civilized dirt road.

"Ah, Troy, did you really think that was a shortcut? Or did you just want to put this poor vehicle through some kind of test drive?" Madge said with a high degree of wonder.

"What's the matter, little one? Goin' soft on me?"

"Wait till we get to the barn, you big jerk, and you'll see how soft I've become! But this 'have to hurry for Eric' nonsense won't fly anymore. If we'd taken Tanners Ridge we'd have been there by now."

"Yeah, probably," Troy responded with a grin, "but it wouldn't have been nearly as much fun. And besides, this way you get to see some new territory."

"Okay, I'll give you that. I don't recognize this road at all." Then Madge added with a laugh, "I don't know, men and their toys and all that stuff!"

Donny jumped in with, "You don't recognize this section of road because it'll bring us in on the backside of the property, which you haven't seen before. We'll come up behind the house, close to the barn, instead of up the front drive."

Rounding a sharp bend, Troy brought the Hummer to a stop in front of a forbidding-looking gate. Chain-link fence topped with concertina wire led into the woods from either side of the eight-foot high steel gate, topped with sharp spikes. Donny hopped out and began entering a code into the number pad embedded in the center casing. A no-nonsense sign stating—Hunt Club. Members Only. No Trespassing—hung from the gate.

"Wow!" Paul said. "This is even more impressive than the front gate. And a lot less friendly!"

"Right," Troy replied. "The only people who would be back here are folks who shouldn't be back here in the first place, so we want them to understand we're serious."

"You've made me a believer," laughed Paul. "How much property actually belongs to The Retreat, aka Hunt Club?"

"We have three hundred and fifty acres. Not all of it's heavily fenced, so people can wander in, but what isn't fenced like this is barbed-wired and posted with unfriendly little signs. And, of course, there are the usual cameras, motion detectors, heat sensors, etcetera."

"You know," Paul continued, "when we were training here last year, I don't think there was any kind of human security on-site—other than you two, that is. So, how, exactly does that work?"

Chuckling, Troy answered, "Well, you can house a lot of folks on three hundred and fifty acres and not make it look like it's anything other than a residential vacation area. We maintain several 'vacation homes' around the perimeter, and they are staffed with rotating security. It gives our operatives a break from some nasty assignments, allows them to maintain their training, and allows us to sleep peacefully whenever we are at the big house, so to speak."

"Well, well, well," Paul said with a shake of his head and a little smile. "Charles forgot to mention all that when we were here before."

"Oh, I don't think he forgot," Donny added as they drove through the gate, which silently closed behind them. "I'm pretty sure he felt you and Madge had been handed enough information about the organization to allow you to do your job. I seriously doubt you've forgotten we function on a need-to-know basis."

Sighing, Paul answered, "No, I haven't forgotten. But just the mention of 'need to know' has my little wife twitching with curiosity. I'm afraid our last year's adventure with the Fast Food Kills murders brought out the dark side of my bride, and now, with people disappearing off the trail and hikers finding human skulls in the woods, I just know she's not going to drive away from Shenandoah in a couple of weeks and forget all about these mysteries."

"Not true. Not true," Madge piped up from the front seat. "And you don't need to talk about me as though I'm not here. I have no intention of poking my nose into places it doesn't belong—as you like to say. Besides, Annie and Gerard are arriving at the end of the week in their rented RV, and I'll be too busy playing tour guide to worry about anything else."

"Uh-huh," Donny said. "Sounds to me like the lady doth protest too much!"

Paul and Donny laughed and knee-slapped as the SUV came out of the woods onto a gravel road that led directly to the back of a huge barn. Troy reached over the visor and punched a remote and they all watched as one of the four garage doors opened. Once inside the barn, Troy cut the engine and announced, "Well, we're here!"

"Wonderful," Madge remarked with mock sarcasm. "Not much gets by you, does it?"

"Is this our workout barn?" Paul asked, looking around at the collection of vehicles parked in the garage area.

"Yep," Troy answered. "You'll know where you are as soon as we go through that door," he said, pointing to a single door off to the left. Moreover, he was right. Once they went through the door, the Franklins saw the mirrored wall, the workout mats, the weight bags hanging from the ceiling, and the door leading down to Troy's pride and joy—the indoor shooting range.

"Who are Annie and Gerard?" asked Donny as the foursome exited the barn and headed up the slight rise to the beautiful C-shaped log home known as the big house.

"Oh, they're great friends of ours from France. They love to travel in the United States and asked if we'd play tour guide for them on an excursion down the Skyline Drive, Blue Ridge Parkway, and into Great Smoky Mountains National Park. The timing worked out for us, so that's the plan. They'll be here at the end of the week. While we finish up at Shenandoah, they'll day-trip around the area. Then we'll head off on our adventure. It'll be nice since we don't have any time constraints. They're going to go on to Middle America, then up through Canada, and over to Alaska, where they'll turn in the RV and fly back to France. Don't know what we'll do after we drop them in the Smokies, but I'm sure we'll find something to keep us out of trouble."

Walking behind Madge and Paul, Troy and Donny looked at each other with raised eyebrows and Troy said, "No plans. That's really interesting."

Madge thought that was a weird remark but, before she could respond, the back door flew open and Eric rushed out to greet them with Charles, Ben, and Bev close behind.

CHAPTER 15

In keeping with his theatrical bent, Eric stopped in front of Madge, and, bowing deeply from the waist, said, "My Lady, your presence gives me great pleasure. I have prepared an exceptional feast in honor of your arrival. Obviously, your consort should join us, but I will leave it to your discretion as to whether or not the masses should be permitted to partake of your midday meal."

Rising to the occasion, Madge squared her shoulders and peered down her nose as she glanced around at Troy, Donny, Charles, Ben, and Bev. "Rise, my good man. I have been gratified by the care with which we were delivered to your door. And, since my gratitude includes the one who extended the invitation as well as those loyal subjects who care for us while we are in residence, it seems only fitting to allow all present to join us at the table," Madge decreed royally as she extended her hand for Eric to kiss.

"Thank you, Eric," Charles interjected as he came forward with open arms to greet Madge. "Glad to see you are still the Madge we know and love," he said warmly.

Then, turning, he shook hands with Paul, saying, "Good to see you! We have quite a bit of catching up to do. As Eric mentioned, lunch is waiting. You know where your rooms are if you need to freshen up before we eat."

Ben and Bev waited by the door with their usual stoic demeanors. However, Madge, being unwilling to settle for handshakes, hugged them both. Being the psychiatrist-in-residence, Bev hugged Madge, then Paul, but continued to look closely at them both. "I'm available anytime if you want to talk," was all she said as she smiled, then headed back into the house.

Before he could escape, Madge grabbed Ben's arm and said to the IT specialist, "If you have some free time while we're here, I'd like to pick your brain on some Internet stuff."

"Hey, girl, I'm on vacation for the next couple of days, but you know I always have time for you," he said with a grin.

Once inside, Madge and Paul carried their bags up to their room. Madge looked around the sitting room and asked Paul, "You want the bathroom first?"

"Okay, I'll be quick," he said as he walked back through the sitting room and shut the bathroom door.

Madge sat on the loveseat and marveled, once again, at the efficiency of the suite. A sitting room with two writing tables, a love seat, two chairs, and the appropriate tables allowed occupants to entertain four. With the bedroom on one side and the bathroom on the other, the privacy of the bedroom was never violated. *Perfect*, Madge thought. *When Paul and I get off the road, this is really about all we'll need—well, except for a kitchen.*

"Next," Paul announced as he emerged from the bathroom. "I'm going on down. I'll see about saving you some food if you don't drag your feet," he said over his shoulder as he closed the entry door behind him.

Madge didn't drag her feet. By the time she got to the kitchen, everyone else was seated around the oddly shaped table in the bay window. The only seat left for her was on the bench facing the window, which left her back exposed to the kitchen. Paul tossed her an evil grin but indicated, with a toss of his head, he would trade places so her back could be to the wall.

Giving him a look, Madge sat down on the bench and surveyed Eric's lunch offering. A clear glass salad bowl filled with mixed baby greens, julienned beets, crumbled goat cheese, bacon bits, and topped with lovely homemade croutons sat on the table just to the left of the wildflower centerpiece. Warm, fresh rolls, soft butter and strawberry jam sat on one side of the salad. On the other side of the centerpiece, fried chicken filled an oval platter flanked by a large bowl of mashed potatoes and an only slightly smaller bowl of creamy chicken gravy.

"Well, there you go. Outdoing yourself again," Madge admonished as she turned her best smile on Eric. "You came through with my favorite salad, and my waistline thanks you. But then you blew it with that danged fried chicken. By the way, what did you fix for the masses?"

Everyone laughed as the food began being passed around and Eric beamed happily at Madge for her kind words.

"I can't believe we were so lucky to hit you at a time when you could be free for a few days," Madge said to Charles as she placed a piece of chicken on her plate beside her salad.

Passing the potatoes to Bev, Charles said rather matter-of-factly, "It does seem fortuitous. I imagine you and Paul would like to go play with the 'children' this afternoon, but perhaps after dinner we could take some time to catch up, as you put it."

"Ah, sure. That would be great," Madge said as she sent a questioning look to Paul.

"Hey, playing would be terrific," Troy chimed in. "You guys want to work out, hike, shoot? We're up for whatever floats your boat."

Putting her fork down and looking around the table at each person in turn, Madge said sweetly, "I'm sensing that something's going on around here that somebody wants to keep under the radar for now. So, being the great team players we are, we'll go along with your little charade. But I expect you to fess up and come clean before I turn in tonight, or I can promise you will sorely regret it!"

"Hear that, Charles?" Donny said. "I think you've just been told!"

That brought laughter all around and whatever tension had been brewing eased away and the meal progressed with the usual banter and good humor of friends. No one turned down Eric's offer of warm cherry cobbler with vanilla ice cream for dessert.

CHAPTER 16

Since Madge and Paul had fired nothing other than Madge's BB gun since they were last at The Retreat, they opted for time at the indoor shooting range. Because this was just for fun and not a training session, Donny and Troy decided to shoot too. The foursome spent a relaxed afternoon in friendly competition with an assortment of pistols. They were surprisingly evenly matched. Madge was the undisputed leader with revolvers and lightweight pistols, and she and Paul tied with Donny for second place against Troy's first place with the big guns.

"Not too shabby," Troy observed as they prepared to clean their weapons. "When we finish here, how about some trap and skeet. Unless, of course, you're too tired."

"That sounds great," Paul said. "The last time I had a shotgun in my hand I had it pointed at people. I much prefer pointing it at clay pigeons. Whaddaya think, old girl?"

"Excuse me. What's this 'old girl' stuff, buster? Remember, I know where you sleep! Zapping some clay pigeons would be a great way to end a beautiful Sunday afternoon. We should be able to get in a pretty good session before happy hour."

All guests at The Retreat looked forward to happy hour. Sometime between five and five thirty every day, Eric put some form of cheese and crackers next to the fresh fruit bowl on the sideboard in the living room. He kept the mini fridge stocked with an assortment of wine, beer, juice, soft drinks, and water, and the liquor cabinet stocked with only the best high-end options. Relaxing in the living room at the end of the day brought everyone together in an informal setting that promoted the camaraderie enjoyed by the various groups that used the facility.

On this particular day, Madge arrived last. She had just settled in her favorite club chair, with a glass of red wine, when Eric appeared. "You're all invited to join me on the patio—if you want to, that is. The baked potatoes and salad are ready, and you're welcome to grill your own steaks, or I'll grill them for you."

"Nobody has to ask me twice," Paul said as he picked up the cheese tray with his free hand and followed Eric out the door.

Madge grabbed the crackers, Bev picked up the bowl of nuts, and Ben carried the ice bucket. Troy and Donny each reached into the mini fridge for an extra cold beer, and Charles brought up the rear after topping off his club soda with a twist of lime.

The flagstone patio overlooked the little wet-weather stream that bubbled out of the woods then trickled down the side yard until it disappeared under a tangle of boulders. An enormous Char Broil grill stood opposite the French doors leading to the kitchen. Two wooden picnic-style tables shared the space with a black, oval, eight-person expanded metal table. A two-foot high rock wall separated the patio from the green lawn sloping gently upward to the split-rail fence that separated the yard from the forest.

A tray of two-inch-thick T-bones sat on one of the shelves protruding from the grill. Eric finished wire brushing the grill, then, using tongs to hold an oil-soaked paper towel, thoroughly oiled the cleaned surface. "Okay, folks. Grill's ready. How do you want your beef?"

"Still mooing is fine for me," came Troy's response.

"Same for me," Donny chimed in.

"Medium rare for the Franklins," Paul offered.

"Medium rare for the rest of us too," said Charles.

"I think the grill master's earned a nice glass of red wine," Madge said as she handed a filled glass to Eric. "A toast," she added, "to our host and his accomplished companions."

"Hear, hear," resounded around the patio as glasses clinked and steaks sizzled.

CHAPTER 17

After dessert, Bev said she and Ben would help Eric with the cleanup, then they were heading to their rooms and would see everyone in the morning. Charles invited Troy, Donny, Paul, and Madge to join him in the living room. As they settled in, Charles asked if anyone would care for coffee or brandy.

"Not just yet, thanks," Madge said. "Maybe later, depending on how this goes."

"Now, Madge. What is it that you are thinking?"

"Oh, I don't know, Charles, but this seems a bit too convenient to be a coincidence."

"How do you mean?"

"Oh, come on, Charles. Please let's not play games. What's going on?"

"All right. Here it is. We did just finish a training session, and, if you had not called us, we would have called you. That plan has been in the works for some time. We knew you were hosting at Shenandoah and were at the end of your commitment there. However, we did not know what your plans were when you leave Shenandoah and were hoping to find out in an unofficial capacity. After all, when you and Paul finished your Fast Food Kills assignment, you said the experience had changed you and that you would have trouble going back to the life you led before you joined our team. You also rejected our offer to talk with Bev, and you turned down the two weeks we offered you here or in Hawaii. While we have, from time to time, checked in on you, we have not actually had any personal contact. So, before we offered you another opportunity to assist us, we felt we should evaluate where you both are physically, mentally and emotionally."

"Well, then. Wow," was all Madge could manage as she looked at Paul for help.

"Don't look at me. I'm just as surprised as you are," Paul said.

"Hey. Wait a minute," Madge said as she leaned forward in her chair. "Are you saying you have an assignment for us?"

Donny, Troy, and Charles exchanged looks. Charles sighed and said, "There is that possibility. We have a situation that we will be monitoring. I really do not want to get into the details, but it would be helpful if you could spend some time traveling up and down the Skyline Drive and the Blue Ridge Parkway between here and Great Smokey Mountains National Park. We do not want to interfere with plans you have already made. That's why we wanted to simply visit as friends rather than contact you as potential employees."

"Oh, you big ole softy. Of course, we'd do anything we could to work with you again. And if you need for us to meet with Bev for a session or two, that will be fine," Madge said with true sincerity while her body language fairly screamed excitement.

"Now, Madge," Charles admonished with a grin, "I can see the enthusiasm, but you need to understand this would truly be nothing more than a courier assignment, if it turns out to be an assignment at all."

"Oh, Charles, who cares? Just to be able to see these two goofballs every now and then and to have a chance to hang out with you and Eric and Bev and Ben—ah, speaking of Ben, do you think I could hook up with him for a bit tomorrow? I have a little issue he may be able to help me with."

"That should be possible. We really are on a break, so it will be up to him as to whether or not he wants to get involved in one of your little issues," Charles replied with a twinkle.

Madge felt Paul's eyes on her and, without even looking at her husband, said, "Paul, you don't need to be giving me the evil eye. I'm not getting involved in anything. I just want some answers to some questions, and I think Ben can help me find them, so bug off!"

That brought laughs all around. "Go ahead. Get your laughs at my expense. See if I care!" Madge huffed while trying to hide a smile. Then she added quite primly, "Perhaps I'll take that brandy now, sir, if you are still offering."

Chuckling, Charles replied, "I am. And, if you and Paul could be available after breakfast tomorrow, we can talk about how you might be of assistance to us during your travels this summer."

"Okay. Tomorrow it is," Madge said, giving Paul a satisfied look accompanied by a bright and happy smile.

CHAPTER 18

While vacation days meant no set schedules, Paul had suggested they talk Donny and Troy into a prebreakfast workout. It didn't take much talking and, by six a.m., the foursome was in the gym warming up for a lightweight mixed martial arts session.

"You two are in pretty good shape for having been bums for the last few months," Donny observed. "But, in all seriousness, we don't want you to pull or strain any muscles. So," looking at Madge, he added, "Mighty Mouse, try to hold back. Paul has good sense and we can trust him. But we know you and I can see you're just itching for a knock-down, drag-out. Maybe tomorrow. But for today, if you need more than Troy and I are willing to do, you can always beat the crap out of one of the heavy bags. Agreed?"

"Agreed," Madge answered more readily than Donny expected. "Contrary to popular opinion, I'm not anxious to damage myself or anyone else. So, while you're right—I'd love to really go for it—I know better and will hold back and," she added with a huge grin, "try not to hurt you."

"Well, thank you very much," Troy added. "I feel much better now."

"Ha-ha," Madge retorted to the six-foot, four-inch, two-hundred-sixty pounder. "I know you probably didn't sleep for worrying about our morning workout. But the real question is: Are we going to work out or stand around talking about it all day?"

"Let's go," Paul said as he and Troy began to spar.

***

The smell of frying bacon, wafting from the kitchen windows, encouraged the foursome to hurry with their showers.

Eric's 'casual' breakfast turned out to be a feast of blueberry pancakes, and bacon and eggs prepared to order for each person as they wandered into the kitchen. Additionally, warm, gooey cinnamon rolls encouraged diners to 'fill up the corners' while sipping on a second—or third—cup of coffee.

Conversation stayed casual and light, with Madge scheduling some afternoon time with Ben without divulging the reason. When the last icing had been scraped from the cinnamon roll plate, Charles noted it was time for Troy, Donny, Madge, and Paul to join him in the conference room, then he changed his mind and said they would be more comfortable in the living room.

"Since no one here is not aware of what we are facing, I see no reason for us to be uncomfortable. Get settled in and the boys and I will brief you on our situation."

Madge and Paul exchanged glances. Madge curled up in one corner of the sofa. Paul pulled the footstool over before sitting on the other end of the sofa and propping up his feet. Then Madge stretched her legs out, allowing her feet to rest against Paul in the hopes of getting a bit of a foot rub.

Donny and Troy each chose the lounge chairs, which left Charles with the club chair.

Looking around the assembled group, Charles began with, "Well, now that we all look comfortable enough, I suppose you would like to know what this is all about."

Sighing deeply, he continued, "As I explained last fall when I briefed you about the mission of our group, we deal with a wide variety of unpleasant and disagreeable situations that frequently fall outside the purview of most of our established law enforcement agencies. Much of what we do is off the books, so to speak, and is privately funded. I am sure you are aware of the threat posed by radical groups outside our borders. We have agencies doing an excellent job managing and containing that threat. However, the unfortunate fact remains that within the borders of the United States many fringe groups operate with the express purpose of creating disruption and chaos. Some of these groups are large, well funded, and well organized. Others are less so but just as dangerous and often even more devious. Now, I am sure you are aware of how the Internet and social media are often used to spread hate and a call to violence." Charles paused and shook his head.

"The NSA does an outstanding job of monitoring that arena. Consequently, some of these homegrown groups have resorted to other forms of communication and are, perhaps, being manipulated by outside sources. We have inserted undercover operatives into various areas of the country where we believe there is or will be trouble. We have a serious concern about the area bordering the Skyline Drive and the Blue Ridge Parkway. That is where you come in—if you are willing. The extensive training of the last six weeks was specifically geared toward developing sufficient agents to insert into Appalachia. Donny and Troy will be mobile within that area as contacts, but we would like to use you for contact service as well. Donny, would you pick up here, please?"

"Sure. Here's the thing. Because the Internet, especially social media, is being monitored so closely, many of these fringe groups have resorted to old-time spy tactics. You know, letter drops, newspaper and magazine want ads and personals, meets at bars, gun shows, motorcycle and auto races and other spots. Troy and I will be getting short-term jobs, or trying to, around the area of the drive and the parkway. We'll check in on our people whenever we can, but we would like for them to be able to contact you, if needed, as you go up and down."

Troy broke in with, "Then you could contact Charles, who would get word to us. All you would have to do would be to stop at designated spots along the way and wait to be contacted, just like you did in Alamogordo and at White Sands."

"Uh-huh," said Madge. "And how did that work out? Seems that was a test we've already passed!"

"This is not a test," Charles said. "On the contrary. This is deadly serious business that could make the difference between life or death, security or chaos, for many innocent people. We could truly use your help and do not see that your participation would, in any way, place you in danger."

Without waiting for Madge to comment, Paul said, "Well, when you put it that way, I don't see how we can refuse. Right, Mata Hari?"

CHAPTER 19

Donny and Troy dropped the Franklins back at their RV late Tuesday evening. They hadn't spent much time talking about the new assignment, but Madge did bid the boys farewell with, "Don't you two go gettin' yourselves damaged. I'd hate to have to hurt somebody just because you forgot to duck!"

"We love you, too, Mom," Troy said with a grin from behind the wheel.

"We're always careful," Donny said as he noogied Madge's head after giving her a warm bear hug.

As the boys drove off, Madge and Paul stood by the picnic table until they could no longer see the Hummer's taillights. Then, without a word, Paul took out his key and unlocked the door of the RV. After all these years, he understood and respected his wife's need for quiet. He also knew if he just gave her the time and space she required, it wouldn't be long before she'd need a sounding board for the conflicting emotions rolling around in her head—and heart.

By the time they unloaded their overnight bags, showered, and were ready for bed, Paul found Madge in the kitchen pouring herself a glass of wine. Looking up, she asked, "Want one?"

"Sure," he answered. "Are we talking or just drinking?"

"Don't know yet," Madge replied.

Paul took his glass from Madge and, looking around, asked, "Where to?"

"Um, think we can go outside in our PJs?"

"Well, why not? Half the park runs around in PJs every morning. Besides, if we sit in the chairs, instead of at the picnic table, we won't be very visible."

Settling into the blue folding chairs snugged against the RV, they quietly sipped their wine and listened to the night sounds.

Because it was Tuesday, instead of Friday, there were only five or six campsites in their area that were occupied, and all of those campers seemed to have turned in for the night.

An owl hooted from a nearby tree and a friend answered from several trees away. Their conversation continued for some minutes and prompted Madge to ask, "Do you ever wonder what they're talking about?"

"Of course," Paul answered. "I like to think they're lovers planning an assignation."

"If that were the case, don't you think they'd at least sit in the same tree instead of shouting their plans to the entire neighborhood?"

"Umm, you have a point. Could be a couple of guys planning a hunting trip."

"Speaking of guys, what do you think of this plan Charles and the boys have come up with?"

"Well, since Charles didn't want to bore us with the details, I don't feel I can judge one way or the other. On the other hand, if there are lone-wolf, loose-cannon types out there, that may not have all their oars in the water, I'm willing to do whatever is necessary to keep them from causing trouble. At the moment, how we can be of any help eludes me. Guess we'll just have to carry-on—go with the flow, as it were—and see how it all shakes out. How 'bout you?"

"Oh, I don't know. I don't like the idea of Donny and Troy being undercover. However, I have a feeling that's what they do when they're not training us or being our backups. Since I can't do anything about it, I might as well move on. Anyway, there's another issue out there." Madge sat a minute before she continued.

"I met with Ben because I wanted to check into just how often people go missing while hiking. Sure, I could probably have done that myself, but he said he didn't mind, and the way he did it made it a really quick search. Paul, over the past ten years, about two women a year have disappeared from various hiking trails throughout the country. Sometimes a man has disappeared too. But in all but two cases, when a man has disappeared, he's been hiking with a woman—who has also disappeared."

Madge stopped talking and she and Paul simply sat for a bit, each lost in their own thoughts.

Finally, she said softly as if to herself, "I wonder if we'll ever know the name of the person whose remains the girls found. Or if it's a man or a woman. Or if he or she was hiking alone. Or, or, or . . . "

CHAPTER 20

Although the Franklins were the only hosts on duty on Wednesdays and Thursdays, those days usually passed with little or no issue. Not having campground problems to solve or campers to counsel gave Madge too much time to think and she got antsy. The remains found by the students were still not identified and the missing hiker was still missing. The more she thought about what she learned when she was with Ben, the more troubled she became. She wanted to pick the brains of her law enforcement friends to see what, if anything, they knew about people—especially women—going missing while hiking, but she was unsure about how to broach the subject. She didn't want to sound like some kind of goofy nutcase, so she focused on planning for the arrival of their friends from France on Saturday.

Their friends loved the United States and traveled there often. They would fly in from Paris several times a year and spend weeks focusing on a small section of the country. They were serious students of whatever area of the world they were in, and, although they studied the usual tourist information, they also looked for the little details that made each town, county, and state unique.

For Madge and Paul, this trip would present the usual challenges of tour escorting, as well as an additional challenge from an RVing standpoint. Annie and Gerard always traveled by car. However, the Franklins lifestyle as RVers inspired their friends to rent a small RV for this adventure. Paul and Madge felt some pressure to make sure the trip lived up to expectations without undue negative challenges.

As Madge strolled the campground on late afternoon rounds, a couple flagged her down. They appeared to be in their mid-to-late fifties and were bubbling over with excitement.

"Hey, Ranger—uh—Madge," the man corrected as he read her name badge. "Do you think you could help us out?"

"I don't know," Madge answered with a chuckle, "but I'll sure try. What do you need?"

"Advice," the woman said quickly. "We're from Iowa, have just retired, and this is our first trip east as well as our first experience with RVs. We want to visit Washington but have heard horror stories about the traffic, the parking, and the crime. Do you know anything about getting around in D.C.?"

"Well, yes," said Madge, "actually I do. What you've heard about the traffic and the parking is true. As far as crime goes, Washington is a big city, and I don't believe the crime rate is any worse than in any other big city. Obviously, there are areas you should avoid. But if you stick to the busy, tourist parts of town you'll be fine. Follow the usual common-sense rules like, don't carry your wallet in your back pocket, if you carry a purse or camera bag sling it across your chest, not just over your shoulder, don't flash big wads of cash, be aware of your surroundings—stuff like that."

"What about an RV park? We looked online and the only one that seems close is called Cherry Hill. Do you know anything about it?"

Laughing, Madge said, "Yes. We've stayed there many times and personally think it's the only way to go if you are RVing. They are on the city bus line, and the bus leaves and returns all day to a stop directly across from the office. You can take the bus directly to one of the Metro stations. The D.C. Metro is wonderfully easy to get around on, and, while it seems expensive, it will save you a lot on parking fees and frustration. But if you haven't made a reservation at Cherry Hill, I'd recommend calling them ASAP."

The couple looked at Madge, so, taking a breath, she continued. "Now, Cherry Hill is more or less on the other side of town from here, which means you'll do some D.C. driving to get there. Closer to where we are now is Prince William Forest Park, which is a National Park Service site. They have a very nice campground, and it's not a bad drive at all to the nearest Metro stop. However, getting a parking place in the Metro lot can be challenging. We've stayed in both places but prefer Cherry Hill since, once there, we don't have to get back into the car. Does that help any?"

"Well, yes, I suppose it does," the woman said. "We'll have to talk about which would be best. I haven't driven the RV yet, but I'm not a good passenger. Heavy traffic scares me."

Madge smiled. "Boy, do I understand that feeling! Traffic is never really light around D.C., but hitting the area between ten and two is probably your best bet. How long are you going to be with us?"

"Oh, we just got in today," the man said. "I hope at least a week. We'll use the showers here, and the rest rooms, except in the middle of the night, and Paula here's going to go with paper products while I'll do all the cooking on the Coleman or the grill, so even without any hookups we should be able to make it for a week."

"Sounds like you are in good shape. Anything else I might be able to help you with?"

"Well, some advice on sightseeing in D.C. would be nice. I mean, there's so much information out there it's hard to sort it out. If you have any ideas we'd be happy to listen."

"Okay, just quickly. I agree about it being confusing. So if you have the time and the money, here's what I would suggest. Right from the start, take one of the guided bus tours. Could be a narrated stay-on-the-bus type or a hop-on, hop-off. But do something that will give you a good overview. Study a D.C. map. Fix the major sightseeing spots and their location to each other in your head. Plan one Smithsonian facility a day. They are extensive and mind-boggling."

Madge paused then continued. "Personally, I think the Capitol tour offered to the general public is a waste. Touring the Capitol is wonderful and an important thing to do, but I think the best way to see it is by contacting your representative or senator and asking if someone in their office can show you around. Usually they'll have a staffer available and you'll get a much more comprehensive tour. Also ask them for tickets for a White House tour. Used to be you could just go stand in line for the tour, but now you have to have a ticket issued by a member of congress. And now is not too soon to take care of that.

"Once you get oriented, you can rent bikes for bike tours, take Segway tours, or go around on your own. Oh—one tour that doesn't get much press is one given by the National Park Service out of Ford's Theater. A ranger plays the role of the lead detective on the Lincoln assassination and you follow him around to different points in D.C. that relate to that investigation. It requires walking from Ford's Theater to the White House, but we found it to be worth every step."

Taking a deep breath, Madge smiled and said, "That's probably more information than you wanted, but D.C.'s my hometown and I do love it. I often go on longer than I should. Sorry."

"Oh, no. Don't apologize. In fact, could we get together some other time and pick your brain some more?"

"You must be gluttons for punishment," Madge said laughing. "But of course you can. I'm always happy to tell folks about my town. We'll be around until Sunday, so anytime you are available I'll be glad to get together. Helping visitors is what we're here for. My husband and I are in the host site in the older section, and the Commers are the hosts in the site that's beside the ranger station. We're all available at any time you have a need. And that's twenty-four-seven, so don't be bashful," Madge said with a big smile as she eased away to continue her rounds.

The couple took the hint, smiled, thanked Madge profusely and headed back to their campsite.

Madge smiled to herself as she walked. *That was nice,* she thought. *I must have needed that. Telling them about getting around in D.C.'s put me in the mood to get busy on planning our trip south. No reason to put it off any longer. Can't do anything about the other stuff, so might as well let that go and take each day as it comes.*

CHAPTER 21

By the time Saturday rolled around, Madge had her thoughts together regarding their upcoming trip south, and Paul felt good about the RV 101 class he planned to give their friends.

"Just one week and a day and we'll be back on the road," Paul said as he and Madge began running the late-outs. "Do you think Annie and Gerard will make it in before we get off work today?"

"I don't know," Madge answered. "They landed Thursday evening and planned to stay in a motel Thursday and Friday so they could adjust to the time change. They were picking the RV up sometime this morning. I told them we wouldn't be off until two, so I hope they planned accordingly. But, if they didn't, that's okay. Brian'll notify us when they stop to check in. Their site is reserved, so it really doesn't matter."

"Were you able to sign them up for the Camp Hoover tour?"

"Yep, them and us. All set for Monday at ten. We haven't been down there in what—ten years?"

"Probably been at least that long. Have you clued them in on any of the history of this place?"

"Actually, no. They're so good at doing their own research I thought I'd wait and see what they'd discovered that piqued their interest. And the museum does such a good job of explaining the history of the park, I saw no reason to belabor the point."

"Hmm, well okay. So what have you been stewing over for the last few days?"

"Things like how far we should try to go in a day. Where we should try to stay. How early we should stop for the night. How long we should allow for sightseeing stops. What stops off the drive or parkway we should consider visiting and whether or not we need to consider staying off the mountain in any commercial parks. Stuff like that."

"Okay then," Paul said with a slight smirk as he glanced over at his wife. "I'm sure glad I asked."

"You don't need to be a smart-ass!" Madge grumped. "That's important stuff to figure out." Then she continued in her most professional voice, "Although it's all flexible, it's good to have a basic structure from which to begin."

At that Paul broke down laughing and said, "I sure do love you, you little goofball."

"Back at you, handsome," Madge said as she elbowed Paul's side.

Chuckling, Paul observed, "Looks like the Tanner party forgot to pull their tags."

"Oh, good grief. That's six sites. I'll hop out and get them. Then we only have our section and we'll be done. Yeah!"

"Only have two sites checking out on our side, so won't be a strain over there."

As they parked at the ranger station after finishing their rounds, Rangers Miranda Jones and Pablo Garza pulled up, parked, and got out.

"Hey, you two have a minute?" Miranda asked.

"Sure. Just let us clear the board and, unless Brian has something he needs for us to do, we have all the time in the world," Paul answered.

"Great. We'll wait out here at the picnic table."

Once inside the office, Madge whispered, "That's odd. Wonder what's up?"

"Guess we'll find out in a minute. Hey, Brian. Board's clear and, unless you need us to do something else, we'll be at the picnic table. Seems Miranda and Pablo want to have a powwow."

Brian looked up from his paperwork, gave Paul a thumbs-up, and returned to his project.

Madge looked at the counter, then took the time to pick up pens and paperclips and file the reservation cards that had piled up in front of the small, olive-green countertop, four-drawer file cabinet. Closing the last file drawer, she said, "Okay, all done. Let's go see what those two have on their minds."

CHAPTER 22

Stepping outside, Madge saw Miranda and Pablo sitting across from each other on the far end of the picnic table. Paul indicated he would sit facing the office, which put him next to Miranda and left Madge joining Pablo on the side facing the Commers' RV.

"Hey, what's up?" Paul asked as he settled on the bench. "It's not like you guys to hang out here. Usually you barge right in for an assault on the candy jar."

"True, true. We learned from the best. That would be you and your 'assault the candy jar' technique," Pablo said.

"Guilty," Paul admitted with a sigh. "But since candy equals energy and this job requires incredible amounts of energy, I offer no apologies. You two, on the other hand, spend your day riding around looking at the scenery with the occasional five-mile search and rescue thrown in to break the monotony."

"Would be true if five mile carry-outs were just occasional," lamented Miranda with a sigh. "Anyway, we thought we could fill you in on some info out here better than in there. What with the phone and the visitors. Besides, some of this isn't for general consumption."

"Okay. Anytime you're ready," Madge said with a tinge of suspicion in her voice.

Taking a deep breath, Miranda began. "The dental impressions taken from the skull led to an identification of the body. The next of kin have not yet been located so, as of now, notification has not been made. Therefore, this is not for publication."

"We understand perfectly. And we have no need to know the name. However, we are very interested in knowing anything you can share," Madge said.

"Right. Okay. We know this will go no further—his name was David Franks. He was twenty-four years old and from the D.C. area. He and his girlfriend, Angela Patterson, were reported missing in September of 2010. The missing person's report says they were spending a couple of days up here. They were staying at the lodge but were big into all-day hikes. Actually, the lodge notified law enforcement they were missing. When they didn't check out of their room when they should have, house cleaning notified the front desk. We started a SAR immediately, but that was a good twenty-four to thirty-six hours after they should have been gone anyway. They had not told anyone where they were hiking. We found their car in the lodge parking lot, so the assumption was they hiked on the Appalachian, although they could have been on any of the trails in this area. Unfortunately, during that time, there was a hard rain, which washed out any clues that might have helped. The SAR continued for several weeks before the incident became listed as a cold case."

Everyone sat quietly for a few moments. Finally, Madge asked, "What happened to the girlfriend?"

"No one knows. She's still listed as a missing person."

"Okay then. We have a couple, hiking along. He 'falls' off the mountain, and she's never seen or heard from again. Were any more body parts found, or was there any way to tell how he died?" Madge asked.

"No more body parts," Pablo said. "And as far as cause of death—well—the back of the skull was bashed in, but that could have been caused by the fall. However, since the girl has never been located, the man's cause of death is listed as suspicious and both cases could be reactivated if new evidence is found."

"Well," Madge observed, "that's troubling and interesting at the same time. Have you ever checked into just how many people go missing—all over the country—while out hiking?"

Miranda and Pablo looked questioningly at each other and shook their heads while saying "No."

"Well, I did. Just this past weekend. And you'd be amazed and maybe surprised to learn that in the past ten years, at least two women a year have gone missing while hiking somewhere in the United States. Oh, men go missing too, but, in all but two cases, they've been hiking with a woman who's also disappeared. Never to be heard from again."

"Interesting," Miranda said.

"That's what I thought. So let's move to our currently missing hiker. Any word on her?"

"Nope. Not a thing."

The foursome sat silently, looking at each other but lost in their own thoughts. The dry leaves around the large oak shading the table rustled as two chipmunks chased each other up and down and a crow cawed loudly overhead. Finally, Pablo looked directly at Madge and asked, "Are you thinking there's some kind of connection?"

"Let's just say I'm not a big believer in this much coincidence. Do I know what to do with this great potential insight? Nope. Do I plan on trying to figure out what to do with this great potential insight? Yep. Will I let you know when I come up with something? You betcha."

Madge took a deep breath and, changing her voice tone, continued and stood up. "However, till then I have places to go, things to do, and people to see. So how 'bout you two coming over sometime this evening and meeting our friends who we'll be traveling with for the next week or so?"

"We can do that," Miranda said as she and Pablo also stood to leave.

"And thanks for the heads up," Madge said quietly.

"No prob. Was pretty sure you'd want to know," Miranda added as she closed the cruiser door and she and Pablo began making their rounds.

CHAPTER 23

"Well, that certainly sheds a different light on things," Madge announced as she and Paul re-entered the office.

"Now, Madge," Paul cautioned. "Try to keep 'places to go, people to see, and things to do' in mind."

"I will. But it won't hurt for this to percolate around in the back of my mind while I act as friend and tour escort. After all, I am woman. I can multitask as well as roar!"

Still deep in paperwork, Brian looked up and grinned as Madge and Paul entered. "'Bout time for you guys to call it a day. When do you expect your friends?"

"Any time now. How about we hang out here for a while. It would be kind of cool to be able to be the ones to check them in," Paul observed.

"Fine with me," Brian answered. "I'm hoping to finish this project today, and any relief from the window will be great."

As he finished speaking, a family came to the open top of the Dutch door and asked for directions to the lodge. Madge smiled and directed them through the picnic area and up the hill. Before she could turn away, she saw a Travel America rental RV pull up and stop at the Stop Here to Register sign.

"Hey, Paul. I think they're here!" she cheered with a grin. "Should we go out to greet them or wait here and look official?"

"Let's wait here. I think they'd get a kick out of seeing us being official."

As they climbed out of their rented RV, Annie and Gerard looked around at the trees, the campsites on their right, and the little log cabin-office. Smiling, they walked side by side up to the open Dutch door and burst out laughing when they realized Madge and Paul were looking back at them from inside the office.

"Yeah!" Madge sang out. "You made it!"

Grinning from ear to ear, Annie answered, "Yes, and I am so glad to finally be here! The RV is a very different experience from a car! We are so far off the ground, and the valley is so far below!"

"I hear you," Madge replied. "But I'm coming out."

She and Paul quickly scooted around to the front of the building to welcoming hugs of the European sort; slight hugs and air kisses on each cheek.

"Welcome, welcome, welcome," Madge said with enthusiasm. "Let's get you checked in and off to your site. Once we get the paperwork done, we are through for the day, so you will have our undivided attention until seven tomorrow morning."

"It will have to be later than that," said Annie. "I have no plans to be awake at seven o'clock! Eight, perhaps, but not seven."

At that point, the Commers stepped to the window. "Hey. These must be your friends from France. We're the Commers—Barb and Don—and you must be Annie and Gerard. Boy, are we glad you finally got here," Barb said with a grin. "Madge's been like a cat on a hot tin roof for the last few days just anticipating your visit."

Shaking her head, Madge said, "She exaggerates, but I have been excited."

The Commers offered to handle the check-in process and Madge and Paul gratefully accepted. The paperwork consisted of filling in the RV's license plate info as well as reading and initialing the food storage policy. Once that was done, Madge and Paul thanked the Commers for their help, then the four friends climbed into the RV and headed for Site D-142.

Paul began explaining. "We reserved a site close to both the bathhouse and the restrooms. Since you will be here for a week, we thought it would be good if you don't have to run to the dump station. You'll be eating most of your meals with us—either at the RV or out somewhere—so you won't have dishes to worry about. If you use the bathhouse instead of the shower in the RV, you'll save enough water that I think you can make it without having to go for a water fill. We'll stop by the dump station on the way out and empty both the black and gray water tanks and fill up with fresh water then. Of course, if for any reason you need to dump or fill before we leave, it's doable. Nothing to worry about. Do I have you completely confused?"

"Not completely. Just mostly," Annie replied with a grin. "With your help, I am sure we will have everything understood before we fly home. We have said if we enjoy the RV, we may continue to use it instead of staying in motels."

Gerard just smiled and nodded. Madge tapped him on the shoulder and asked, "Gerard, are you still at the listening but not speaking stage?"

Glancing around at Madge, Gerard just grinned and nodded yes.

Everyone laughed but Madge added, "We're not laughing at you. We're laughing with you. And since I know very well you understand everything we say, I'll be careful not to plan your demise in your presence."

"*Merci,*" came the jovial response from Gerard.

CHAPTER 24

"You guys ready?" Madge called as she jogged into Annie and Gerard's campsite on Monday morning.

Sitting at their picnic table in the early morning sun, Annie closed the map she had been studying. "We have been doing our homework," she said. "But I could find very little on this Camp Hoover tour you have scheduled. Will we walk?"

"Oh, no," Madge replied. "We're taking the ranger-led tour leaving by van from the visitor's center. While it's only a four-mile hike round trip, and the two miles downhill make for a pleasant hike, the two miles back up—not so much! It was President Herbert Hoover's answer to Camp David. This particular location was chosen for several reasons: close to D.C., great trout fishing, and an altitude that's just a bit too high for mosquitoes. Guess Hoover didn't mind gnats since they have no problem with the altitude," Madge added as she fanned her hand around her head to chase away the gnats attempting to access her eyes and ears. Continuing, she said, "Paul thought it might be fun to take the nature trail and walk to the visitor center. It's only about a mile, and often we run into wildlife along the trail."

"Deer are fine," Annie offered, "but not bear. I only choose to see bear from the car."

Laughing, Madge said, "Annie, I promise I won't let any bears bother you. You're way too skinny for our bears to see you as a food source. Our bears like well-fatted Americans!"

"Not to worry, Annie. She's just teasing you," Paul said as he stepped around the fire pit into the picnic table area. "Our bears are gentle, friendly little guys—unless, of course, you've dipped yourself in honey or make the mistake of getting between mom and her babies."

"I do not plan to do any of those things," Annie stated with great conviction. "When we were in Yosemite the bears would break into cars and we were warned to be very careful of them."

"Well, our bears have better manners," Madge said with a chuckle. "But unless we want to double time it to the VC, we'd better get going. Can I do anything to help you close up?"

"Thank you, no. Should Gerard carry these in his messenger bag?" Annie asked, pointing to the stack of maps, books, and brochures on the table.

"I think you'll be okay leaving them here," Paul replied. "You won't need them on the tour, and when we get back it'll be time for lunch, which we'll grab at the Wayside before hiking back here. Madge and I have bug spray, so all you need to worry about is having water, your camera, and binoculars if you want them."

Within minutes, the four friends began walking through the campground to the connector to the nature trail. As they hiked past several walk-in sites, Annie observed, "It is so different than in Europe. Your sites are designated. Whereas at home, we can pitch our tents wherever there is space. When we were young, we had no problem with that. However, now that we are older and have traveled so much in your country, I think we might find our way not so inviting."

Smiling, Paul asked, "Does that mean you're ready to turn the RV back in and buy tenting equipment?"

"No," came the instant reply from Gerard, which brought a laugh from the others.

"Shhhhhhh," cautioned Madge.

Whispering and gesturing, she pointed through the trees into a small meadow. There they saw a mother bear turning over a log while her two young cubs looked on. The foursome stopped, and, as they watched, the mother bear sensed their presence. She turned, looked at them, and somehow signaled to her cubs because the little guys suddenly scampered quickly to the nearest tree and climbed to the top. Then mom went back to what she was doing seemingly unconcerned by the humans not sixty feet away. Annie and Gerard were snapping away with their cameras and cell phones while Madge and Paul smiled.

Paul signaled that it was time to move on and, after moving a significant distance down the trail, said, "See? No problem with the bears. And they provided the perfect Kodak moment."

"I do not think I know what to say," Annie remarked. Then she grinned wickedly and added, "I think you may have planned for them to be there."

"Absolutely!" Madge answered with a perfectly straight face. "Our bears get paid to be in particular spots at particular times each day. How else could we keep the campers happy?"

Annie and Gerard looked questioningly at each other before the joke hit them and they burst out laughing.

The air smelled fresh and clean and a stream on their left gurgled happily as the water hurried along. By the time they crossed the little wooden footbridge, they could hear cars on the drive and knew they were nearing their destination. Emerging from the trees, they could see the stone front of the VC, the parking lot with the National Park Service van, and their ranger guide waiting for them. A few tourists gathered around the beautifully sculpted bronze statue of the shirtless CCC worker standing with his shovel. Without the efforts of the CCC, the Skyline Drive would never have become a reality. The Park Service dedicated a considerable amount of time, energy, and museum space to the recognition of that fact.

As the foursome climbed aboard the van, their conversation was drowned out by the unmistakable growl of several Harleys pulling into the adjacent parking slots. Madge looked over at the group and suppressed a smile when she thought she recognized a familiar shape. The suppressed smile morphed into an honest grin as one of the bikers removed his helmet and Donny Banks appeared in all his biker-dude glory. Continuing to stare hard at Donny, Madge willed him to look her way. And, as was his practice, he skillfully surveyed the area. Perhaps sensing her, or simply out of habit, he glanced toward the van and their eyes briefly met. Neither of them overtly acknowledged the other. However, as Madge sat down, she smiled knowingly—aware that since her friends were on the job, she and Paul were back in spook mode too.

CHAPTER 25

M adge and Paul's host site needed to be cleared by noon to accommodate the new hosts. Nevertheless, the Franklins packed up early, said their goodbyes and were heading south on the Skyline Drive by ten that Wednesday morning. Following behind, Annie and Gerard kept in touch by using the walkie-talkies the Franklins provided. Although the plan was to just slowly pull into each overlook and stop only if Annie or Gerard wanted to, Madge did have one stop scheduled. It was at the Doyles River overlook, the last place the missing hiker had been seen.

As the two RVs pulled into the overlook, Paul asked, "Well, Sherlock, what now?"

"I don't know. It's been—what? Almost two weeks? I don't know. I just want to hike a little way down the trail—maybe in both directions. It won't take long, but it's just something I feel like I need to do."

"Hey, it's not a problem," Paul said gently. "I understand, and, knowing you, you may pick up some vibes that no one else could tune into. So don't apologize," he added with a smile as he gave his wife's shoulders and neck a good rub.

"This is so lovely," Annie crooned as she climbed from the RV. "It is unfortunate we are so early. What a wonderful place to share a meal."

Looking around, everyone agreed. The overlook hugged the east side of the drive and hikers on the Appalachian Trail had to hike through the overlook to stay on the trail. In the meadow, a large spreading oak tree grew out of the narrow grassy median separating the overlook from the main roadway, and one could see that the long shadow cast by the oak's wide branches would create an invitingly pleasant spot for a picnic.

"I want to hike just a bit down the trail," Madge announced. "Company's fine, or you can just hang out here and visit."

"I'm hanging," Paul announced as he looked over at their friends.

Gerard already had his camera out and appeared to be in full photo mode.

"If you do not mind hiking alone, I would like to stay and take some pictures," Annie offered. "The light is quite nice now. It is making the flowers glow. I am afraid it will change before you return."

"That's fine. I won't be long," Madge answered as she walked slowly toward the south end of the asphalt and entered the forest on the Appalachian Trail.

Not far into the woods, she stepped off the trail into a small open area on her right. Then she turned to look back toward the overlook. She could see everyone and both RVs quite clearly, even though she was reasonably sure they could not see her. She stood quietly and watched as another smaller RV and a car pulled into the overlook. She looked behind her and realized she could see a decent way down the trail but thought that she was probably not visible from that direction either.

Hmm, interesting, was her only thought as she returned to the trail and walked slowly back to the overlook.

"Well, that was quick," Paul observed.

"Yeah, didn't go far. Now I want to look at the other section. Back in a jiff."

No one seemed to mind as she walked north on the black-top to meet the other section of trail. This also became quickly enclosed in trees but also curved downhill and around to the west so that there seemed to be no place to comfortably or easily step off the trail and still see the overlook.

Again, her only thought was *interesting,* and, after going only a short distance, she turned around and returned to the overlook.

"So, Sherlock, what did you learn?" Paul asked as he ambled toward her from where he had been leaning against the tree.

"Not sure that it means anything, but there's a spot on the south side of the trail that affords a great view of the overlook without a person being seen from any direction. If she was grabbed while sitting under the tree, it would have been smarter for the driver to be heading south rather than north. But that would suggest this was a planned abduction rather than an abduction of opportunity." Shaking her head, Madge added, "Just gives me food for thought. That's all."

Annie and Gerard's cameras were back in their camera bags and, as they walked over to Madge and Paul, Madge said with a grin, "If you two are through with the photo shoot, let's get this show on the road!"

"Photo shoot?" Annie inquired quizzically but grinned and nodded as the meaning clarified itself in her brain. "Of course! I will have to remember 'photo shoot.' But, Madge, you did very little hiking. Please, do not let us keep you from your walks."

"Oh, you're not," Madge assured her friend. "I just wanted to check on a couple of things. A young woman went missing almost two weeks ago, and she may have been abducted from this overlook. I was just curious about the area and wanted to have a look for myself. Just a bad case of nose trouble, I guess."

Annie and Gerard looked at each other and shrugged before Annie said, "We do not understand how someone going missing from here has caused your nose to hurt, but nevertheless we are sorry about both situations."

"Thank you," Madge laughed. "But my nose is fine. Nose trouble is an American idiom for being curious."

At that everyone laughed, climbed back into their respective RVs, and proceeded south on the Skyline Drive.

CHAPTER 26

Less than an hour later, Madge keyed the mic on the walkie-talkie to announce they were leaving the Skyline Drive and beginning their 469-mile journey down the Blue Ridge Parkway. Announcing the change was a good idea since it can be challenging to tell where the drive ends and the parkway begins. Both follow the crest of the mountains, and both are operated by the same National Park Service guidelines. Both have maximum speed limits of thirty-five and forty-five miles per hour.

"Because it's getting on toward lunchtime," Madge continued, "we'll stop at the Humpback Rocks picnic area. Then we can check out the visitor center and other exhibits before heading to our campsite at Sherando Lake."

"Copy that," came the reply, which caused Paul to laugh so hard he nearly crashed the RV.

Once she and Paul finally stopped laughing, Madge asked, "What do you think the chances are we'll be contacted here?"

"Not likely," Paul replied. "I doubt there's been enough time for one of Charles' plants to have established a trust relationship with potential evildoers. But, who knows? We're here. We'll follow procedure, and, if we're contacted, we'll do what we've been trained to do, right?"

"My goodness. Your name must be Bond, James Bond. I kind of liked my husband, but you might be all right too," Madge said as she looked askance at Paul.

"Okay, Miss Smarty Pants. You have a better idea?"

"No, but you just sounded so—I don't know—unPaul like. It was kind of interesting," Madge said as she looked at Paul with a twinkle in her eye.

"Are you flirting with me?"

"Umm, yep."

"Maybe Annie and Gerard could tour the visitor center for a while on their own before we have to check out the farm," Paul suggested hopefully.

"Hold that thought, handsome. Right now we need to park this bad boy in that there picnic area over yonder."

"Uh-huh," Paul grunted as he maneuvered the RV to the curb in front of a meadow where a cluster of picnic tables nestled. Perhaps because it was the middle of the week, enough space remained for Gerard to pull his RV in behind the Franklins. Both couples stepped out onto the grass at the same time.

"Hey guys, this look okay to you? Or should we just eat in our RVs? It's nice and level here, so the refrigerators will be happy. What's your pleasure?" Madge asked.

Annie and Gerard conferred for a moment, then Annie answered with, "We think eating in the open would be refreshing. Perhaps we could put our food on the same table and share. I think you call it potluck?"

"Absolutely!" Madge replied. "And potluck it is! The boys can pick a table and dust off the seats while we gather up the grub," she added with enthusiasm.

With that Madge disappeared into the RV to return in no time with a basket filled with a tablecloth, napkins, paper plates, and an assortment of crackers, cheeses, pickles, apples, and cookies. Annie added additional crackers and cheeses as well as some lunchmeat and grapes. By the time the table was set, the boys had taken drink orders and returned with bottles of cold water for everyone.

A few puffy white clouds drifted lazily across the sky. Several deer browsed on the wildflowers at the edge of the meadow, and a pair of chipmunks begged for handouts, but at a safe distance from the picnic table.

"We are not supposed to feed them, are we?" Annie asked.

"Definitely not," Paul replied. "They're way too habituated as it is. With all the picnic areas, it's hard to avoid. Even if folks don't actually feed them, food always gets dropped. Same thing happens with the birds. So we'll try to be careful and they'll just have to be disappointed."

The friends took their time with lunch, and, when all was cleared away, Madge suggested they drive to the visitor center and check out the recreated 1890s Appalachian mountain farm.

"I hope they have costumed interpreters who demonstrate mountain life at the turn of the century," Madge told the group. "Actually, there'll be a lot of that between here and Cherokee, but for me it's always fun and I usually learn something new. Besides, it makes me appreciate all the modern conveniences I have even more."

As the foursome perused the exhibits at the visitor center and the farm, Madge and Paul made an effort to wander off from time to time to make themselves available for contact by any of Charles' people. Evidently, Paul's thoughts must have been correct as no one approached them or in any way indicated any interest in them.

"Well, that was fun," grumped Madge as she closed the door on the RV and Paul started the engine. "Hope we don't spend the entire four hundred-plus miles being useless."

"Better to be useless than to be the bearer of ill tidings regarding evildoers plotting evil deeds," came Paul's sage reply.

Sighing, Madge gave her husband a look, then smiled and said, "That's one of the things I like so much about you. You really are a good person."

CHAPTER 27

Later that day, as the foursome set up camp at Sherando Lake, one of the groundskeepers approached Paul saying, "Wow, that's some fancy rig you're in!"

Smiling, Paul replied, "Well, thank you. I think. But for us, it's home. We're full-time RVers and have no other place to live."

"Well, sir, guess that makes a big difference, but that looks like a pretty heavy piece of equipment."

"It weighs in at around thirty-four thousand pounds, so I guess you could call it heavy."

"That's heavy, all right. Do you get nervous when you have to cross bridges?"

"Not really. Why?"

"Well, sir, haven't you heard? The bridges in this country are in a sad state of disrepair. You take that little bridge over on twenty-seven that crosses Tomlyn Creek. Not much to it, but if anything happened to it the folks in Sydell would be in a world of hurt. I think you're pretty brave to be driving something that heavy." With that, he tipped his hat and added, "Nice talkin' to you. Have a good one," and walked away.

Paul looked after the man for a moment then shook his head and decided he'd best share that very strange conversation with Madge. She listened quietly, then said "Hmm, that really is odd. You'd better call it in. Better to bother Charles with nothing than to let something like that fall through the cracks."

As Madge left the RV, Paul pulled the satphone from the linen closet and placed the call to the Brookville Travel Agency. However, he was surprised to hear Charles answer and he wasted no time in relaying the odd conversation with the groundskeeper. Then Paul asked if calling this in was a waste of time because it made no sense to either him or Madge, and there had been no prior conversation to check or verify identities.

Charles paused briefly before responding. Then he said, "Our people have been made aware to look for you and Madge in your RV. They know the make, model, year, color, etcetera, and have seen pictures of you both. So, there will usually be no need for verification. Now, Paul, I will give you a brief summary of what we are up against. Someone out there, somewhere, is using the white supremacy agenda to inflame those of like minds to become lone-wolf disrupters of small, local, hometown festival events. Aside from that being reprehensible in and of itself, it appears there is an attempt to make this a coordinated, nationwide effort. We are talking about a desire to disrupt things like local craft fairs, carnivals, apple festivals— things that are held nationwide during September and October. Because the plan is to concentrate on small-town events, the idea is to also limit the ability of first responders to access the scenes. Blowing small bridges over streams, causing rockslides on access roads, tossing explosives into those little out-of-the-way electrical substations, destroying first-responder equipment where it is housed—all in an effort to create chaos, confusion, and fear. The really scary part is that it will also appeal to an element we are unable to monitor—the sociopaths, the confused, and those that, for whatever reason, feel disadvantaged or alienated from mainstream society."

"Come on, Charles. That's a tall order. So how do these folks even hope to be successful?"

"That is where our undercover operation comes in. The people this group is targeting tend to tune into the same type of magazines, newspapers, and webpages. That gets the idea out there. Then Joe Blow reads an article and mentions it to his buddy or cousin. It either snowballs or dies right there. While there may be other targeted venues, we have discovered that truck stops, biker bars, tattoo parlors, and gun shows seem to be fertile ground for discussions about this kind of disruption. Our teams work nationwide, and we are seriously concerned that this fall will see this concept come to fruition."

Stunned, Paul said, "Okay, I can understand how the idea gets planted. But implementation? Not so much."

"Actually, the concept is clever. Remember I told you earlier that because of how effective the NSA is with phone calls and e-mails there has been a movement to return to World War Two style spy work? Well, it was effective back then and it is effective now. The only drawback is that it is considerably more labor intensive. It requires some serious coordination, which another branch of our organization is dealing with. Our responsibility, right now, is for the operatives we have inserted up and down the Skyline Drive and Blue Ridge Parkway to pass anything they learn on to either Donny or Troy or to you and Madge."

"Okay, so that strange message I got from the fellow here at Sherando is applicable to all of this?"

"Yes, Paul, it is. Our man obviously does not have specific dates—yet. However, he knows the bridge over that creek is scheduled to be blown. Now we can act to see that that does not happen. So, thank you. This is only the beginning. Keep up the good work."

"Thanks, but—" Paul went no further when he realized he was talking to an empty line.

After putting the satphone away, Paul found Madge sitting outside at Annie and Gerard's RV. After giving Madge a look and an affirmative nod, he sat down at the picnic table and asked Annie and Gerard, "What do you think so far about RVing?"

As expected, Annie answered. "Um, I like having my own bed and not having to shop every day for groceries. However, I am not yet comfortable with being so high up off of the road. As long as we do not go too fast, I think I will adjust. Gerard says he enjoys driving the RV and likes not having to pack our suitcases into a motel each night."

"Well," Madge chimed in, "fortunately you can't go too fast on the parkway and when, and if, you take the RV on the interstates, they are, as you know, very wide, mostly smooth, and not very curvy. I think you'll be just fine. Now, since it's my turn to cook dinner, I'm going to excuse myself, and I will call you when dinner's ready to be put on the grill, which my better half will get out of storage and have ready for chicken within the next fifteen minutes. Until then, relax and enjoy the wine and cheese, but don't eat enough to spoil your dinner!"

With that, Madge marched off and the others raised a toast to the evening's chef.

CHAPTER 28

After breakfast the next morning, as the two couples sipped coffee by the lake, Madge explained the plan for the day. "We're not driving very far today. Not even a hundred miles. That will give us plenty of time to stop at overlooks, hike, and visit the James River Visitor Center and Canal before getting to the campground at Peaks of Otter, where we'll spend tonight. It's a really pretty drive, and it will be an interesting day for several reasons, one of which is that we will go from the lowest point on the parkway, at six hundred and forty-nine feet, to the highest point on the parkway in Virginia. I think that's somewhere around three thousand nine hundred and fifty feet, and we'll make that elevation change in less than twenty miles. Just the change in vegetation in that short distance is, at least to me, fascinating. I guess this is as good a time as any to talk a bit about the difference between the Skyline Drive and the Blue Ridge Parkway," Madge added.

"I did not realize there was a difference," Annie said. "They are both national parks and they are both drives that follow the mountaintops."

Smiling, Madge replied, "That's right. But there's more to it than that. The Skyline Drive, in and of itself, is not a national park. It is simply the only road through the Shenandoah National Park, whereas The Blue Ridge Parkway is a National Park within itself. When we were on the Skyline Drive, we only had four places where we could enter or leave the park. There were many, many places along the Skyline Drive where we could access the hundreds of hiking trails within the park. As we travel down the Blue Ridge Parkway, notice that at many places the parkway is only as wide as the road itself and is bordered, not by woods and forests, but by farms and homesteads owned by private citizens. There are many little roads leading off the parkway. There will also be sections bordered by national forests. Those sections are administered by the National Forest Service, not by the National Park Service. The National Park Service falls under the larger umbrella of the Department of the Interior, and the US Forest Service falls under the larger umbrella of the Department of Agriculture. Both are government agencies, but both have different mission statements."

At that point Paul gently interrupted with, "Madge—TMI."

Looking at the glazed-over expression on the faces of their friends, Madge said, "Oh dear. It looks like I've overwhelmed you with too much information. I'm so sorry. I guess I just get carried away sometimes. Don't worry about it. You'll see what I mean as we travel along. Then this afternoon we'll day-trip to Bedford and visit the D-Day Memorial."

"It is strange that your D-Day Memorial is not in Washington, where so many of your memorials are located. This seems an out-of-the-way sort of place to put something that is so very important," Annie observed.

"Yeah, I wondered about that too. Then I found out that Bedford was chosen because it's the town that lost more men, per capita, in the D-Day invasion than any other town in the country. Placing the memorial there honors Bedford's sacrifice as well as the sacrifice of all those who perished on the beach at Normandy. We appreciated the tour you took us on of Normandy. I've often wondered if this memorial would have had the same impact on me had I not been to the actual site. But this memorial actually hits me harder. It's so condensed. The bronze statues just rip at my heart. Especially the ones depicting the top of the cliff. The ones that are just a bayonet stuck in the ground with a helmet on top. It's hard for me to talk about it. It affects me the same way our visit to Pegasus Bridge did."

Annie smiled sympathetically. "I remember. When we told the woman who owns the little store there that you were Americans and she began to cry, hugged you, and thanked you for saving France, you just hugged her back and cried too. It was a very moving moment. We will be honored to visit your D-Day Memorial here."

"Thank you. Our countries have a long history of coming to each other's aid. I'll be so glad when that's no longer necessary," Madge said matter-of-factly. Then she added, "Don't know why people can't just get along. It would all be so easy if we would just stop the hating."

Everyone nodded. After a short and somewhat awkward silence, Paul announced, "Ah, you know, we could think about getting on down the road. I know we don't have far to go, but even a journey of only a hundred miles begins with a single whatever."

Madge chuckled. "Good icebreaker there. Let's head 'em up and move 'em out."

"What?" asked Annie.

Laughing, Paul explained. "That saying is a throwback to the cowboy days in the Old West when herds of cattle were rounded up and driven hundreds of miles to a railhead. For some reason, it's one of Madge's favorites. You might as well get used to it. You'll probably hear it again." Then he added softly, as if to himself, "And again and again . . ."

Madge grinned as she sashayed off toward the RV singing, "Home, home on the range . . ."

***

The drive to the campground at Peaks of Otter proved pleasant and uneventful. The group enjoyed some short, easy hikes and marveled at the James River canal that helped promote settlement of the area when it was the last frontier. As the foursome returned to the parkway, after visiting the D-Day Memorial, Annie commented on the beauty of the rhododendron and mountain laurel.

"Just wait," Madge said. "This has been a cool spring, so we have a late bloom. Pretty soon, we'll be driving past what looks like a solid wall of rhododendron. In fact, there will be many places on the parkway where the rhododendron are so tall and so thick they remind me of the noise abatement walls we build along some of our interstates."

CHAPTER 29

Their overnight at Peaks of Otter included the bus tour up to the peaks themselves as well as a visit to Polly Woods' 1840 tavern and the Johnson Farm. Upon leaving the Johnson Farm, Annie observed that she found the difference between the first farm they visited and the Johnson Farm quite striking.

"Well," Paul said, "that shows the difference between the early life of the hardscrabble farmer-pioneer and the later era middle-class farmer. Remember, in the early to mid-eighteen hundreds, this was, quite literally, the wild frontier. End of the line, so to speak. Most of the settlers came from Scotland, Ireland, and Germany. Many by way of Pennsylvania. Then added to that mix were the African blacks—both slave and runaway."

Grinning, Madge added, "When we get to the Blue Ridge Music Center, you'll see how that particular blend of cultures influenced today's music."

"I will look forward to learning how the music we hear today began here almost two hundred years ago," Annie stated with her usual intensity.

"And you will just have to wait 'cause I'm not spilling the beans!" Madge teased.

"I do not understand how spilling the beans relates to music," Annie queried.

"Ah—another American colloquialism," Paul offered. "Means telling secret information—more or less. Kind of like you're planning a surprise party for someone and you don't want anyone to let the secret out, so you say, 'don't spill the beans.'"

"Don't spill the beans. I will remember to use that at the correct time," Annie said with a laugh. "We love American colloquialism."

Since they were only going a little over a hundred miles that day, Paul suggested Annie and Gerard take the lead and set a pace that would be good for them. The foursome would regroup at the Rocky Knob picnic area at lunchtime. Then, after lunch, they could explore Mabry Mill together. Both families needed groceries, and Madge figured she and Paul could swing into a grocery as they passed through the Roanoke area.

Swinging into a grocery was not the easiest thing to do in a large RV with a Jeep hooked on behind, but, after so many years, the thought no longer traumatized Paul. As they pulled into the grocery lot, Paul said, "Hey, take a look at that panel truck."

"Yeah, so?"

"Nothing, except they were at Big Meadows."

"Ah, okay. And that's a problem because?"

"It's not. I guess. Did you talk to them?"

Madge thought for a moment before saying, "Well, no, not really. I tried, but they're not too social. I think it's a mom and adult son—or at least I hope that's what it is. He may have some learning disability or something. He acts really shy, and his mom seems overly protective. We didn't do more than the usual 'Mornin' nice day' stuff. Why?"

"I don't know," Paul answered. "Just something about them doesn't compute as the camping, outdoor type."

"Well now, who are you and what have you done with my husband? He's not usually into people analysis."

"Yeah, you're right. But there's something there that just seems out of place. Anyway, we're here," Paul said as he reached for a paperback. "Do you need me to go with you, or can I hang out here and see what kind of trouble Lee Child's gotten Jack Reacher into?"

"As far as the noncampers go, maybe they're just down on their luck," Madge said. Then she added, "I think I can handle the grocery on my own, so read away, my good man. You and Jack enjoy. I'll be back in a flash."

With that, Madge hopped out of the RV and began her hike into the grocery. As she looked around the parking lot, she reaffirmed the observation she and Paul had made after visiting so many different parking lots all over the country. It appeared you could tell the socioeconomic status of an area by the number of grocery carts left willy-nilly in the parking lot. In this instance, nearly all the carts were neatly placed in the cart-return area, suggesting the area to be reasonably affluent. That also suggested to Madge that she would be able to find some of the more upscale treats she and Paul enjoyed—like yummies from an olive bar as well as a good selection of cheeses and artisan breads.

Meanwhile, back in the RV, Paul made himself comfortable in his recliner. Because Madge loved grocery stores, the chance of her coming 'back in a flash' wasn't a remote possibility. Consequently, Paul jumped when the door opened and Madge called out, "Hey, could use some help out here."

"Did you forget something?" Paul asked as he hurried to her aide.

"No. But this would go faster if you would take the bags as I hand them up to you. Then I can return the cart."

"Wow. How'd you do this so fast?" he said as he reached for the bags Madge handed him.

"Wasn't all that fast," Madge answered. "You and Jack must have really been into it. I didn't have that much to get," she said as she handed him the last bag and began pushing the cart back to the cart-return area.

Once back on the road, Madge said, "I did run into that lady and her son. You know, the ones in the panel truck."

"And?"

"Seems they are SAG support for something called The Appalachian Trail Appreciation Team. The woman, Sharon, said the team is made up of people who would like to hike the trail but for a variety of reasons can't. So they act as support for actual hikers. She said she's in charge of the Skyline Drive and Blue Ridge Parkway teams, which is why—from April to the end of October—she and her son drive up and down from Front Royal, Virginia, to Cherokee, North Carolina. So, evidently, we'll be seeing a lot of them for the duration of our trip."

"Really," Paul said matter-of-factly. "Don't you think it's strange we've never heard of this group?"

"Yep. But the soup aisle at the All Goods didn't seem like the appropriate place for an in-depth interview. I'm sure we'll have several good opportunities to find out more about this group," Madge remarked before asking, "So, how's old Jack doin'?"

"Up to his ears in it, as usual. Lee Child knows how to spin a yarn. What an imagination."

CHAPTER 30

By the time Madge and Paul pulled into the picnic area at Rocky Knob, Annie had a picnic table covered with a cloth, paper products stacked on one end, and cheese and fruit waiting in the middle for the French bread Madge picked up at the store.

"Hey guys," Madge called. "Have you been waiting long?"

"Not at all," Annie replied with her usually sunny smile. "We drove very slowly and stopped at all of the overlooks. The road felt very narrow, so Gerard drove with great care. We especially enjoyed the views of the Roanoke Valley. Having spent a great deal of time in both Scotland and Ireland, we understand how the settlers from those countries would have felt very much at home here. We tried to imagine the valley without so much civilization—as it would have looked so long ago."

"You'd need a good imagination to do that," Paul said as he settled at the table. "Try as I might, I just can't visualize an area the way it might have been seen by people a hundred or more years ago. That's why I need those recreated areas with costumed interpreters. Like Mabry Mill, where we'll be going right after lunch. I'll unhook our Jeep and we'll all go down in it. Parking at Mabry Mill is not so good for RVs. There's space behind the main building, but I'm not sure how the Park Service feels about RVs parking there."

By then Madge's smile had turned into an actual grin. "Mabry Mill holds a special place in my heart," she said. "When I was a kid, we spent a lot of time running up and down the Blue Ridge, and Mabry Mill was my dad's favorite spot on the parkway. Over the years, the Park Service expanded the exhibits and seems to phase costumed interpreters in and out. It will be interesting to see what the current policy is regarding costumes.

Personally, I think the rangers spoil the experience if they have to be in their green and gray uniforms. But that's just me."

"How will Mabry Mill be different from the two farms we have already seen?" Annie asked.

"Well, in the first place, it's not set up as a farm. Back in the dark ages, when I was a kid, the mill itself was the only thing I remember being there. It's a wonderful old working mill and the setting is quite lovely. As the years have gone by, more buildings have been brought in from different places, and the last time we were there, costumed interpreters actually worked at different jobs in different buildings. A ranger worked in the blacksmith's shop. Another ranger was weaving in one of the cabins, and a costumed volunteer was spinning wool in another cabin. There's a gift shop and a restaurant, which is always terribly busy and crowded. I think the locals like to come up here and, once you see it, I think you'll understand why."

"Our reservations for tonight are only thirty miles down the road from the Mill, so we can spend as much time as we like watching, asking questions and just soaking up the atmosphere," Paul announced as he finished the brie off on a hearty chunk of French bread.

"Thanks for sharing that last hunk of brie," Madge said sarcastically as she glared at Paul.

"Oh, did you want some?" he asked with wide-eyed innocence.

Laughing, she replied, "No. I just wanted to give you a hard time, but you were smart enough not to take the bait."

Just to be sure Gerard didn't miss out on the fun, Annie translated the exchange as she and Madge packed up the leftovers and the men collected the trash. Once the lunch items were stored in the two RVs, the foursome climbed into the Jeep and drove the short distance to Mabry Mill.

As they pulled into the parking lot, Madge paid close attention to the group of motorcycles clumped together in one of the parking slots, but none of them looked like the one Donny had been riding. *Oh well*, she thought with a sigh. *Hope my boys are okay.* Shoving that thought aside, she announced, "Let's go have some fun!"

CHAPTER 31

As he hiked the AT between Great Valley Overlook and Purgatory Overlook, he wondered how many times he would need to walk the roughly ten miles before he would hear the voice. He'd begun today's hike shortly before noon. It was now after four, and he had yet to meet anyone other than three men, all hiking alone. Two northbound and one southbound.

Then he heard the voice.

"Stop. Sit. She is coming from the south. Wait for her."

He found the stump of an oak tree and settled down to wait. He removed an apple from his backpack and pulled his water bottle from its holder on his belt. He had been taught that when waiting he should look like a hiker taking a break.

The only sounds he heard were the occasional *caw, caw, caw* of a highflying crow and the rustle of leaves as both squirrels and chipmunks went about their daily business.

Then he heard it. The unmistakable crunch of hiking boots on leaves and rocks as well as the merry tinkle of bear bells attached to either a backpack or a hiking pole.

Get ready, he thought as he took a bite out of his apple and unscrewed the lid on his water bottle.

She rounded the corner to his left and slowed when she saw him. He was huge and could have been a wood troll just sitting munching on an apple. He tucked his head and smiled shyly when he saw her. He'd been told looking shy made people more trusting.

She slowed as she neared him. Then she stopped in front of him. "Hi," she said. "Looks like you found the perfect spot to take a break."

He smiled back at her as he rose and said, "If you need a break, you can sit here. I'm ready to go anyway."

She laughed softly and said, "No, thanks anyway, but I need to keep going. I want to get to Bearwallow Gap by dark. Which way are you headed?"

"The same as you. My mom's picking me up at Purgatory Overlook."

She nodded in understanding and said, "Well, see you," as she swiftly continued on her way.

He waited only a brief heartbeat before following her. She moved quickly over the roots and rocks with long, measured strides. He stayed a reasonable distance behind her until he heard the voice again.

"It's time."

He quickened his stride. Coming up behind her, he plunged the syringe into her neck and caught her as she slumped into his arms.

A hundred yards ahead, a white panel truck sat in the overlook with its back doors open. The woman waiting by the truck helped assist the groggy hiker into the back of the truck and climbed in after her. The man who had been on the trail got in the driver's door, started the engine, and drove away.

CHAPTER 32

Unlike many of the information centers on the parkway, Mabry Mill lacked a traditional visitor center. Instead, a one-story gray building housing the restaurant and gift store sat adjacent to the parking lot. A group of people stood chatting on the sidewalk just outside of the entry. They appeared to be a bit older than Madge and Paul and were dressed more for an afternoon at the country club than for hiking in the mountains. When Madge saw the beautifully coiffed women, her hand automatically flew to her hair, where she ran her fingers through her tousled curls. *That was silly*, she thought. *I like my hair just fine! Just the way it is*! Smiling, she took Paul's hand, skirted the group, and entered the building.

The front door emptied into the small waiting and cash register area for the restaurant, which, considering the crowd, made getting to the gift shop somewhat like running an obstacle course. Once in the gift shop, Annie said matter-of-factly, "I am glad we have already eaten. It appears there is quite a wait to get seated in the restaurant."

Laughing, Paul replied, "I've never seen it any other way. The food may be outstanding, but we've never had the inclination to face the crowds to find out. Can somebody tell me why we are in here to begin with?"

"Mainly for postcards," Madge answered. "I told Annie they might have a good selection since they always have so many visitors."

"Good. Then you won't mind if Gerard and I get started on the tour," he said as he looked at Gerard and indicated, with a jerk of his head, that they should attempt to exit the building.

Gerard grinned, nodded in the affirmative, and led the way back outside.

"I knew he could understand everything we said," Madge observed with a chuckle. "And I understand why he's hesitant to try speaking. So it's okay. Anyway, I think he and Paul will enjoy being off without us for a change."

While Annie purchased a small collection of postcards, Madge browsed in the locally made pottery section. She could seldom resist uniquely made local pottery, but this time found nothing that piqued her interest.

"Ready?" she asked as Annie slipped the bag containing her purchased postcards into her purse.

"Absolutely," Annie replied. "I am pleased with the selection, and I hope I will be able to find a place to post them tomorrow."

"That won't be a problem," Madge said. "We'll scoot into Hillsville for breakfast, and you can mail them at the post office there. Let's see if we can find the boys."

As the two began their trek down the path to the restored buildings, Annie stopped to admire the setting of the gristmill.

Nestled on the bank of a beautiful pond, the mill wheel turned slowly, seemingly not disturbing the pair of swans and the assorted ducks sitting as still as decoys on the smooth water.

"Are they real?" Annie asked as she pointed to the birds.

"I think so," Madge answered. "They always have been."

Just as she spoke, one of the swans shook its head and paddled to the other side of the pond.

After taking several photos, Annie continued down the path with Madge close behind. They crossed the bridge over the stream that fed the flume and proceeded into the mill itself. It smelled of freshly cut wood and freshly milled corn with just an occasional hint of machine oil.

The costumed docent explained that Ed Mabry, the original owner, used the power of the waterwheel to not only grind corn but to also cut wood. So the mill, built around 1905, did double duty. Ed ended up working mostly in the sawmill, while his wife, Lizzie, became the miller. Their water supply kept the mill wheel running at such a slow speed they lost customers to faster mills in the area. However, when the corn was ground too fast, it often overheated and ended up with a burned taste. Therefore, the Mabry's mill became noted for the quality of its cornmeal as opposed to the speed at which it could be produced.

After chatting for a while with the docent, they continued around the dirt path, which wound artfully through and around huge old oak trees. When checking out the cabin with the weaver, the ranger there made a point of asking if they knew why the doors were so low that the Park Service felt it necessary to post a Watch Your Head sign. Madge smiled and stayed silent while Annie thought for a moment before observing, "I would imagine the height of the door adequately met the needs of the people of the time because I believe they were of a smaller stature than most people are today."

"Well said," came the reply from the ranger.

Eventually, Annie and Madge discovered the boys in the blacksmith shop, where Paul and the blacksmith were in deep discussion.

"There you are!" Madge announced as she slipped her arm around Paul's waist. "I should have known this would be where we could find you. Have you learned anything you didn't already know, or were you interviewing for a job?"

"Um, no to both questions. However, if I were looking for work, this is something that would be very attractive. Especially in cold weather," he added while taking out his handkerchief and wiping his brow. "It's pretty toasty in here right now."

He thanked the ranger for taking so much time with him, then the four friends followed the trail back to the millpond, where they stopped to simply enjoy one of the most photographed spots on the parkway.

Finally sighing, Madge said, "This has been wonderful and for me a great walk down Memory Lane, but I think it's probably time to head on down to Fancy Gap. We'll be spending two nights there at a RV park with full hookups. No more dry camping for a day or two."

As the foursome neared the building with the restaurant, a group of women, who were quite obviously seniors, came pouring out the door. Laughing and chatting, they all wore fancy red and purple hats varying in style from ball caps to wide, floppy brimmed sun hats. Annie reached for Madge's arm and pulled her aside.

"Do you know anything about that group?" she asked in wide-eyed wonder. "Why are they wearing those—hats?"

Madge laughed. "Yes, actually I do. They call themselves the Red Hat Society, and they were inspired by a British poet by the name of Jenny Josephs. She wrote a poem titled "Warning." I first learned about it in the mid-eighties. However, it wasn't until 2001 that Sue Ellen Cooper turned Jenny Joseph's concept of the proper attitude for middle-aged-plus women into an organized movement."

"I do not understand," Annie replied.

"Well, it's all about enjoying life on your own terms and having a sense of humor. You are already there with your attitude and sense of humor, but I'll give you a copy of the poem anyway. I'm pretty sure you'll get a kick out of it. It begins:

When I am an old woman I shall wear purple
With a red hat which doesn't go, and doesn't suit me.

"Well, their sense of humor seems to be firmly intact," Paul observed as the bevy of red hats melted away into various cars. "If Madge was a joiner she'd fit right in."

"Hmm, I guess I'll take that as a compliment," she said. "Not sure how it was meant, though."

Madge still pondered the idea as they climbed into the Jeep for the trip back to the Rocky Knob picnic area.

CHAPTER 33

After returning to the RVs, the drive from Rocky Knob to the campground at Fancy Gap proved to be uneventful but scenic. They entered an area of the parkway that alternated between farm fields, oak forests, and those rhododendron walls Madge mentioned earlier. Both couples had programed their GPSs with the address of the campground, so Madge and Paul continued to let Gerard lead.

"This is a most interesting drive," Annie commented into the walkie-talkie. "Your country is so big it is difficult to realize how far we have come and yet are still in the United States. Of course, now that we are no longer required to stop at border crossings when going from country to country, Europe feels much larger than it used to."

"Yes, I know. I sometimes wonder how we would cope if we had border crossing stations between each state," Madge replied.

"I am sure you are grateful that you do not," Annie added then broke into a chuckle. "With that wall of rhododendron on the left, I understand and agree that it does resemble a sound reduction wall. How nice it would be if those walls could actually be so beautiful!"

"Yep. As a frequent visitor to our country, perhaps you could suggest some beautification programs to the different highway departments."

"I do not think they would be impressed by the observations of a French visitor," Annie answered with a laugh.

Soon Gerard signaled they'd arrived at their turnoff. The RV park had a Fancy Gap address but was located just off Interstate 77, which made for a drive of several miles from the parkway exit. By now, Gerard's comfort level had increased to where he felt he could handle the RV in just about any situation, and the two RVs moved along much faster than they would have a few days earlier.

The men waited outside of the office while Madge and Annie handled registration. They'd been able to get side-by-side sites and, after getting parked and hooked up, met at the Franklin's picnic table. The weather seemed warmer than usual for late June, and Annie suggested the pool looked inviting. The weekend crowd had not yet arrived, so there were no children swimming.

"It is not that we do not like children," Annie observed. "Of course we do. However, we find swimming in a small pool with many children less pleasurable than it would be right now."

Laughing, Paul answered, "Couldn't agree more. What do you say, Madge old girl? Should I crank out my Speedo?"

"Oh, I hope not!" came the emphatic reply. "I'm so glad those awful things seem to be a product of years gone by." Then stretching, as if to remove muscle strain, she added, "A swim might be just the thing after a hard day of heavy-duty sightseeing."

"That is a joke, correct?" Annie asked with wonder. "We do not feel we have had a hard day."

"Neither do we," Paul assured her. "And, yes, Madge was just kidding. Actually, it's been a very good day. One I have enjoyed very much. No rush. No hurry. Very pleasant."

As they were about to go to their RVs to suit up, a young man walking by gave them a long, hard look, then broke into a big grin and shouted, "Aunt Madge!" as he walked into the Franklin's campsite.

Madge and Paul stopped in their tracks, looked inquiringly at each other, then looked back at the young man. Tall, slender to the point of being almost skinny, his hair was pulled back in a loose, blond ponytail. He wore a small hoop earring in his left ear and a skull and crossbones stud in his right. He wore low-slung, faded jeans with all of the appropriate rips and tears, and a well-worn lightweight black leather vest over a bare chest.

Encased in flip-flops, his very clean feet suggested they had been recently removed from shoes.

"Aunt Madge," he repeated with enthusiasm.

"I'm sorry," Madge replied. "You seem to have me confused with someone else."

"I don't think so," he said with conviction. "You are Donny Banks' Aunt Madge! I'm Greg. We met at that BBQ Eric had for Donny's birthday. I guess there were so many people there you wouldn't remember everyone, but you are hard to forget. The way you outshot all the men when they had the skeet shooting competition just blew me away." He paused briefly, glanced apologetically at Annie and Gerard, then continued. "Sorry. I didn't mean to startle you, but it sure is great to see you again. What do you hear from Donny?"

CHAPTER 34

Madge and Paul recovered quickly from the shock of being 'recognized' and Madge said warmly, "I am sorry for not remembering you, Greg. But you're right. There were a lot of people helping Donny celebrate turning thirty. Please," she added as she pointed to the picnic table, "won't you join us?"

"Well, I don't want to interrupt," he said.

"Not at all. We were just going for a swim," Annie offered as she and Gerard moved toward their RV. "If we do not see you later at the pool, we will come over after dinner."

"Sure. Great," was all Madge managed with a wave.

"Well, now," Paul said as the threesome settled at the picnic table. "Can we offer you anything to drink? We have iced tea, soda, good water, or there's also beer, wine, or wine coolers."

"That's quite a choice," Greg answered. "I wouldn't mind a beer—as long as you're offering."

"Not a problem," Paul said. "How 'bout you, sugar," he added as he turned to Madge.

"Nothing right now, thanks. Maybe later."

Settling her elbows on the table, Madge said, "So, Greg, I'm not sure how this works. Maybe you could lead the conversation."

"Okay," Greg answered as he looked around. He'd placed himself at the picnic table with his back to the RV, which gave him a good view of the area. Several rows away, a group of motorcycles were in front of three tents pitched close together.

"I'm with the group camped over there," he said as he indicated the tents and motorcycles. "I've just recently hooked up with them, but we've been stopping regularly at spots off the parkway. At each stop I've heard talk about the 'need to shake things up' or the 'need to teach the suckers a lesson.' Nothing

106

concrete. But the word is out there that something needs to be done to wake the 'peasants up to the realities of life.' The guys I'm with don't seem to be of that particular mindset, but maybe they just don't trust me yet. My best guess is that, as of now, whoever is behind this is involved primarily in a mind game. Getting the seeds of action sown. I was told to be on the lookout for you and, if I had the chance, to approach you as 'Aunt Madge' from Donny's birthday party."

"What kind of places are you talking about?" Paul asked as he returned with a couple of beers.

"Mostly biker bars. Thanks," Greg said after taking a long pull on the frosty Dos Equis Paul handed him. "But a couple of times we went into gun shows and, once, at an outdoor hot dog stand, I heard someone saying that it would be 'interesting' if more than fireworks went off over Fourth of July.' The group the guy was with thought that was very funny, but no one made any other comment that I could hear."

Sitting by Madge with his back to the road, neither Paul nor Madge heard the person walking up until he was almost at the picnic table. Greg raised his beer and called out, "Marco, you'll never guess who I ran into."

About the same age as Greg, except for his clothes, Marco was the polar opposite. Short, stocky, and complete with the beginnings of a respectable beer belly, Marco said, "That's cool, man, but I wanted you to know we're riding into Hillsville for dinner. Out of here in thirty. Just so you know."

"Thanks. This here's my friend Donny's aunt and uncle." Holding up his beer, he continued, "Be right there."

Nodding his head, Marco said, "See you," as he turned and walked back to his campsite.

The threesome sat quietly for several minutes. Finally, Paul said, "We'll get hold of Charles with what you've shared, but that really doesn't tell us much more than we already know."

"Not specifically, no. But for the ideas to be spreading so rapidly—without the use of social media—suggests a well-organized, structured plan from someone who understands the angst and frustration of the fringe elements. I'll keep my ears open. If I pick up anything tonight, I'll catch you in the morning before you leave."

"Actually, we'll be here for two nights," Madge said. "We're going to Mount Airy tomorrow and will be there all day. How about planning to get together again late tomorrow afternoon?"

"Good idea," Greg said as he stood, put his empty beer bottle on the table, slapped Paul on the shoulder, and walked off.

CHAPTER 35

As Greg and his new friends departed, a lone biker rode in and stopped beside a large fifth wheel attached to a Dodge Ram pickup. A dilapidated white panel truck sat in the parking area beside the fifth wheel. The motorcycle rider parked his bike and removed his helmet and his gloves. He placed his gloves in his helmet, hung his helmet on a handlebar and looked around. Satisfied no one seemed to be paying him any attention, he walked to the door of the fifth wheel, knocked lightly twice, then disappeared inside.

The biker closed and locked the door, turned right and walked up the two steps to the living room, which, in this model, rode over the bed of the pickup. The biker joined a man and woman already seated in the living room. The men, in their early forties, looked enough alike to be twins. They were big men—burly and broad-shouldered with shaved faces and heads. Both wore small earrings in each ear. The only distinguishing difference in the two was the twisted star tattoo on the back of the right hand of one and the heart with a dagger in it on the right bicep of the other.

In her mid-fifties, the woman's build was slight enough to make her look almost frail beside the two men. Her heavily lined face suggested she had been a heavy smoker for years. Her eyes showed a hard edge, suggesting she would not be someone you would want to cross.

Local news played on the TV. As he walked toward an empty chair, the biker picked up the remote and turned off the TV.

"Want a beer?" the woman asked as the biker sat down.

"Later," came the reply. "Let's get down to business. Where's the last catch?"

"In the back," the woman answered. "Rolph'll make the transfer tomorrow."

The biker said, "Then we need to set up another meet for tomorrow night. I'm heading north to check on the units working the Shelby area, and there's a good chance I'm going to need the cash. Where are you making the exchange?"

Rolph, the man with the star tattoo, replied, "Handoff's scheduled for two out of Meadows of Dan. No reason you can't be hanging out there looking at the scenery. I can give you the cash after our contact leaves."

"Karl, are we set for the Selby test?" the woman asked the biker with the heart and dagger tattoo.

Giving her a disgusted look, the biker said with exaggerated patience, "Sharon, that's why I'm going there. If it goes well, and I expect it will, we will need to step up our collections. I have teams waiting for instructions for the September and October events, but they will need cash to purchase their supplies." Continuing to address Sharon, he added, "You have not been as successful as we had hoped. Why?"

"Why? Well, darling brother, because I was under the impression we wanted to stay under the radar, and every time a hiker goes missing, staying under the radar becomes more and more difficult," she said with a forced smile as her words fairly dripped with sarcasm. "If you haven't checked, the Appalachian Trail doesn't touch much of the parkway, so locating hikers on the parkway turns out to be tricky. I am not about to run the risk of 'collecting' anymore from the Skyline Drive this year. They have too much law enforcement patrolling the drive."

Looking long and hard at Sharon, the biker finally said, "Fine. But if we run short of cash, darling sister, what would you suggest?"

"That you should have been less spendy to begin with?"

"Well, since that horse has already left the barn, what would you suggest?"

The man with the twisted star tattoo, said, "Knock it off, you two! Everybody's sick of your bickering! We have a job to do and you two wallowing in your ancient sibling rivalry is a waste of time and energy. Papa wants this done and I'm not stupid enough to disappoint him."

The brother and sister sat glaring at each other until finally Sharon asked, "You want that beer now?"

CHAPTER 36

The next morning, as the couples climbed into the Franklin's Jeep to drive into Hillsville for breakfast, Annie asked, "Did you have a nice visit with that young man? I felt as though you were unsure as to how he knew you."

"Unsure is an understatement!" Madge replied. "I'm floored that he remembered me—us—from a party with so many people."

"He commented on your ability with some kind of a gun. We did not know you were proficient with firearms," Annie continued somewhat hesitantly.

"Um, well, yes. I love to shoot. At targets," Madge said matter-of-factly. Then she added with excitement, "But we won't be doing any of that today. I'm looking forward to showing you around Mount Airy, North Carolina. When you've watched American TV, have you ever seen a show called *Mayberry RFD* or *The Andy Griffith Show*?"

"Yes. We have seen both. We like the America portrayed in those shows."

"Well," Madge continued, "the town in those shows—Mayberry—was modeled after Mount Airy, North Carolina, where Andy Griffith lived. The Andy Griffith Museum used to be in his home but is now in a proper museum. Personally, I don't think it's as much fun, but that's just me. Anyway, the town is very 'Andy Griffith' friendly. We can take a tour in a vintage patrol car, have fried pork sandwiches at the Snappy Lunch, check out Floyd's Barber Shop and Wally's Service Station, or just enjoy wandering in and out of the shops downtown. There's a great sock shop there where you can get top-of-the-line socks at a real discount."

After pausing briefly to catch her breath, Madge continued, "Mount Airy is famous for more than Andy Griffith. It was also the home of Chang and Eng Bunker, the original Siamese twins, and there's an extensive display about them in the museum. While Mount Airy likes to be known as The Friendly City, it's also known as The Granite City since the world's largest open-face granite quarry is there."

While pausing again to catch her breath, Paul quipped, "If we get tired of traveling around, I do believe you could get a job with the Chamber of Commerce."

"You don't have to be snide. I happen to like Mount Airy and think it's cool for a town so small to be so famous for so many different things, and most people don't know about them," Madge said with conviction.

Laughing, Paul said, "I'm just teasing. I love it when you get all worked up about something—good, bad or indifferent—your passion is contagious."

Frowning, Madge said, "Thank you, I think. Ah, Annie, I could use some help here."

Annie and Gerard had been trying to control their laughter but, at that point, gave up and burst out laughing. "Oh, Madge. You and Paul are the funniest people. It is our pleasure to be able to travel with you and I am sure our day in Mount Airy will be memorable. But what is a pork sandwich?"

Now it was Madge's turn to laugh. "Nothing good for you. That's for sure. But it's a classic, and the tour buses all stop there so folks can have the experience. As for what it is, well, it's a nice piece of pork, fried on a grill and served on a bun. You'll want to order it 'all the way,' which includes slaw and I can't remember what else. However, I do remember that it is unbelievably messy and delicious."

"Yum," Paul noted. "Now I'm hungry."

"Well, you won't have long to wait for breakfast," Madge noted. "The coffee shop is just around the corner, and you can pig out on yummy food and great coffee."

As they left the café, Annie said, "Madge, you were correct about the food and coffee. Gerard and I truly enjoyed breakfast. It seemed much more European than some place like McDonald's or Denny's. And the coffee selections were excellent. So, thank you."

"No prob," Madge said. "We found this one time when I wanted a mom-and-pop kind of place and this turned out to be perfect. Locating it was a hoot. I'd seen the billboard on the road but hadn't gotten the address. So we stopped at several local places, like the barber shop, and asked where a good mom-and-pop breakfast place was. Everyone said there wasn't one in town. I was about to give up when I saw a woman come out of a door carrying a to-go cup of coffee. And low and behold, she was coming out of the café. I ended up telling the owner he needed better PR. I should have added he might consider shortening the name. 'DT's Blue Ridge Java Coffee Shop & Café' is quite a mouthful! Anyway, glad it worked. But I was pretty sure it would," she added with a grin.

CHAPTER 37

Later that day, as the sun disappeared behind the mountains, the moonless sky filled with the brilliance of a trillion stars. Although the late June air was softly warm, campfires—some small, some not so small—danced merrily at almost every occupied campsite.

"Okay, Annie, if you had to do an instant replay of one thing you did or saw today, what would it be?" Madge asked as the foursome sat around their own low campfire after supper.

Sighing, Annie thought for a while before she said, "I think the way I felt in the original downtown area. I felt a sense of calm and peace we do not experience in many American towns and certainly not in the large cities. There was no hurry in anything we did. Nor did the store clerks act harried. Everyone was friendly and seemed to have all the time in the world to chat and visit. It was a most pleasant experience."

"How about you, Gerard," Madge pressed as she turned to him. "Would you share your impression with Annie so that she can pass it on to us?"

"Yes," Gerard said with a smile before reverting to French.

"He says," Annie explained, "that he enjoyed the entire day but, if he had to choose, he liked the granite quarry and was then able to understand why so many of the houses have granite as part of their construction."

"I agree," Paul added as he stood to poke the fire. "But I think my favorite is the museum. I like to watch TV, and I loved seeing some of the artifacts and props that had been used in the shows."

Sitting back down, Paul pointed toward the road. Casting a long look at Madge, he said, "Here comes Greg."

"Should we return to our RV?" Annie asked.

"Absolutely not," Paul replied with conviction. "We're not close friends, and I don't imagine our conversation will be anything other than casual. He seems to travel in a different subculture than we do, so we may just get a view of how the others live."

"Hey, Greg," Madge called out. "Can you join us?"

"Not tonight," he said. "My friends and I are going to check out a bar that features local musicians. The guys I'm riding with play guitars and are heavily into bluegrass, which seems to be pretty big around here. We had talked about getting together tonight and I didn't want to just run off and seem rude. Are you leaving tomorrow?"

"Yes," Paul answered. "And our first stop is the Blue Ridge Music Center. Might be a good place for your friends to check out too."

"That's a real possibility. Maybe I'll see you guys there in the morning. Well, need to be going. Have a good evening."

With that, Greg turned and walked quickly back to the road.

"Goodness, that was fast," Madge observed. "I wanted to find out where this bar is. We might want to check it out ourselves. Maybe Annie and Gerard would enjoy some local bluegrass in an authentic setting," she added with a twinkle in her eye.

"If you think that it would be safe and appropriate, we would be glad to go with you," Annie replied with some hesitation.

Shaking his head and giving Madge a disapproving look, Paul said, "No, Annie, we're not going to the biker bar. Madge was trying to get a rise out of you, and it looks as though she succeeded. I'm sure it would be perfectly safe, but we would probably look very out of place. Besides, tomorrow we'll be at the Blue Ridge Music Center, where you can steep yourself in the history and the culture of—not only bluegrass—but also American music as it has developed into what it is today."

"Well, aren't you just the most learned tour escort around," Madge teased. "That was a pretty good summary. You make Mamma proud!"

"Thank you, ma'am. Every now and then I actually pay attention," Paul stated with pride as he placed another log on the low-burning fire.

Gerard reached for the wine bottle and, with a smile, ceremoniously refilled each glass. He then raised his glass in a toast and said, carefully in English, "To friends."

CHAPTER 38

With only about 110 miles to travel on Sunday, the group decided to enjoy a lazy morning. They planned to enjoy breakfast in their RVs and head out for the day's adventure no later than ten o'clock. However, when Paul checked the morning news, he learned the East Coast was being battered by an early tropical storm and the weather service predicted the rain would make its way to the Blue Ridge by late afternoon. Calling Annie, he asked if they could change plans and be ready to leave by nine.

"Of course," she replied. Then teased, "We do not make breakfast as complicated as the English and Americans."

"Yeah, but you enjoy pancakes and eggs as much as I do," Paul teased back. "Madge is finishing up in the kitchen, and I'll have us unhooked and ready to roll by nine. Have Gerard fall in behind us today."

By leaving an hour early, the group arrived at the Blue Ridge Music Center before it opened at ten. As Paul pulled into the first RV slot, he silently said a 'thank you' that he and Gerard were the first RVs to arrive. Getting out would be so much easier than if had they been in the far back slot.

Once out of their RVs, the friends grouped together to look around. Surrounded by rolling, grassy meadowland, the main building appeared to sit atop a small knoll, while a portion of the building seemed to be built into the knoll itself. A pathway led to an amphitheater where weekend visitors could enjoy a variety of free concerts. But at this time of day, the only sounds were birds chirping, bees buzzing, and the growing-ever-closer growl of motorcycles. Madge and Paul glanced at each other with suspicion as Greg, Marco, and three other riders cruised into the lot and parked their bikes.

Removing their helmets, Greg hailed Madge and Paul with a hand wave and called out, "I'm glad you're here. We were actually hoping to catch up with you. Marco wants to talk to you, if you have time."

"Sure," Paul said. "Let's go sit over at those tables. I think we have ten minutes or so before we can even get in."

While walking over to the tables, introductions were made and, because the tables were four-seaters, Annie and Gerard indicated they would stroll down the path and look at the amphitheater. Marco and Greg sat at one table and their three friends sat at another.

"What's up?" Madge asked.

"Well, Marco doesn't like some of the stuff he's been hearing. I'm going to be taking off and won't be hanging with them after today. But I suggested you guys might be able to advise him as to what he should or shouldn't do."

"Can you be more specific?" Paul asked.

Greg looked at Marco and said, "Go ahead, man. I think they're okay."

Looking long and hard at both Paul and Madge, Marco finally said, "We're bikers. A lot of bikers have a real bad rep. And some of it's deserved. There're some bad asses out there. Some are in clubs and then there are some that are loners. Sometime the loners are the worst of the bunch. Us, well, we just want to be able to ride and make our music. We're proud to live in a country where we can live the life we do."

He stopped as if searching for words and Madge prompted him with, "Okay, how can we help?"

"There's talk," he said. "Talk we don't like."

"What kind of talk?" Paul asked innocently.

"Talk about causing trouble. Things like how much fun it would be to blow up a bridge or an electric relay station or a firehouse. There's even talk about messing with people's heads by disrupting local events like fairs and festivals. Hearing it once seemed like just some local misfit spouting off. That was more than six months ago. But now you hear stuff everywhere. From the North Carolina coast to the Virginia mountains. Ugly

119

stuff. Somebody needs to look into it. Greg thought because you travel so much you might have heard something too. Or maybe you'd know who to tell."

"That's pretty scary, all right," Madge offered. "It's kind of weird that different people would be talking about the same kind of thing in so many different places. Must be a big Internet thing. You know how crazy stuff can go wild on the Internet."

"No, that's just the thing. Whenever it's mentioned, the person always says something like, 'If you want in, pass it on person-to-person. Don't use the phone or the net. You know Big Brother is everywhere.' Then laughs like the whole thing's just a big joke."

"Hmm," Paul said. "Well, Madge, what do you think?"

"I think this could be a real problem in the making. Marco, have you ever seen the same person making any of these suggestions?"

"Only once. Early on. Saw him first down in Harkers Island, North Carolina, then again with a group out of Stanley, Virginia."

"Can you describe him?" Paul asked.

"Not really. Nothing special. Regular looking biker." Then he paused, looked hopefully between Madge and Paul, and asked, "Shouldn't somebody do something?"

"Yeah," Madge said. "Somebody should. I have a friend who may have some ideas about what to do. Look, let us give you our contact information. It's probably best if you don't challenge these folks, but you should feel free to contact us anytime you hear stuff that you feel should be passed on. I'm not sure my friend can help, but at least it's something. I'm sorry we can't offer any kind of instant solution, but, at this point, it sounds like what you're talking about is just rumors."

"Yeah," Marco said, "let's hope it stays that way. Well, thanks for listening and thanks for your contact info. We don't want any trouble. Just want to ride and make our music."

"We understand," Paul said sympathetically. "If you haven't been in the museum, I'm absolutely sure you will enjoy it. I certainly did. I was amazed to learn that bluegrass music had its roots in the music brought to this area by the folks who came from Germany, Scotland, and Ireland, and the slaves from Africa. They combined the music and the musical instruments of their homelands and, eventually, out came bluegrass. Then from that grew jazz, pop, rock, and on and on. Who knew? Such a cool history!" Paul chuckled before continuing. "I keep saying I'm going to learn to play the banjo, but guitar didn't work so great for me so, more than likely, I'll pass. Hey, look who's back," he said as Annie and Gerard came up to the table.

"I think the museum is now open," Annie offered. "Are you going in with us?" she asked looking at Marco and Greg.

"Well, we're going in," Greg answered. "I think the museum is probably self-guiding, but I'm sure we'll keep bumping into each other," he added with a laugh. "I probably won't be seeing you after today. I'm heading on south and need to move along faster than Marco here is willing to travel. So, even though we'll be bumping into each other in the museum, I'll say my goodbyes now. It was great seeing you again, and be sure to give Donny my best the next time you talk to him."

"Will do, and you take care," Madge said as Greg and Paul shook hands and the two groups worked their way up the steps, through the door, and into the museum.

CHAPTER 39

As the foursome exited the museum, they found themselves buffeted by strong gusts of wind and noticed dark clouds boiling westward from the eastern sky.

"Uh-oh," observed Paul. "Looks like we may get caught in a downpour. Maybe we can outrun it. But, if we can't, how do you feel about shopping and sightseeing in the rain?"

"What do you mean?" Annie asked.

"Well, we'd planned to stop at the Moses H. Cone Memorial Park, which houses one of the premier craft centers on the parkway. Their products are exquisite, and Madge has purchased several pottery pieces there that she's very fond of. Then wandering around the town of Blowing Rock is always fun. It's quaint and very up-scale, with some delightful restaurants. It's what we think of as the high-rent district with down-home charm," Paul explained.

While clamping her hand on her head to keep her ball cap from flying away, Madge said, "Those two places are pretty much together and about eighty miles south of here. Let's see how things look when we get down there. Even if we miss Moses Cone, we'll still be able to get to the Folk Art Center, and I don't think, as well traveled as Gerard and Annie are, that missing Blowing Rock will be the end of the world. Even though we're dry camping tonight at Linville Falls, I'd rather not arrive in howling wind and torrential rain. Anyway, that's my vote. Wait and see. Then keep going if the weather is really awful."

"I am in favor of doing things as Madge suggested," Annie offered. "We have no need to purchase many things, and not driving the RV in heavy wind and rain would be our choice."

"Good plan," Paul said. "Let's get on the road. We can pull into an overlook for a quick lunch. I'll watch for one that will hold both RVs. A ten-minute stop should take care of the lunch needs for me. Gerard, can you eat and drive at the same time?"

Annie started to translate but Gerard had already nodded that yes, he could drive and eat.

"Knew he understood," Paul said as he and Gerard grinned at each other.

By the time they reached the turnoff for Blowing Rock, the weather had deteriorated to high wind, sprinkles, and dark skies. At that point it was a no-brainer to just keep going to the campground at Linville Falls. Madge hoped the storm would be fast-moving since they only had a one-night reservation at Linville, and they were expected at Pride RV Park in Maggie Valley, North Carolina, the next day. Of course, she could get on the phone and shuffle things around, and, since it was the beginning of the week, staying another night at Linville Falls would probably not be a problem but, dang, what a pain. She hated it when she had to rearrange her already established reservations.

"Hey, pretty lady. What's with the sour face?" Paul asked when he glanced over at his wife.

"Oh, just thinking about reservations and stuff," Madge grumped. "Sorry, it'll be okay. I don't know why I make such a big deal over such small stuff," she said with a forced, fake smile.

Chuckling, Paul was wise enough to just smile and keep driving.

Eighteen miles later he led the way into the campground at Linville Falls. The sky still spit light rain, but that didn't stop Madge from hopping out to handle the registration, and before long both RVs were safely parked in pull-through sites. No longer grumpy, Madge felt very pleased that she'd been smart enough to reserve pull-throughs for both units. No messing around with back-in directions or unhooking the Jeep.

The original plan was to do some hiking after they got in and set up. However, considering the weather, they decided to simply hunker down in their respective RVs and spend the time reading and relaxing. Tomorrow would be soon enough to venture onto the trails. Also, not being committed to group activities allowed

Madge time to place a call to Charles and bring him up-to-date on all that had happened with Greg and Marco. Charles' parting comment to Madge was, "Good job giving Marco your contact information. I hope he can provide something concrete we can follow up on. Keep up the good work."

CHAPTER 40

On Sunday morning, the hiker left her car on the parkway at the trailhead. Even though dark clouds boiled overhead, she wasn't worried. Storms often blew in at this altitude and, even if it did rain, she thought it would probably be a fast-moving event. The parking permit on her dashboard allowed her car to remain at the trailhead until sundown on Tuesday. Being given Monday and Tuesday off had been an unexpected gift, and she had no intention of letting the threat of a little rain interrupt her three days of back-to-nature alone time.

Five hours later, she found she was pushing herself harder than she wanted to. Even though she'd gotten her poncho out before the true downpour began, it offered no protection below the knees. Her rain-soaked boots squeaked and sloshed with every step. She could feel the blisters beginning to blossom at her heels. She hated pitching her tent in the rain, but no shelters existed within any reasonable distance. She needed to pitch her tent as soon as possible. But not here. Too much shrubbery. The rhododendron, laurel, and blueberry bushes created an impenetrable wall on each side of the trail. Feeling cold, miserable, and somewhat disheartened, she trudged on.

The trail led to a narrow dirt road, which she followed to a meadow, where several trailheads converged. The vault toilet there was a welcome sight—until she opened the door and discovered previous hikers had used it as a dumping ground, rendering it completely unusable.

She considered just turning around and going back to her car, but it was so late in the day she would have to hike after dark.

All right, she thought, *there was no good spot to tent between my car and here. So there's no point in turning around. Camp-*

ing here isn't permitted, and I still have two hours of daylight. Surely these shrubs have to give way to some tent space. I'll hike down the trail until I find a reasonable spot and pitch my tent. When the sun comes out tomorrow, I'll stay put, dry everything out, and head back then. It's Sunday and only a one-day hike back to the car. My permit is good till sundown on Tuesday, so no prob.

As she prepared to walk through the meadow to continue on her chosen trail, a woman with an umbrella stepped out from the back of a tired-looking panel truck. The woman called to the hiker, saying, "Hey, you look like a wet puppy. I can't offer you much beyond a dry place to change your boots and socks and a hot cup of coffee or tea, but you'd be welcome company. I'm waiting for my son, so I'm not going anywhere anytime soon."

The hiker thought for only a very brief moment before thanking the woman and following her into the truck.

CHAPTER 41

Madge woke early the next morning and decided to take advantage of some alone time by going for a walk. Not wanting to disturb Paul, she left the blinds in the RV down. The thick cloud she encountered when she opened the door took her by surprise. The cloud vapor was so thick she could barely make out the RV in the adjoining site. This didn't trouble her. She was used to being socked in at Shenandoah. Frequently the clouds hung low over the mountains early in the day. By the time the sun reached midmorning, the clouds lifted and gave way to beautiful sunny skies. She hoped that would be the case today. Still, there was nothing like walking through the woods wrapped in a cloud. She remembered the time at Shenandoah when their then very young grandson had been excited to walk from the campground to the Wayside 'inside a cloud.' Even after going home he would ask his mom when they could go back to the restaurant in the clouds.

As she walked the campground, she began to calculate the time frame needed for that day's driving and stopping.

Four and a half to five hours for the one hundred thirty-five-plus miles at thirty miles an hour. An hour at the Museum of North Carolina Minerals. Another two hours at the Folk Art Center and, somewhere in there, time for lunch. Eight hours minimum, with a lot of that driving time.

Hmm, she thought. *It's six now. Annie and Gerard are usually early risers, so they're probably already up. If we can get out of here by eight—shucks, that won't help. The mineral museum doesn't open till nine and it's only about ten miles south. Okay. Let's say we leave by eight thirty. Cut the museum time to thirty minutes. No matter how we slice it, it's going to be a long day. We're getting into the really high, curvy section of road. Lots of great views and scenery. I'd like to have time to stop at Craggy Gardens and even walk up to the top of the mountain there—if the clouds have lifted. But, we really can't go anywhere till things clear up here. Actually, if the sun hasn't broken through by eight thirty, we might as well just plan to stay here till tomorrow. We can do the mineral museum today as well as hike the trails here and, if we want to, we could even drive back to Blowing Rock for supper. Means unhooking the Jeep, but that's no biggie. Okay. Executive decision made. We're here for another night. If we do the mineral museum today, and there's no cloud cover in the morning, we can leave at o'dark-thirty and not feel rushed at all. Good plan, old girl.*

Feeling very pleased with herself, she continued to wander the campground. She loved the quiet of the early morning. Something almost magical happened to sound when the clouds—or fog, as most people thought of it—were so thick. All the usual sounds seemed to be sucked up in the cloud. Her footsteps were muffled. The normal rustle of leaves was hushed. Even the usual sounds of other early risers stoking up their last night's fire didn't penetrate the mist. No birds chirped their early morning songs. Even the noisy squirrels and chipmunks, always so busy chasing each other and scampering for nuts, were silent. Madge smiled contentedly. *Does it really get any better than this?* she wondered as she headed back to the RVs to share the new plans with the group.

Surprisingly, everyone seemed relieved to have a whole day to just poke around. Annie and Gerard found being enveloped in a cloud delightful—as long as they didn't have to drive in it. They were accustomed to fog but had not expected to find themselves in the clouds on the Blue Ridge Parkway. Madge explained it was not unusual, especially at this time of year.

The cloud cover had not lifted by nine o'clock when the foursome left for the Museum of North Carolina Minerals. Located just west of the parkway, the museum showcased the twenty-five-mile-long mining district centered around Spruce Pine, North Carolina. The mountains around Spruce Pine contained some of the richest deposits of minerals and gems in the entire world.

Madge couldn't help but give notice that she was a closet rock hound and that Annie and Gerard should feel free to haul her away when they had had their fill of rocks and minerals.

"I just find it beyond fascinating," she offered, "that right here, in little ole Spruce Pine, under them thar hills, rest deposits of some of the purest quartz in the world. In fact, it's so pure that they say most computer chips manufactured worldwide come from Spruce Pine quartz. If I remember correctly, sometime around 2009, a ton of Spruce Pine quartz went for fifty thousand dollars a ton. Besides minerals, this area produces lots of gems. In fact, there are places along the highway where you can buy a bucket of dirt and mine for emeralds, rubies, amethysts, and garnets. We've done that a couple of times. Found some cool stones that we've had faceted. Since we have all day, we can work that in if it's something you think you would enjoy."

"Thank you, Madge. We will think on that," Annie said with a smile. "However, I think if, when we return to the campground, the air is clear enough, we would enjoy hiking to the waterfalls."

"Hey, that works for us too. We can choose between several hikes of varying difficulty. The only one Paul and I have actually done is the easy one, but we're up for whatever you think you would enjoy."

The group spent more time in the museum than Madge had expected and it was close to lunchtime when they finally returned to the RVs. By then the sun had burned away the clouds, the sky was a nearly cloudless blue, and a gentle breeze helped remove the last visage of rain from the leaves overhead.

After reviewing the different hikes available to the falls, Annie and Gerard decided on the easy one that Madge and Paul had done in the past. Listed as flatter than the other trails, this one hugged the stream and brought hikers to the top of the falls on the southeast side of the river. Since they had all afternoon, the friends walked slowly. They walked mostly in silence as good friends who are comfortable with each can do. It was an afternoon to enjoy both the beauty of the area and the solitude afforded by a lack of visitors. The sounds of the river, the falls, and the forest itself proved sufficient stimulation, and the foursome returned to their RVs feeling revived in mind, body, and spirit.

CHAPTER 42

It wasn't quite o'dark thirty when the group left the Linville Falls Campground the next morning, but they did get away by eight o'clock sharp. Yesterday's clouds were history and the two RVs drove the parkway in pure sunshine and crystal clear mountain air. As tour guide, Madge determined their first stop would be Craggy Gardens. While only fifty miles south of Linville Falls, the drive included high mountains, twisty roads, and awesome views. The recent rain created some serious waterfalls that poured out of the rock cliffs on the side of the road. Madge had mentioned they would see 'weeping rocks' and was gratified that, because of the rain, Mother Nature wouldn't be letting her down.

Because the scenery was so outstanding, Paul suggested Gerard lead once again. That way they could go as slowly as necessary to enjoy the views. Consequently, the fifty-mile drive became close to a two-hour event.

Tucked in among the rocky outcroppings, the rhododendron bushes in the Craggy Gardens area provided a riot of color. Many of the balds—areas barren of trees—were covered by rhododendron bushes, creating a pink to purple haze as far as the eye could see. Even before the two RVs got parked, Annie keyed the walkie-talkie to announce, "This is truly spectacular!"

"I thought you'd like it," Madge answered as Paul shut down the engine. "You might want a light sweater or jacket. We're up over five thousand feet and it's usually cool and breezy. Be out as soon as I grab my wrap."

Stepping out of the RV, Madge spread her arms and inhaled deeply. "It's at times like this that I just want to wrap my arms around the entire world!" she said to Paul as she stood with her arms outstretched and the sun on her face.

"I know, Missy," Paul said gently as he stood behind her, slipped his arms around her waist, and rested his cheek on her head.

The two stood quietly, gazing at the westward view when Annie and Gerard announced their arrival with a clearing of throats before Annie asked respectfully, "Are we interrupting something?"

Laughing, Paul answered, "No, no not at all. We were just enjoying the view. These are called the Craggy Mountains for good reason. It's all about the rocks. The few trees here are mostly gnarled sweet birch and mountain ash. The bald areas between the rocks are called heath and are covered with a combination of rhododendron, wildflowers, and blueberries. Later in the summer, the wildflowers are almost as spectacular as the rhodo are now, and, in the fall, the clusters of deep red berries on the mountain ash will blow you completely away."

"My, my, aren't you just the poetic one," Madge teased with a giggle.

"Hey, just because I'm a guy doesn't mean I can't wax poetic now and then," Paul said defensively.

"I support Paul's point of view regarding men and poetry," Annie said. Adding with conviction she continued, "Many of our greatest poets have been men. The scenery here is sufficiently breathtaking as to inspire poetic rhetoric."

"Well, now that we've covered the academic as well as the emotional fine points of our location, let's check out the physical side by hiking into the visitor center, then up that ole mountain to the trail shelter. It's only about three tenths of a mile, but, as you can see, it's a pretty steep climb. Once we get there, we can decide if we want to continue."

Between the altitude and the steepness of the climb, the group decided not to do anymore hiking at Craggy Gardens. By the time they got back on the road, it was eleven o'clock and Madge suggested they go on to the Folk Art Center and the Blue Ridge Parkway Visitor Center. She was sure they would find a spot to fix lunch somewhere between Craggy Gardens and US 276, where she planned for them to exit the parkway.

The inn at Mt. Pisgah used to be one of her favorite places to eat. However, because of its proximity to Asheville, it had become way too popular, and she had no intention of getting into the crowd there. Besides, after talking about it, neither she nor Paul could remember any room for the RVs. They planned to take Annie and Gerard to several attractions in the Asheville area but decided day-tripping from Maggie Valley would work better than trying to either take the RVs or finding a place to park them and unhitch the Jeep.

They were nearing the highest section of the parkway and the views were spectacular. When Paul saw an overlook where both RVs would fit, he pulled in. Although he felt somewhat guilty about the two RVs taking up most of the view, he knew they would eat quickly, so he pushed the guilt aside and turned off the engine. Facing south and pulled to the east side of the road, the tables in both RVs faced the awesome view. While Paul settled himself at the table, Madge pulled some spinach-artichoke dip out of the fridge and grabbed the box of Ritz crackers. "Water or Coke Zero?" she asked.

"I'm fine with water," Paul said. "By the way, have you told Annie and Gerard that we're getting off the parkway at 276?"

"Yep," Madge answered as she sat down, picked up a cracker and spread it with a very generous portion of dip. "They understand the reasons and are fine with day-tripping. I just think the parkway between Soco Gap and Wagon Road Gap is so awesome that Gerard doesn't need to be bothered with driving. This way, he and Annie can ride with us and be more relaxed. We'll take the parkway when we do the Cradle of Forestry but go up the interstate when we visit Biltmore." Pausing to spread another cracker, she continued, "We will also take the parkway when we go down to Cherokee so they will actually get to drive or ride the entire four hundred and sixty-nine miles."

"You're such a good tour escort," Paul quipped. "Want to make this a career?"

Giving Paul a sideways glance, Madge thought for a moment before saying, "Maybe. This is kind of fun. I love seeing the excitement on their faces when we're doing something that's new to them, and reexperiencing some of our favorite places with someone else doubles the fun for me. So, maybe not a career, but I wouldn't mind doing this again in some other part of the country with someone else sometime. Maybe."

Looking at his wife, a smile spread slowly across Paul's face. "You never cease to amaze me," he said while slowly shaking his head from side to side. "So, where's our next adventure?"

"Not so fast, Mr. Smarty. We have to finish this tour thing then head back the way we came, playing super sleuths before we can plan anything else. Goodness knows where this—whatever you want to call it—gossip, rumor, whatever—will lead to. I can't believe we're going to be of any real use to Charles, but I'm willing to hang in. If there's even the teeniest chance we could help stop a disaster—well—you know," she said, looking over at her husband.

"Uh-huh, I sure do know, and I also know you're just itching to get yourself right in the middle of whatever it is. I also know whoever is behind this is not a nice person and is recruiting more not-nice people. So, Sweet Pea, I think it's great if we can help out by passing along news or messages. But," he added while giving Madge his most serious look, "that's where it begins and ends."

Nodding her head, Madge said, "Absolutely! Absolutely!" as she smiled and began clearing away the crackers and dip.

CHAPTER 43

Before starting up again, Paul wanted to talk to Gerard about how he felt about driving off the parkway. The distance wouldn't be that far, but Paul wanted to be sure Gerard was comfortable with driving the RV in traffic. If he said he wasn't, then Plan B was to recruit Madge to drive the rental—even though she wasn't on the 'approved driver' list with the rental company. Also, he hadn't mentioned Plan B to Madge and hoped he wouldn't have to. Driving RVs was not one of her favorite pastimes. Fortunately, Gerard said he had no problem driving the RV, and Paul chuckled remembering how comfortable Gerard had been driving the van they had all chipped in to rent when Annie and Gerard toured the Franklins around France.

The pair exited the parkway at US 276 heading west. Fortunately, traffic was light. Both drivers had the address programed into their GPSs, so even if they became separated, Paul felt they would be okay. He breathed a small sigh of relief when, after maneuvering through Waynesville, Lake Junaluska, and Dellwood, he saw Gerard in his side mirror with only one car between them. Once into the outskirts of Maggie Valley, they made the right turn onto Jonathan Creek Road and shortly thereafter turned right into the entrance of Pride RV Park. Once again, Madge and Annie hopped out and took care of the registrations.

It pleased Madge that they had been assigned pull-in sites on the riverbank. The front of each RV faced a lovely, grassy area that bumped up to the south side of the shallow, rocky, bubbling river. Called a river, right now it looked more like a large stream. Madge knew—from experience—it had the capability of becoming a raging river. Once before she and Paul had been parked on the riverfront when, during an especially brutal storm, the 'stream' overflowed its banks and the swollen waters came within a couple of feet of the front of the RV. Scattered along the edge of the river were an assortment of well-spaced picnic tables, Adirondack chairs, and even a couple of porch swings hung from frames staked to the ground.

By the time both men had the units hooked to the utilities, Madge and Annie had the insides of the RVs 'nested' and ready to use. Madge had also gotten their outside rug down and arranged four folding lawn chairs and two little folding tables neatly under the awning. As Madge opened a storage compartment to pull out their outside candles, Annie came over wearing a giant smile.

"This is lovely," she said as she turned in a full circle to take in a 360-degree view of her surroundings. "We will enjoy our time here. Thank you for finding such a pleasant location."

"I'm glad you like it. We've enjoyed many happy weeks here. It's not quite five o'clock, but I think it would be all right if we sipped on a wine cooler. What do you think?"

Laughing, Annie agreed and offered to provide the wine.

"Nope. Not this time," Madge said. "This is a 'house specialty,' so it's on us."

"How do you make your wine coolers?" Annie asked.

"With whatever the current house red is and diet tonic water over ice. Then the secret ingredient—a twist of lime. Yum—and soooo00 refreshing. Probably not very French, but then it's also not very alcoholic," she added with a laugh. "Sit down, relax, enjoy the ducks, and I'll be back in a jiff," Madge said as she went into the RV. Paul went in right behind her to wash his hands and, when he saw what she was doing, asked if he could help.

"Nope, got it," was all Madge said with a grin. "Go keep our guests company. Oh, wait, you can take out a couple bowls of nuts. Good to munch on something while drinking," she announced with authority.

"Yes, ma'am!" Paul replied as he pulled the container of mixed nuts out of the cabinet and filled two plastic bowls. "Anything else?" he asked.

"Nope, all done," she said as she put four glasses on a tray and headed for the door.

Outside, Annie and Gerard were quietly chatting away in French, but Annie switched to English as soon as Madge and Paul joined them.

"We were just talking about what you have planned for us while we are here. Would you mind telling us again? I am afraid neither of us committed everything to memory, and I did not write any of it down," Annie said apologetically.

"Not to worry," Madge said with aplomb, "my plan was to go over all the options with you. There are many, many, many things to do and see in this area, and much of it we're going to leave for the two of you to do—or not to do—on your own. I've already checked with the folks here, and you can stay for up to two weeks if you want to. Do you want to do this now of after supper?"

"I think now would be good," Annie said with a nod of her head.

"Okay," Madge agreed. "Let's move to the picnic table. I'll get a map and we can go over the options together."

Once settled at the table with a couple of maps, Madge launched into her plan.

Pointing to the map, she said, "We are south of Asheville. We definitely want to go with you to the Biltmore Estate and to the Cradle of Forestry. Each one of those outings could take an entire day. However, if we leave early enough in the morning, we could do both in one day. That's something we can play by ear. Then we want to go with you to Cherokee. The Cherokee area is worth a week, in and of itself, so you might want to actually take the RV there for a few days, but you'll be able to figure that out after the four of us do a recon trip there." Switching from the parkway map to the map on the back of the Smokies Guide, Madge continued. "See how from here there is only one logical way through the Smokies?" she asked as she pointed to US 441, which bisected the park from north to south. "Notice that Cherokee is on our side—as it were—and Gatlinburg, Tennessee, is on the other. Now, to do justice to the area, you need to spend time on both sides of the park. I'm not a big fan of going back and forth, so when we do the Cherokee area we usually stay in Cherokee and then move to Townsend, Tennessee, to catch the north side of the park. While we are here, we'll catch the Asheville attractions, do the recon into Cherokee, and take you to the Cataloochee area of the park to see the elk. Then you can decide just how much more time you want to spend in the area, where you'd like to spend it, and whether or not you're going to continue in the RV or go back to moteling it."

Pausing, Madge looked at Annie and Gerard, who had begun quietly conferring in French. "Are we correct in feeling that you and Paul may be leaving us at the end of the three or four days you mentioned?" Annie asked with concern.

"That's a possibility," Paul said. "But it will depend, in part, on what you and Gerard decide to do and how you decide to do it. If you want to turn in the RV, rent a car, and revert to motels, we will let you go on your way. However, at this time, all options are open, and I think we should just focus on the next three or four days. We are both reserved in here for five days, which gives us ample time to both tour and chill. Right, Madge?"

"Yep. And I'm looking forward to doing both—chilling and touring," Madge said with a wicked grin. "Furthermore, I'm looking forward to not cooking tonight. So, Annie and Gerard, would you please do us the honor of being our guests at a local eatery?"

Looking at each other, Annie and Gerard answered at the same time with, "Thank you," and "*Merci.*"

CHAPTER 44

Madge and Paul awakened Wednesday morning to the sound of the sawmill across the river. Smiling at each other, they dressed while the coffee brewed, then took their filled cups outside and breathed deeply the scent of freshly cut wood.

"I hope Annie and Gerard aren't annoyed by the sawmill," Madge said. "It doesn't operate every day, but I forgot to mention that sometimes the mill starting early in the morning was a possibility."

"I wouldn't worry about it," Paul said. "They're pretty easygoing. Not much seems to bother them, and, as much of the world as they've traveled, I imagine they've dealt with worse than being awakened by the sound of a sawmill."

As he finished his observation, Annie appeared around the front of the RV with her own cup of steaming coffee. "Good morning!" she sang out. Taking a deep breath through her nose, she added, "What a delightful way to begin the day. I love the aroma of freshly sawn wood, and to think it is available here along with the music of a babbling river."

"You're kidding, right?" Madge asked suspiciously.

"Not at all," came the assured response. "This is typically local and semirural America. We love it!"

"See, told you," Paul chided.

"Hey. I'm just glad you're not annoyed," Madge said happily. "They don't operate every day, but the early morning buzzing could happen again."

"We are not annoyed at all," Annie assured her. "And we are looking forward to the relaxed day you have planned. It will be nice to get some laundry done this morning, and a picnic supper with the elk will be a new experience for us," she added with a grin.

"Well, we have plenty of time. I think leaving around three will be fine. We can both get laundry done and, after that, it will be nice to just sit for a bit and read a book. Paul's into the new Lee Child book, and I have a Mitch Rapp that I've been wanting to start. Did you guys bring any fun, light reading with you?"

"I am not sure what you call 'fun, light reading,' but we do have several books on the history of different sections of the United States that we would enjoy reading before we get to those places. We have one that we have been reading in the evenings. It is called *The Trail of Tears*. I feel we should try to finish it before we go to Cherokee."

"Yeah, well, that's not a pretty story, and you can see first-hand how painful it would have been to be forced out of this beautiful land, let alone being force marched more than halfway across the country. Pure evil is what it was, and it just breaks my heart!" Madge said angrily.

"Whoa, girl," Paul said as he put his hand on Madge's shoulder and looked at Annie. "The treatment of our native Americans by our forefathers is a touchy subject with Madge. She somehow feels responsible, even though the abuses occurred over a hundred years ago."

"You don't need to talk about me as though I'm not here," Madge said. "I know I'm not responsible, but that changes neither the facts nor the tragedy. Too many of the consequences of our collective stupidity still manifest themselves today in the way we continue to manage our 'Indian' affairs." Shrugging, she continued, "Obviously, I don't have the answers to these very complex issues. If I did, I'd be doing something about them." Then, as if to herself, she added, "Don't know why people can't just get along!"

By then Gerard had joined the group and Paul mentioned that he and Madge had not yet had breakfast. Annie and Gerard grinned and said they'd eaten and they would take a walk while Madge and Paul ate.

"Good plan," Paul announced as he stood and motioned for Madge to join him in the RV. "We'll track you down after we eat. I believe some calories would be good for my girl about right now."

"Do I sound like my blood sugar's low?" Madge asked with a frown.

"You could say that," Paul agreed sagely. "I'm cooking. Scrambled eggs with cheese, V8, and dry sourdough. Sound good?"

"Yum," came the somewhat gloomy response.

Less than an hour later, Madge and Paul found Annie and Gerard sitting in one of the porch swings at the far end of the campground, almost at the fence separating Pride from the RV park next door. The fence was more of a formality than anything else. Low, with large open-wire squares, the fence afforded a clear view into the adjoining property and allowed small critters, both wild and domestic, ready access to both parks.

Greeting Annie and Gerard, Madge and Paul pulled a couple of Adirondack chairs over to the swing and made themselves comfortable.

"We had a stimulating walk around the campground, then decided to enjoy the swing. Now that the sawmill is no longer running, we can readily hear the music of the river. It is most soothing," Annie observed.

"You're right," Madge said. Then, looking over into the other RV park, she furrowed her brow, squinted her eyes, pointed her finger, and said, "Is that Marco over there messing with his bike?"

Three sets of eyes looked in the direction she pointed and, nodding, Paul said, "Sure looks like it to me."

"Well, I'll be darned! It really is a small world, and looky over there. If that's not a beat-up white panel truck I've never seen one. World's getting smaller all the time."

"You gonna hail Marco or let it go?" Paul asked.

"Um, I'll walk over to the fence and give him a wave. If he sees me, that's great. If not, I'll just let it go."

Standing at the fence, Madge raised both arms and waved them back and forth over her head.

"Don't say a word about how stupid I look," she cautioned the group behind her as she heard the snickers they were trying to control.

About then Marco looked up and saw Madge waving to him. As a smile of recognition crossed his face, he acknowledged her with a nod of his head, then stood and walked over to the fence.

"Hey, Madge," he said. "Didn't expect to find you here."

"Well, same here," she responded. "What are you guys up to?"

"We're actually playing at one of the clubs here. There's a big biker rally here this weekend, and we're part of the entertainment for that too. How 'bout you?"

"Just here for a few days showing our friends the area. Don't know if we'll be around this weekend or not, but, if we are, where can we hear you guys play?"

"You sure you want to do that?" he asked suspiciously.

"Absolutely," Madge said. "Look, we're up for all kinds of experiences, and I have no problem with a biker rally. Paul and I have enjoyed visiting Sturgis during bike week, so I can't see why a little ole bike rally in the North Carolina mountains would be an issue."

"Well, okay then," Marco said. "There'll be a tent set up in the field behind the motel that's at the corner of Jonathan Creek Road and 19. Parking could be a problem for you, but there's no charge to come into the tent. We're sharing the stage with several other bands. Music is scheduled for most of the day on Saturday and Sunday—from ten in the morning until whenever. I'll let you know if I find out anything more definite about times. If you're not around, I'll just leave a note on your rig."

"Works for me. Good to see you again," Madge said as she took a step or two back to indicate they'd said all that needed to be said. "Take care," she added as they both turned and walked away.

"Well, well, well," she announced as she returned to the group. "We may be hanging out here until Sunday, at least. I'll fill you in on the way to Cataloochee, but, right now, I think we should follow through on the things we talked about," Madge said as she ticked a list off on her fingers. "Like doing the laundry, eating lunch, packing a picnic supper, and starting a book. We can still be on the road to the elks by three. Okay?"

The other three just grinned, shook their heads, and began walking back to their respective RVs, leaving Madge to do a little jig in order to catch up.

CHAPTER 45

Paul chuckled as everyone loaded into the Jeep a few minutes before three o'clock. Annie and Gerard seemed content to let Madge structure their time and thanked Madge when she handed them the printout she'd pulled off the Internet on Cataloochee.

"This is one of our favorite outings," Paul remarked as he climbed into the driver's seat. "As you can see from the printout Madge gave you, around 1910 the Cataloochee Valley was a thriving community of some twelve hundred people. They farmed, planted commercial grade apple orchards and ended up involved in a light form of tourism. But by 1943, most residents had left the area due to the establishment of the national park. That was in 1934, but some residents didn't want to leave their land, so they were given lifetime occupancy rights. There are a number of buildings there that have been preserved. If you are interested we can visit them. But our main interest is the elk."

"We love the elk!" Madge announced with enthusiasm. "I love to look at them, watch them do their elk thing, watch the bulls bellow, and they taste really good, too."

"Madge!" Paul admonished.

"Well, they do taste good. Especially with raspberry sauce."

"Anyway, they were reintroduced into the park in 2001 and have been so successful that you can see them in the Oconaluftee area now as well as here. I thought a new group had been introduced down there, but, the last time we were here, one of the rangers told me the ones at the Mountain Farm Museum were ones that had wandered down from the Cataloochee area."

"What do you find so interesting about the elk?" Annie asked.

"Oh dear, I was afraid you were going to ask that. I'm not sure except that they are so big and their rear ends are so cute and their faces have the dearest expression. We were in Yellowstone one year during the rut and we had the best time watching this bull defend his harem. His stomach would go in and out, in and out, before he would bellow to let any other nearby males know who was in charge. He had his harem in a meadow, and there were two or three other males at the meadow's edge who acted like they were thinking about challenging him, but I guess he either sounded pretty fierce or something, because none of the others worked up the nerve to actually enter the meadow."

"That would be a most interesting sight to see," Annie observed.

"Another time, again in Yellowstone, we had some close encounters with elk at Mammoth Hot Springs. Then again in Canada and, well, lots of places, I guess. They're just a favorite critter of mine."

Annie shook her head in understanding then asked suspiciously, "Will we be taking the entrance road listed in the printout or the scenic route?"

Laughing, Madge said, "Not to worry. We're taking the entrance road. It's bad enough. I wouldn't take you over the scenic route. The printout doesn't exaggerate the challenges of that road, and, personally, I don't think it's that much more scenic."

As she said this, Paul turned onto a gravel road and began the climb up the narrow, winding road to the valley. Twenty minutes later they passed the campground and, shortly after that, entered the meadow where the elk gathered for their early morning and late afternoon visits.

Heavily forested, steep mountain slopes bordered each side of a long, flat, narrow meadow. A dirt road, just wide enough for two cars to pass side by side, traversed the length of the meadow leaving two-thirds of the meadow on their left and one-third on their right. Portable orange plastic fencing running parallel to the road cut off access to off-road parking. Additionally, both rangers and volunteers patrolled the road to discourage close contact between the elk and humans.

"In the beginning," Paul said, "we would come here, drive down to the church, spread our blanket on the ground and have a nice picnic while watching the elk, who kept their distance. Now, you'll notice, there are park rangers and volunteers trolling the road to protect the elk from us. We know better than to feed the guys. But a lot of folks either don't know or don't care. Now the elk have become so habituated they are a potential danger to tourists. The last time we were here, we had the windows down, like now, and when we were on the way back out got stuck in a traffic jam. We were just minding our own business when a female elk rather unceremoniously stuck her head in the backseat passenger window, presumably looking for a handout. Madge was the one sitting there. She had to work hard at not reaching out to pet the elk, but she also pretty much ended up in our friend's lap. It was scary, exhilarating, and exciting all at the same time."

"That will not happen today, correct?" Annie asked while reaching for the window button.

"Can't say one way or the other," Paul replied with an evil little grin. "But there's no need to roll the window up just yet. We'll pay better attention to what's going on today."

A young, female ranger, standing just a few feet from the road's entrance, signaled for them to stop and asked if they had been here before. Paul said this was one of many visits and that they understood and appreciated the rules. After a brief exchange, she signaled for them to proceed and they entered the realm of the elk. Because it was not yet four o'clock, there were no elk to be seen. Knowing this, Madge had planned to drive out the other end of the meadow to where there were some hiking trails, do some walking around, then return to the meadow at 'elk time' and see if there was any chance of picnicking there. If that didn't seem possible, they could always go to the campground area and find a nice spot for dinner.

As they drove past the church on their left, Madge wondered aloud if the piano was still in the church. Continuing down the road, they reached an area where several cars were parked at a trailhead on their right. Everyone agreed a walk would be a good thing to do, and, as they exited the car, a flock of turkeys, led by a strutting tom, marched across the parking lot and into the cornfield.

Annie laughed, saying, "That is an ugly bird. I think the eagle was a much better choice for a national symbol. It is a good thing Benjamin Franklin did not get his way."

"Wow, Annie, I'm impressed that you know that little known fact of American history."

"Aside from the fact that Mr. Franklin was a great friend to France, Gerard and I have very much enjoyed your play *1776*."

By the time they returned from their walk, turned the Jeep around, and retraced the drive back to the church, it was going on six o'clock. Elk had begun to wander into the meadow and cars were just barely moving in the roadway. Everyone was stopped to watch the elk.

Paul said, "I don't believe parking and picnicking here is going to be an option. So my suggestion would be that, since we have no choice but to go with the flow, let's relax and enjoy the ride."

"As long as I do not have an elk's head in my lap I will certainly relax and enjoy the ride," Annie said with a smile and her hand on the window-raising button.

They crept along while different groups of elk moved around munching sprigs of grass or rolling in the dust wallows. About halfway through the meadow, there was a break in the fence, and, as they came alongside, an elk stepped through the break and stopped in front of the Jeep. Annie quickly rolled up her window and Gerard began clicking away with his camera. The elk looked the Jeep over then moved to the side-view mirror on the driver's side and checked out her reflection. Paul quickly rolled his window shut, which seemed to discourage the elk from further inspection. She gave the Jeep a gentle shove with her shoulder, ambled back through the break in the fence, and rejoined her friends in the meadow.

"Wow, now that's a first," Paul remarked as he pulled forward and picked up a bit of speed. "If you've seen enough elk for today, I'll just point this buggy toward a picnic table."

"Good plan," Madge said. "Had enough?" she asked and was rewarded with a resounding yes.

Not far from the meadow, the road climbed steeply upward and curved sharply to the right. A small parking area on the left led to a set of stairs cut into the mountain. The stairs led to a stone observation deck complete with a stone picnic table. As they spread their evening meal on the table, several birds began to hop around the stone wall that protected the deck from the sheer drop to the valley floor below.

As the sun began to sink lower in the western sky, the friends enjoyed a satisfying supper of shaved, chilled hard salami, room temperature triple cream brie, perfectly ripe pears, good French bread, and even better French wine. With a satisfied sigh, Paul announced, "Up here it feels like God's in his heaven and all's right with the world."

"Amen to that," Madge said. "Amen to that."

CHAPTER 46

After their encounter with the elk, Madge thought a day of sophisticated sightseeing would offer an interesting change of pace. By nine the next morning, the foursome piled into the Jeep to take Interstate 40 east to Asheville and the Biltmore Estate.

"Now I know Biltmore won't have the same wow factor as the restored European castles or certainly not Versailles, but it does support a considerable amount of cultural history, especially about this area," Madge explained. "Because this probably wouldn't have been on your to-do list if you were on your own, this is our treat. And that is not up for discussion!" she added emphatically. "So, having done a good bit of research on the US, what do you know about Biltmore? This is not a test. I just don't want to bore you with background you already know."

Annie and Gerard looked at each other, conferred briefly in French, then Annie explained. "Not very much. We understand it was built by George Vanderbilt in the late eighteen nineties and is representative of life in the Gilded Age of the Industrial Revolution."

"Actually, that's a pretty good mini description," Madge offered. "Other members of the Vanderbilt family built their retreats close to the ocean. However, George fell in love with the mountains and the Asheville area. His dream was to create a self-sustained estate reminiscent of the large, self-sustained estates of Europe. He created a village where his servants and estate workers could live, shop, and go to school. There was even a hospital there. He planted trees for lumber and crops for food. He raised beef cattle, milk cows, sheep, pigs, and chickens. Until he died unexpectedly in 1914, it looked as though his dream just might become a reality. After he died, things got tough. To maintain the house, George's widow sold off sections of the property. Actually, much of the forest area became the Pisgah National Forest."

"Pisgah. Didn't we drive through a section of that on the parkway?" Annie asked.

"Absolutely," Paul responded. "The campground there is one of our favorites on the parkway. We've had great times there. Once when we were there, in a pop-up camper, we had a skunk stand directly under our bed and spray the folks in the next campsite, who had been foolish enough to throw a frying pan at him. Thought we were going to throw up. None of the spray got on our camper. However, being that close was worse than awful. But then—that's the stuff memories are made of!"

"Thank you, but that is a memory I will be happy without!" Annie said with a laugh.

"Well, once was enough for me, too," Madge said.

As they drove into the parking area, Paul pointed to the house. "Interestingly, a portion of that big old house was used as a residence until as late as 1956, when it began operating as a historic house museum. I believe it's still owned by one of George's relatives, a grandson or great-grandson maybe. Hard to keep all that straight. I'm sure we can pick up a brochure that will have all that history in it," he said.

"This is our fifth visit," Madge said. "We've been here in the spring, at the height of summer, in mid-October, and over Christmas. To be completely honest, I just don't know when I like it best. Vanderbilt hired an awesome landscape architect— um—something or other Olmsted—"

"Frederick Law," Paul interjected as he pressed the lock button on his key fob.

"That's right! Argh! How do you remember that stuff?" Madge exclaimed. "Okay, Frederick Law Olmsted, who came up with the whole landscape plan. The three-mile approach, the wonderful formal gardens, the farms along the river, the commercial timber forest—well, just all of it. Personally, I think he was a genius and I'm so glad it's being maintained. I don't even mind the entry fee, which seems to increase every time we come."

"It is beautiful," Annie observed, "but since you have been here so many times, why did you feel it was important for us to come?"

"Um, well, could have been the only excuse I could come up with to justify coming back," Madge admitted with a grin. "However, in truth, because Vanderbilt had such a tremendous influence on, not only this area, but the development of forestry in this country, I think it's historically important to see where it all started. I suppose we could have just gone straight to the Cradle of Forestry and skipped the house and gardens, but what would be the fun in that?" she said as she spun around pointing to the house, the grounds, and the gardens.

"Besides, if I remember correctly, one little girl grew up here all by herself except for mommy and daddy and one hundred servants. I try to imagine rattling around in that house as a kid. I was an only child and know what it's like to live in a house full of adults. Was she able to use the indoor pool and the bowling alley? Did she have anyone to play hide-and-seek with? Did she slide down the banisters? Was the house spooky at night?" Madge asked rhetorically as she skipped up the walk.

"Annie, it's all right if you and Gerard want to pretend you don't know us. I'm accustomed to my wife's undignified behavior. However, if you are embarrassed by it, you should feel free to step away, point, and say something like 'Look at that strange woman!' I will understand," Paul said with a straight face.

Not knowing quite what was expected of them, Annie and Gerard looked at each other, shrugged, then burst out laughing. "Oh, Paul, it is quite all right. Madge is her own person, and we are most fond of her just the way she is," Annie stated with warmth and understanding.

At that Madge grinned and waved as she trotted away to purchase the tickets for their self-guided tour of George Vanderbilt's dream home.

CHAPTER 47

Once they finished lunch, the group drove the parkway back to US 276. Only this time, instead of going west, they turned east for the four-mile drive to the Cradle of Forestry. Madge was determined that Annie and Gerard see the birthplace of American forestry. She told them how impressed she had been on her first visit.

"I don't know why I'd never thought about forestry management. But I hadn't. I suppose I just thought forests grew, got cut down for lumber, paper, or firewood, and grew back. It was just something that never crossed my mind. Well, of course I knew about big lumber companies. My great-grandfather was a lumberman here in North Carolina at about the turn of the century, when this school was established by a forest specialist brought in from Germany." She paused, and then continued, "Anyway, I never gave the idea of managing a forest even the tiniest thought. Then we toured here and I gained a new world of understanding and a deeper appreciation and respect for George Vanderbilt, his vision, and his understanding of the need for resource sustainability."

"Madge, it sounds as though you should consider volunteering here. You seem truly passionate about the message the facility promotes," Annie observed.

"I am. And we have. Considered volunteering here, that is. So far, it just hasn't worked into our schedule, but we certainly haven't rejected the idea."

As they pulled into the parking lot, Paul said, "There is a visitor center, a café, a gift shop, and several trails. The exhibits are mostly geared toward school-age kids, but we still enjoyed them. Where we learned much that we didn't know about was on the trails through the area of the school. I would hope that by now, as a people, we would have come to an understanding of forestry management, but I shudder to think what would have happened to our forests had Vanderbilt not had so much foresight. I read somewhere that Captain John Smith, when he was poking around here, noted in a diary or letter or something that a squirrel could go from what is now Maine to South Carolina without touching the ground. Must have been an incredible sight!"

"Perhaps we could start by taking one of the trails," Annie suggested. "We always enjoy a walk in the woods, and if that is what you enjoyed most here, it is perhaps where we will spend the most time."

The afternoon sun filtered softly through the trees as the friends wandered the self-guiding trails. Although they had no fixed time schedule, Madge wanted them to return to Maggie Valley via the section of the parkway they had not yet traveled. She urged them not to dawdle, and two hours later they were back in the Jeep once again headed south on the parkway.

Climbing to over 5,000 feet, Paul pulled into the parking lot at Graveyard Fields.

He turned to Annie and Gerard and explained. "This is one of the most popular hiking areas on the parkway. It's easily accessible, has awesome flora and fauna and has trails that lead to some nice waterfalls. It looks as though there's some kind of problem going on here now. Look over there," he said as he pointed to several law enforcement vehicles pulling into the parking area from both directions. "It's really unusual to see LEs on the parkway—other than at some of the visitor centers. For there to be so many here and coming in with their lights and sirens on . . ." His voice trailed off as Madge opened her door.

"I'm not going to bother any LEs," she said disgustedly before Paul could admonish her. "But I'll just bet some of those lookie-loos over there know what's going on."

As casually as she could, Madge strolled over to a cluster of college-age people in full hiking gear. She stood for a moment before saying, "Excuse me. We just pulled in. Would you happen to know what the fuss is about?"

153

"Actually, we do," one of the young women responded. "It seems a hiker has gone missing from here. Her car is here, but no one has seen her in a couple of days, so they're forming a search and rescue party. We're sticking around in case they need extra people."

"I see. That's terrible news. You say she's been missing for a couple of days?"

"Well, we don't know exactly," a young man said. "We haven't actually talked to any officials, so what we know is word of mouth, and you know how that can be," he paused, as if searching for the right word, then said, "confusing or inaccurate."

Madge smiled. "Yeah, I sure do. Thanks for the information. It's terrific of you to be willing to stick around. We can only pray for the best," she added as she turned and walked back to the Jeep.

"Well, dang," she said as she returned to the back seat. "Seems another hiker has gone missing."

She and Paul exchanged looks in the rearview mirror before Paul said with resignation, "Well, all we can do here is get in the way, so say a prayer that the hiker will be found safe and sound and we'll just move along."

"Does this happen with regularity?" Annie asked.

"Not with regularity," Paul responded, "but certainly much too often."

CHAPTER 48

When the Franklins said goodnight to Annie and Gerard, Madge felt sure it was still early enough for her to make a phone call. Rooting in her black box of contact information, she found Miranda's phone number. As she punched in Miranda's number, Madge hoped her friend wasn't still on patrol.

On the third ring Madge heard Miranda's familiar voice-mail message: "Probably out keeping the world safe for small children. You know what to do."

"Hey, it's Madge. Need to pick your brain. Call me. Doesn't matter what time."

Paul looked at his wife and shook his head. "You're getting involved, aren't you?"

"How can I? I'm just seeking information," she said defensively as she picked up a paperback, plopped into her chair and pretended to read.

"Uh-huh," was all Paul said as he continued to shake his head. He waited several minutes before asking, "How's the book? That's one of Patterson's I haven't read. What do you think about it?"

"Don't know yet. Hard to read with so much chatter going on in here," Madge groused without looking up.

"It's even harder to read when the book is upside down," Paul observed with a smirk.

Looking at her husband, then down at the book in her hands, Madge announced, "Sometimes you are a beast!" Then she smiled, turned the book right side up, took a deep breath and relaxed. "But I love you. No matter what—"

Cut short by the ringing of her phone, Madge greeted her caller with, "Wow, that was quick! Do you have catch-up time right now? . . . Yes? Awesome. Let me get a glass of wine. . . .

Okay. I'm back. Settled outside in a comfy chair, looking up at a sky full of stars. How's life? . . . That good! I'm glad things are going so well. Can't believe you've had no SARs or carry-outs, but I don't want to jinx you by talking about it. . . . Hey, young trainees couldn't do any better than catching you for a training partner. How's the love life? . . . My advice would be to keep him guessing. But you never know. Hey, gotta ask. Any word on either the skull that the girls found or the missing hiker? . . . Really? Nothing at all? . . . We just heard about the missing hiker on the parkway. . . . What? There was another one? Where? When? . . . But we were just in the Roanoke area. Wonder how we could have missed it? . . . Yeah. I guess. We haven't always had good TV and we've really concentrated on our friends and not worried about the news. . . . Yeah. We're having a great time. They're a ton of fun and so easy to be with. We will probably be heading back up the parkway to your part of the world in a few days. We'll cut them loose so they can explore on their own. . . . I heard. You gotta go. Hope it's not my fault for mentioning carry-outs! Be careful. Take care of yourself and call me when you can. . . . Hugs back at you. Bye."

Disconnecting and going back inside, Madge knew Paul would be anxious for a report on what Miranda had to say. As she closed the door, he looked up from his book and said, "Well?"

"Well, what?" Madge asked with wide eyes.

"Come on. You know what." Then he added with casual disinterest, "How's Miranda?"

"Oh you!" Madge said sitting back down in her chair. "Miranda's fine. She's been assigned a trainee fresh out of FLETC and she's enjoying breaking in a newbie. As far as I'm concerned, the trainee's the winner. He'll get broken in right by the best. Let's see. She's dating a new guy. Not sure she's interested in making it long-term so I suggested she keep him guessing. We didn't get into a lot of detail because she got called to a carry-out, but I did learn they have nothing new on the skull or the missing hiker, known as Sunshine, that we don't already know. The day after we were at Peaks of Otter, a hiker went missing somewhere around Goose Creek Valley overlook. No word on that hiker either."

Paul gave her a concerned and questioning look as Madge paced slowly back and forth in the limited space the RV offered.

"What are you thinking?" he asked.

"I don't know yet. Just stuff mulling around. That's three disappearances in—what—the last month? That doesn't track with the stats. And then we have a bunch of crazy goofballs wanting to create chaos for the peasants in the villages? Too much. Too soon. Too concentrated an area."

"Yeah. Coincidences?"

Giving Paul her most disgusted look, she said, "Neither one of us believes in that old adage. As frustrating as it is, guess we'll have to wait till something actually happens before we can really focus. Umm, then again, something has happened. Somebody is making people disappear."

"Could be they'll turn up because they just got lost or hurt," Paul offered with virtually no conviction.

"Well, we're not buying into that theory either," Madge answered as she paced. Then stopping, she looked at Paul and said with determination, "I think the sooner we cut Annie and Gerard loose and head back up the parkway and drive the better. At least we'll be paying attention this time to hikers instead of scenery!"

CHAPTER 49

The next day, as the group sat by the river sipping their morning coffee, Madge broached the subject of them not being together too much longer.

"We understand completely," Annie said. "We did not expect to be together more than two weeks, and you have been most generous to give us as much time as you have."

"Annie," Madge admonished, "being with you two is a joy! It's just that some things have come up that may need our attention. We may need to head back up the parkway and the drive to check on some stuff. It's still up in the air. But since we may have to leave before Wednesday, we should probably plan our time accordingly. Also, we need to talk about all the cool stuff you could end up doing on your own."

"Gerard and I are accustomed to being on our own, so having you and Paul guiding us along has been an extra treat. Of course, we will miss you, but you have not left yet. We will not become sad until that time arrives," Annie offered in her usual matter-of-fact way.

Laughing, Paul announced, "Said like a true teacher!" Then he added, "Madge, what did you have in mind?"

"Well, first of all, what would you think of packing some overnight bags and moteling it for one night in Cherokee?" Madge asked.

Paul looked shocked and said, "Whoa, where did that come from?"

"Well, there's so much to see, do, and talk about over there, I just thought this might be the best way to handle it. I can't see us driving back and forth, and, this way, we can at least enjoy some of the area with Annie and Gerard. If we left, say, within the hour, we'd have plenty of time between now and tomorrow night to get a lot done."

Looking at Annie and Gerard, Paul asked, "Well, guys, what do you think?"

After a brief consult in French, Annie said matter-of-factly, "We think we will accept Madge's leadership. If she feels an overnight without the RVs is appropriate, then that is what we will do."

"Oh, good. I'll see about getting us a reservation for tonight, and Paul and I can be ready in no time at all. Right, buddy?"

"Sure. Of course. Anything you say, oh great leader lady," Paul said with a twinkle and grin.

As the group broke up and headed to their respective RVs, Paul remarked to Madge, "Sure is a good thing they're so flexible, but a heads up to me would have been nice."

"Sorry. It just sort of popped into my head right then. You're okay with it, though, right?"

"Of course," he said as he hugged her to him. "I actually think it's a rather brilliant idea. Where does that leave going to the music thing with the bikers?"

"Well, they're playing Saturday and Sunday, and, as of now, Marco hasn't left any info about when he or his group will be on, so, when we get back tomorrow we'll just see. If they're playing tomorrow night, maybe we'll run over. If not, there's always Sunday. Not worried about it either way."

"Well, okay then," Paul said as he closed the door behind them, then asked, "One bag or two?"

Frowning, Madge said, "Two, I guess. I'm just throwing some toilet stuff and a partial change in a tote bag. If you need a tote, I have one I can let you use."

"Really? You have an extra tote bag?" Paul said incredulously.

"Woman can't have too many tote bags," Madge snapped as she tucked a pair of flip-flops into the side of her bag and announced, "All done!" as she dialed in the number for the Oconaluftee Lodge.

"Me too," said Paul has he zipped his supersized dopp kit that also served as an overnight bag. "Got us reserved?"

"Yep, at weekend rates but still reserved. So we're good to go."

By the time they locked the RV, Annie and Gerard were waiting by the Jeep with their own overnight bags in hand.

"I'll stow the bags in the back," Paul said. "Then we will be off on another adventure. By the way, Madge, where to first?"

"I think taking the parkway to its end would be in order today. Then, when we come back, we can either come back via Cosby or So Co Gap, depending on where we end up at the time."

Then, directing her attention to Annie and Gerard, Madge continued, "This section of the drive is almost entirely in the Cherokee Reservation. It's quite beautiful, but there are at least three tunnels that we can't go through with our RV. I think you'll see what I mean as we drive along."

"If you weren't aware," Paul said, "Madge has special ties to this part of the world, and she has strong feelings about the way the Cherokee people have been treated at the hands of the whites."

Looking at Madge, Annie said, "No, Madge, we were not aware of any special ties you had here. Do you feel comfortable telling us about them?"

Sighing deeply, Madge answered, "Of course, I feel comfortable. It's just that I can get pretty emotional when it comes to the subject of Native Americans—whether here, out West, in Alaska, or anywhere else. I guess it's really the treatment of indigenous people by settlers or conquerors or whatever they want to call themselves. See, I'm already getting emotional."

Taking a deep breath before continuing, Madge explained, "I spent the first ten summers of my life in Cherokee. My folks loved the outdoors, and, while we spent most of our daylight hours hiking and fishing in the newly established Great Smoky Mountains National Park, we stayed in the only motel around, which was in Cherokee. Now, raised in Wisconsin, my dad grew up in a close relationship with the Chippewa people. He held them, their beliefs, and their original way of life in high esteem. His respect for them transferred to the Cherokee and ultimately influenced me greatly. My heart hurts when I think of the terrible injustice we inflicted on these kind, gentle people."

Unable to continue without breaking down, Madge sat quietly looking at the scenery. Finally, pulling herself back together, she said, "See, I get all weird and I don't explain it very well. That's partly because I get so angry about the way we've treated each other. But, you know, it's still going on—what with all the war-ravaged, displaced people looking for a place to live that will give them a better life. When you think about it, we came here—way back when—looking for a better life and disrupted and displaced the locals. I guess it's no different now. The displaced are still looking for a better way of life. Only this time, the established locals are stronger. Seems to me the only answer is for us to stop hating each other!" Then with a rueful smile, she added, "Guess I've said that before."

"Yeah, guess you have, Little One," Paul said. "Maybe if you say it often enough it'll catch on."

CHAPTER 50

U pon reaching the end of the parkway, Paul turned right onto US 441 and entered Great Smoky Mountains National Park. Madge thought going through the park to Gatlinburg, Tennessee, might be a good option. But when they got as far as the Tennessee line at Newfound Gap, if they decided to turn around, that would be okay too.

Their first stop was the Oconaluftee Visitor Center and Mountain Farm Museum. Annie and Gerard always enjoyed ranger presentations as well as museum exhibits, and Madge was hoping they would be arriving when both would be available. Even though this had once been the home of the Cherokee, the park information centers focused primarily on the role the white man played in the area. Madge believed this was because of all the information and activities in the town of Cherokee itself—the Museum of the Cherokee Indian, the Oconaluftee Indian Village, and the outdoor drama "Unto These Hills." The Cherokee people did an excellent job of telling their own story.

Parking appeared to be impossible. When Paul grumped, Madge patiently explained, "It's a beautiful Friday, at the end of June, with the rhododendron and mountain laurel still in bloom. What did you expect?"

"I know. It just felt better to gripe," he said with resignation. He suggested everyone get out at the visitor center and he would track them down once he found a place to park. That happened sooner, rather than later, and Paul quickly rejoined the group. He was surprised to see Annie getting in line to pay for some purchases from the bookstore. Madge explained that considering the press of people, Annie and Gerard had decided the crowds were more than they wanted to deal with.

Turning to Paul, Annie explained, "I will buy some books, pick up the *Smokies Guide* put out by the Park Service, and learn about the park as we go."

"Works for us," Paul said as they worked their way through the crowds to the door. "We'll do what we can to give you an overview of our most visited national park. However, I think the heavy visitation, in some part, may be because US 441 is the only road through the Smokies. If you are trying to go east or west on 441, you have no choice but to pass through the park."

Once back in the Jeep, Madge said, "Since we skipped the VC, let's go ahead and take a mini tour. I'll narrate, as best I can, as we go along. But first let's get oriented."

Picking up her copy of the *Smokies Guide*, she pointed to the map and said, "See, we are here on the south side of the park. You can see how the road bisects the park almost right down the middle. With Cherokee on one side and Gatlinburg on the other, most of your major trailheads are off this road. I don't think hiking is an option for today. I'm suggesting you and Gerard bring the RV over here, spend a few days in Cherokee, then move over to Townsend, Tennessee. That's a great little town from which to do justice to the Cades Cove and Elkmont areas of the park as well as checking out Gatlinburg, Pigeon Forge, and Sevierville. Then, if you feel like hiking, you will have all the time in the world without any worries."

Annie and Gerard nodded in agreement, then, pointing to the map, Annie asked, "Would it not be wise, for today, to only go as far as that gap in the middle of the park? Then Gerard and I can do the other section on our own. That way we will not have to rush."

Laughing, Paul answered before Madge could by saying, "Annie, you are a gem. We all hate rushing, even Madge, but sometimes we do try to pack too much into a day. Thank you. Decision made. We only go as far as Newfound Gap! Right, Madam Tour Guide?"

"Excellent idea. Amazed I didn't think of it myself," Madge said sarcastically.

Starting the engine, Paul announced with something of a flourish, "So we are off! And, Madam Tour Guide, you are on!"

Clearing her throat, Madge began. "Created in 1934, Great Smoky Mountains National Park, was, as we've said, originally the home of the Cherokee Indians. However, in 1839, after much turmoil, the locals were rounded up and marched off to Oklahoma. We will learn more about that when we see the play. But that event completely opened the area up to settlement by the whites. Areas in several of the valleys developed into small farming communities and eventually the logging industry flourished and pretty much stripped out all of the old-growth forests."

Pausing to collect her thoughts, Madge added, "On a personal note, when I was a little girl and we would come up here at this time of year, there were huge rectangular sections of the mountains, often several side by side, vivid with purple rhododendron blossoms. Back then, when you drove past a cemetery you would see the rectangular human graves covered with fresh flowers. That always impressed me and those huge areas of blooms, side by side, on the mountain made me think I was seeing the graves of giants. It was an amazing sight. But, of course, now I understand that what I thought were the graves of actual giants were, in fact, the graves of old-growth forests." She paused for a moment before adding softly, "So, in a way, they were giant's graves. Mother Nature does a great job of taking care of her own, and now those areas have reforested themselves. The park was established before all of the old-growth forests were destroyed. So, fortunately, there are a few stands left. I hate to think what this area would have turned into had it not become a national park." Then, matter-of-factly once again, she continued. "Okay. Moving on. Paul, please turn into Smokemont."

As Paul turned right and crossed the little bridge over the babbling Oconaluftee River, Madge said, "This campground is huge. It is also where I spent most of the first ten summers of my life. If you don't mind dry camping, it's an option for you. That is, if there are any openings. Otherwise, there are numerous campgrounds in Cherokee as well as on the other side of the mountain. We probably don't need to drive through the whole campground, but I wanted you to see this much to get a feel for what it's like as well as how convenient the location is. I do love to be close to the river, and the forest here is wonderful. The sites are level and reasonably spacious. I wonder if the bears still wander the campground at dusk looking for food," she said then added with a laugh, "That was a biggy back in the day."

"Okay, moving on," she said as they returned to the main road. "Watch for any place you might want to stop. Since we'll be coming back this way, we can check it out later. There are several quiet walks. These are short, like a few hundred yards at most, little strolls into the woods. Some go to a view. Some to water. Maybe we'll try one of those. Anyway, we do need to eat lunch. You guys decide between stopping at a river turnout or waiting until we get to Newfound Gap."

They rode along quietly for a while as the road climbed steeper and steeper up the mountains. Signs announcing Heavy Traffic Ahead served as a clue to approaching a trailhead, and seeing both sides of the road packed with cars validated the signs. Often the Park Service had sections of the shoulder roped off with orange cones to offer some protection to the resource. Hikers crossing the road from both sides slowed traffic even further.

"Gerard and I are amazed at the amount of traffic," Annie offered. "We have visited many of your national parks and have never seen anything like this."

"Like Paul said, most visited."

The road became more curvy and Paul carefully maneuvered a couple of hairpin turns. Gerard said something in French and Annie translated.

"He said he is not eager to drive this road in the RV. We will see if we can turn it in while we are in Cherokee and we will rent a car. I am sure the town of Townsend will have some type of motel."

Chuckling, Paul said, "Yes, they do. But if you can't get a reservation there, Pigeon Forge is motel central."

As they arrived at Newfound Gap they were horrified to see the devastation left by a recent forest fire. "Yeah. It's worse than I imagined," Paul said. Sighing deeply, he continued, "Back in the fall of 2016, a couple of fourteen-year-olds were hiking on the Chimneys Trail. We understand they admitted to throwing lit matches into the woods as they walked along. I don't know that they were attempting to be destructive. Just doing something completely stupid that turned into a major disaster. We were told that the small fires they started were being fought when the wind came up—somewhere I heard over eighty miles an hour. Sparks flew everywhere and what had seemed controllable turned into a wildfire. In the end, seven hundred homes and businesses in downtown Gatlinburg and some fifteen thousand acres of forest within the park were destroyed. Cottages and forests around Pigeon Forge were also affected."

Walking around to the back of the Jeep, Madge opened the hatch and pulled out the picnic basket she kept there. Paul picked up the small ice chest and, instead of trying to find a picnic table, they settled on the low stone wall that separated the parking lot from the sheer drop to the valley below. Paul passed out water bottles and Madge spread out choices of protein bars, granola bars, peanut butter crackers, and cheese crackers along with a can of mixed nuts and several bags of dried fruit.

"This may not be the ideal lunch, but it will stave off starvation until we get to a proper restaurant," Madge offered as an apology for the limited selection.

"You do not need to apologize," Annie assured her as she reached for a protein bar. "This is the perfect lunch for Gerard and me. You know we do not supersize anything when it comes to food." Then, looking around, she added, "I am sad to see the scarred land, but, as you say, Mother Nature will heal it. We do not know enough yet to know how much time we will want to spend here. It is beautiful, even with the terrible fire damage. After tomorrow we will understand better and will be more prepared to make plans without the two of you."

"Yeah, splitting up will be sad for us, but you'll do fine," Paul said as he began to repack their lunch. "Let's head back down and check out Cherokee."

As they started back down the mountain, Annie asked, "Why are these called the Smoky Mountains? Are they not part of the Blue Ridge?"

"Yes, they are at the tail end of the Blue Ridge, which, themselves, are a part of the larger Appalachian Range. As to the name, well, let's see. How best to explain. Umm—the park covers about eight hundred square miles of mostly mountains. These mountains range in elevation from just a few hundred feet above sea level to over six thousand feet. That change is often compared with driving from Georgia to Canada and promotes an incredible variety of vegetation. In fact, the forests here are so diverse they are considered the best example of deciduous forests in the entire world. There are more native species of trees here than in northern Europe. So, what does that have to do with the name? Everything. The water and hydrocarbons produced by the trees create a fog that gave the mountains their name. Don't you think Smoky Mountains is a better name than Foggy Mountains?" she asked with a huge grin.

"Most assuredly," Annie replied with a chuckle. "It appears there is more to learn about these mountains than we thought. I am looking forward to studying the books I purchased as well as doing some hiking. Perhaps the trails will be less crowded during the middle of the week."

"Somewhat, maybe," Madge said. "But getting out and walking is really the only way to get a proper feel for any of our national parks. I hope you'll find the time and the opportunity. Over here, I especially like the Rainbow Falls trail, and, on the other side, I've never failed to see a bear on the Laurel Falls trail. There are many trails out of Cades Cove, and hiking around Elkmont is always fun. Oh, you'll have so many choices. Just enjoy! And always take a picnic lunch. There are just so many lovely spots, it's sad to have to go into a town when you can eat in the shade of a beautiful tree by the laughing waters of a rushing river."

"Madge, you are quite poetic," Annie observed with a nod. "We will be sure to always pack a lunch, and we will offer a toast to you and Paul with each sip from our water bottles."

CHAPTER 51

At breakfast the next morning, Madge and Paul chuckled when Annie ordered pancakes and sausage and Gerard ordered eggs, ham, grits, and toast. "We're going to have lunch today," Madge teased.

"We know," Annie said. "We do not usually indulge in such a heavy breakfast, but neither did we wish to be rude by ordering only a bit of toast and a soft-boiled egg," she added with a twinkle in her eye.

"Of course," Madge agreed. "We would never expect you to be rude."

They all had a good laugh. Then Annie said, "Going to see *Unto These Hills* last night was a good way to spend the evening. It is such a terribly sad story. I must have taken much of it to bed with me because I had troubling dreams. Nothing that I can remember, exactly. But dreams of sad people searching for something. I will be pleased to learn today of the success of the Cherokee."

"Well, it really is a success story. Those Cherokee who resisted and hid in the hills emerged to establish the Eastern Band of the Cherokee Nation and have had great success. Even so, as great a name as *Unto These Hills* is, a Trail of Tears would have worked too. Actually, there is a Trail of Tears National Historic Trail in the Missouri-Oklahoma area. You might want to check it out—at least online," Paul suggested.

They ate in silence for a while and everyone seemed surprised when Madge's phone rang. Not recognizing the number, Madge's 'hello' had a definite question mark behind it.

"Madge, this is Marco. You said to call anytime. I went by your rig but saw your Jeep was gone. Thought you might have gone out for breakfast."

"Yes. Well, we did, Marco. Only in Cherokee. We came over yesterday and spent the night. Of course, you can call anytime. What's up?"

"I wanted to let you know we are not playing until quite late tonight. We go on at ten, and I didn't know if that would be too late for you. We are also playing tomorrow from noon to two, if that would be better."

"It's really sweet of you to get back to me on this. Ten isn't too late, but making it tonight will depend on how we feel when we get back. We have a day of heavy-duty sightseeing planned." Then Madge added, "Have you heard any more rumblings?"

"Some, but nothing other than what we've already talked about. This isn't the kind of venue where stuff like that's yammered about. Besides, we're either on stage or hanging with other musicians, so it's not likely I'll hear much. But I'll let you know if I do."

"Thanks, Marco. Paul and I will definitely make it to one of your shows. Thanks again for remembering. See you tomorrow for sure. Take care."

As she hung up, Paul gave her a quizzical look and asked, "What was that all about?"

"Just info on show times. More than likely, we'll get there tomorrow. Now, let's talk about today!"

Annie said, "Gerard and I will be coming over here on our own, so you do not need to spend much time today here if you would like to get back to Maggie Valley early."

"You're sweet, but I'm too selfish. To be here and not do the two things I enjoy the most just won't work for me. When you come back, you should check out the welcome center and maybe even the chamber of commerce. We're going to hit the Museum of the Cherokee Indians this morning, then, after lunch, we'll visit the Oconaluftee Indian Village. It's a recreated village that demonstrates the way the Cherokee lived way back in the eighteenth century. A docent, who explains what is happening at each stop, will be our guide. The actors play their parts wonderfully well and interact with each other as if they really have stepped back in time. Now that I think about it,

169

we'll switch that plan. Let's do the village this morning while the docents and demonstrators are fresh. I think that will work better. Doing the museum this afternoon will be fine. It is so awesomely well done, you may want to revisit it when you come back. When you come back, you absolutely must go to the Qualla Arts and Crafts Mutual. The craftsmanship is amazing, and you will be able to buy items that you know are authentic."

Motioning to the server, Paul asked for the checks as the girls excused themselves to the restroom, saying they would be back in a minute.

Though small, the women's room contained three stalls with only one being occupied. Madge selected the stall next to the one that was occupied and was startled when she heard a female voice say, "No, I don't think that's such a good idea. Someone will notice you dropping a backpack on the ground then just walking away." . . . "If you're really going through with this, you should use something that people won't think is so odd if left by itself." . . . "I don't know. Maybe like a stroller." . . . "Hey, I'm not in a good place to talk right now. I'll get back to you. Try not to do anything stupid."

Madge heard the toilet flush and could hear the woman pulling up and zippering her pants. At that point, being so anxious to get a look at the woman, Madge simply flushed the toilet she had not used and hurried to the handwashing sinks. She and the other woman reached the sinks at almost the same time, which allowed Madge to look over at the speaker and smile without it seeming out of place.

Madge saw a young woman about her own height and weight but who couldn't have been more than in her very early twenties. She wore torn, low-slung blue jeans held up with a wide black leather belt. A small, silver belly button ring lay against her well-toned belly. Tied in a knot in the center of her chest, her yellow, sleeveless cropped top did nothing to hide the swell of ample breasts. Or perhaps, Madge thought, she was wearing a well-designed push-up bra. Giving her hands a quick once-over, Madge scooted out of the restroom ahead of the girl.

Paul and Gerard still waited at the table and, as she approached, Madge whipped out her cell phone and began snapping pictures. She said, "Smile" to Paul and Gerard, then turned and snapped a picture of Annie as she exited the restroom. Interestingly, the phone girl, as Madge began thinking of her, just happened to be in the line of sight and got photographed instead of Annie.

"Don't ask," Madge hissed to Paul as she plastered a phony smile on her face and exited the restaurant. She stopped beside the Jeep and, grabbing Paul's belt, kept him from getting in the open driver door.

"Shhhh," she hissed. "Pretend we are talking."

"Why can't we just talk? Why do we have to pretend?" Paul asked.

"Because I'm working!" Madge snapped.

"Okay, then. How about I let Annie and Gerard know we'll be with them in a minute?"

"All right," Madge said with a tight smile on her face as she watched the phone girl exit the restaurant and get into the driver's side of a tired-looking pickup.

"What kind of pickup is that?" Madge asked Paul. "Over there. The one backing out."

"Looks like about a 1994 Ford Ranger," Paul said. "You want a license number?"

"You bet I do!" came the enthusiastic reply. "Can you see it?"

"Maybe. Plate's really dirty. Looks like a Maryland vanity plate. Hottie—maybe."

"Yeah, well, that fits," Madge said. "I need to find a way to get this photo to Charles. We didn't bring the satphone—stupid mistake and I don't know how to—wait—I'm going to try something. I remember the number of the Brookville Travel Service. Let's see if it works with regular cell phones." Then, realizing she and Paul were still outside the car while Annie and Gerard were waiting inside, and probably wondering what on earth was going on, Madge said, "I'll try to call from the village. Let's not keep our friends waiting any longer."

With that, she and Paul climbed into the Jeep. Too polite to ask, Annie and Gerard remained silent as Madge tried to think of a plausible excuse for their odd behavior. Finally, Madge asked, "Annie, did you notice the girl that walked out of the restroom just before you?"

"Yes, why?" Annie asked.

"Let me ask you another question first," Madge replied. "Did you hear her talking on her cell phone in the bathroom?"

"Yes, and I thought her conversation most odd," came the carefully measured reply.

"So did I, which is why I took her picture when she came out and why Paul and I were trying to get the license number on her truck. With so much terrorist activity around the world, we've been asked to report anything that we run across that seems out of place. And that certainly seemed out of place. So, I am going to report it. I have the number of a—I don't know—probably some kind of terrorist clearing house that I'll call it in to from the village. Hopefully there is cell service there." Then, taking a deep breath, Madge said, "Wowzer! That was something! I'll be glad to get into the eighteenth century, where life was much less complicated!"

CHAPTER 52

U pon arriving at the village, Madge said she would attempt to make her phone call while everyone else got their tickets. They had just missed a tour and the next one would start in fifteen minutes. She felt sure she would be able to finish her call before their group left for the tour.

Edged by thick forests, the parking lot offered many spots where Madge felt she could make her call without being overheard. A wooden fence that closed off the interior of the village from the parking lot also blended in with the surrounding forest. Checking her cell phone, Madge was relieved to see she had three towers. She walked over to a section of the fence that angled away into the forest and found a spot where she was invisible from the parking lot. Taking a deep breath, she dialed the number of the Brookville Travel Service and was rewarded by a ringing that was immediately answered with "Brookville Travel. How may I direct your call?"

"My name is Madge Franklin, and I need to speak with Charles Benson."

"Certainly. However, our records indicate you are calling from a cell phone. Can you explain?"

"Of course. We didn't think of bringing the satphone when we left the RV for an overnight in Cherokee, North Carolina. Now I've come across some information that I need to make Charles, or someone else, aware of. Please," she added sounding uncharacteristically desperate.

"Certainly. Please hold."

Sooner than she expected, Charles came on the phone. "Madge. What seems to be the problem?" he asked gently. "I cannot imagine you would call on an unsecured phone unless something was truly serious."

"I believe it is," Madge said sincerely. She then related the events at the restroom and asked if Charles wanted her to forward the picture and the license plate information.

"Yes. Of course. You can simply text all of that to the number you called. We will take it from there. Madge, that is good work—as usual. How very opportune that you happened to be in that particular restroom at that particular time. Actually, quite amazing. Again, good work! If there is nothing else, I will let you be on your way."

"No, nothing else. Thanks, Charles. I guess Troy and Donny are doing all right."

"Madge, those two can take care of themselves. And, yes, as far as I know, they are fine. Now, you go enjoy the rest of your day and continue to keep your ears and eyes open. We will talk again soon. My best to Paul."

"Oh, okay. Bye, Charles," Madge said before she realized she was talking to an empty line.

Rejoining the group, Madge said quietly, "All taken care of," as she sat beside Paul on the wooden bench, which backed against the stockade fence.

A young Indian woman, in a buckskin dress and wearing moccasins, chatted pleasantly with different people who were waiting for the tour to begin. At precisely fifteen minutes after the hour, the young woman raised her voice in greeting by saying, "Good morning and welcome to our home. My name is Naomi, and I will be your guide today as you visit my village. We ask that you remain on the path at all times, hold your questions until the end of each presentation, and respect the sacred nature of our council house."

Naomi led the way through a stockade-style gate, and the four friends fell in with the other five people signed up for this time slot. Madge felt having such a small group would greatly enhance the experience for Annie and Gerard. She knew it certainly would for her.

The dirt path curved comfortably through the forest until, on the right, the forest fell back just enough to house a lean-to, where a man sat working on a clay pot. Naomi introduced the crafter and began explaining how the Cherokee pottery being made today was made the way it had always been made—without the benefit of a potter's wheel. Dug locally, the clay was pounded into a fine dust, then rehydrated with water and other materials that would increase the strength of the pot. Initially shaped by coiling, the potter could finish the item by using any number of methods and materials. Designs could be drawn with twigs or feathers, and, when satisfied with the result, the potter would 'fire' the pot in a wood fire. When everyone's questions were answered, the group continued down the path to the next lean-to.

They visited the bead maker, the mask maker, the flint napper, and the basket weaver.

They observed ten minutes in the six-month process of creating a thirty- to forty-foot dugout canoe with a uniform one-inch thick hull.

They learned about blowguns and darts made of wood and thistle. They learned about 'the little brother of war'—stickball.

At the council house, they learned the name of each of the seven clans as well as the responsibilities associated with each. Additionally, they learned how a tribe member could or could not move between clans.

In the end, they joined the cast in a dance around the sacred fire.

Exiting the tour through the gift shop, they waited while Annie indulged in several postcard purchases. Finally, back in the Jeep, Madge asked, "Well?"

"That was quite wonderful!" Annie said sincerely. "It was one of the most well-done representations of an indigenous people's original way of life that we have ever seen. Much of the credit, though, for a truly enjoyable experience, goes to the individual docent, and Naomi excels. We thank you very much for making sure we did not miss this experience. I need to say, though, that I was sorry to see teepees in town. That is a misrepresentation of reality since the Cherokee were not a nomadic people and did not live in teepees. Gerard and I did know that, but, as the young man at the council house said, many Americans do not. It is unfortunate everyone does not come here to learn the truth about the lifestyle."

"Couldn't have said it better myself," Paul offered. "Anybody hungry?"

"Well, not starved, but certainly hungry enough to eat," Madge said. "It's such a pretty day, how 'bout Subway to-go and finding a spot along the river?"

After conferring with her husband, Annie said, "Gerard says he likes that idea."

"Off we go, then," Paul said as he started the Jeep and headed it down the hill back into town.

The late June sun peeked softly through the leaves of the stately old sycamores growing along the riverbank. Annie spotted a large, flat rock just at the river's edge where Paul spread the blanket he'd toted from the Jeep. They didn't talk as they arranged themselves on the blanket, pulled their subs from their packages, opened their chips, and uncapped their water bottles. The recent rain swelled the Oconaluftee River to its banks, and the water, rushing over the rocks, drowned out the sound of the cars on the nearby street. Conversation seemed unnecessary as a quiet peace settled over the couples. Gerard finished his lunch, smiled at the group, stretched out on the blanket, and closed his eyes. Paul took the hint, but put his head in Madge's lap. Madge and Annie just smiled at each other. These were precious moments to treasure. The museum wasn't going anywhere. It would be there when Annie and Gerard returned. So the four friends let the warmth of the sun and the song of the river renew their innate connection with the earth.

CHAPTER 53

Madge and Paul rose early the next morning. It was Sunday, and they wanted to enjoy the biscuits and sausage gravy being served in the clubhouse before attending the church service held in the social hall. Annie and Gerard decided to use the morning planning their next few days. They had decided each couple would do lunch on their own and meet at one to go hear Marco's band perform. They thought an hour at the biker rally would be sufficient. And it would have been except that Marco's band was quite good, as was the band following his, which turned out to be the final act and marked the official end of the rally.

Instead of rushing out of the tent, Paul struck up a conversation with some of the bikers wearing Tail of the Dragon T-shirts. "So you guys tamed the dragon!" Paul said.

Laughing, one of the bikers said, "Not exactly. We rode it, but I don't think anyone can actually tame that beast!"

"I don't know," Paul said. "We've only done it in a truck, but our first time climbing the tail coincided with a downhill race. We couldn't believe they hadn't closed the road to uphill traffic. Bikes were laid down to the point we were afraid they were going to slide right under our truck."

Shaking his head, another of the bikers said, "We're not into that kind of biking. I actually like living. I'm a lawyer, and my friend here's a judge. We do this strictly for fun and leave the crazy stuff to the youngsters."

"Good plan," Paul said. As the crowd thinned, he added a "Stay safe" and waved a friendly goodbye to the men.

Several other brief conversations ensued before all four friends worked their way outside, where they ran into Marco.

"I've been watching for you," he said. "I saw you from the stage. I'm glad you made it."

"Yeah, so are we," said Madge. "You guys are great! How much longer will you be in the area?"

Marco said, "Actually all summer. We were picked up by one of the local clubs when their regular band broke up. So we're off the road for the next two or three months and hope someone who comes to the club will be looking to hire us or record us or showcase us."

"You're going to live in tents for the entire time?" Madge asked incredulously.

"No. No. We're looking for a furnished rental, but we need to work for a few weeks before we'll be able to pay for the deposit plus the first month's rent. Shouldn't be more than a couple more weeks before we have enough. Not to worry. We're fine," he said with a big grin.

"Okay," Madge said. "We wish you nothing but the very best, and I hope you will continue to stay in touch about your own lives. Not just—you know."

"Thanks. I will. You guys take care now," he added as he gathered his backpack and guitar and melted into the thinning crowd.

As they walked to the Jeep, Annie asked, "What is this dragon that motorcycles try to tame?"

Laughing, Paul answered, "It's called The Tail of the Dragon. It's a road, US 129, I think, that's at Deals Gap. If I remember correctly, it has three hundred and eighteen curves in eleven miles and is the number-one motorcycle and sports car road in the country. It is one crazy road! And, yes, thirty years ago I'd probably be on my bike trying to tame the dragon."

"Not if I had anything to say about it," Madge stated firmly as she hopped into the back seat behind Paul.

"So, Annie, what did you come up with when you were planning your future?" Madge asked.

"Gerard has decided to drive the RV over the mountain, so we made reservations for four days in Cherokee at the KOA starting tomorrow night. Then, on Friday, we go to Townsend for a week at Big Meadows RV Park. We will rent cars in both places so as not to have to hook and unhook the RV. We have become rather accustomed to the convenience of not living out of a suitcase. And, although we have eaten out quite a lot, I do like being able to prepare proper French meals from time to time."

"Yeah! We've converted you!" Madge cheered.

Then she suddenly became very quiet. Her eyebrows knitted as she squinted at the big silver Hummer parked beside her RV. The corners of Paul's mouth turned up as he glanced at Madge in the rearview mirror.

"Looks like we may have company," he said while trying to suppress a grin.

"No. No. That's not possible," Madge stuttered. "No way."

But, sure enough, sitting in two of the folding chairs under the awning were no other than Donny Banks and Troy Sheldon. When they saw the Jeep, they each raised a beer bottle in a salute.

In an attempt to remain calm, Madge began taking very slow, deep breaths, which prompted Annie to ask, "Is something terribly wrong?"

"On the contrary," Paul said. "You are looking at two of our favorite people. The blond one is the 'Donny' of the 'Aunt Madge' saga, and the good-looking giant with him is his best friend, Troy. Madge thinks of both of them as her 'boys' and is simply in shock at seeing them here."

Still looking askance at Madge, Annie responded with a tentative, "I understand. I think. Seeing them here is a good thing?"

Now grinning broadly, Paul said, "Oh, yes. A very good thing. Just don't be shocked at the way they greet each other. Sometimes their behavior is—well—unorthodox."

By now, Madge had exited the Jeep and was standing with hands on hips and toe tapping in front of her 'boys.'

"I suppose you two have a good reason for simply showing up out of the blue!" she snapped.

Both men rose as Donny announced with a grin, "Of course. Gotta keep my 'Aunt Madge' out of trouble."

The three simply stood grinning at each other for a moment. Finally, Madge squealed in delight as she hugged first one and then the other. "I don't know what to say," she stammered. "Why are you here? How did you find us? What are you doing here?"

"Seems you found plenty to say," Troy said with a grin. Then looking over at Annie and Gerard he added, "We can get into all of that later. How about an intro here?"

"Oh my goodness. I am sorry," Madge said. "Annie, Gerard, may I present Donny and Troy. You could say we are very close. And, boys, please meet our very dear friends Annie and Gerard. They are visiting us from France. Annie was an English teacher there. Her English is better than yours, so watch what you say and how you say it. Gerard, on the other hand, is hesitant to speak English. However, he understands our language perfectly, so there is no need for you to dumb down your vocabulary. Assuming that would be possible," she added with a smirk.

After acknowledging the introductions, Annie said she and Gerard would like to spend some time at their RV and suggested they could all get together after supper. Madge appreciated Annie's thoughtfulness but said, "I have all the fixin's for a true American cookout: burgers, dogs, baked beans, mac salad, chips, ice cream, and cookies. And I'm sure the boys here can supply the beer," she added knowledgeably. "It's four now, why don't you and Gerard come back over around six thirty and we'll send you off with the most basic of American spike-your-blood-sugar, clog-your-arteries dinners."

"Sounds lovely," Annie said with unusual sarcasm. Then she laughed and added, "No, it really does sound wonderful. And we will bring the wine."

CHAPTER 54

As Annie and Gerard walked away, Donny jerked his head toward the inside of the RV, and the foursome silently adjourned to the living room. Troy suggested Paul lower the thermostat in order to get the AC going. Although it was unlikely anyone walking by the RV could hear them talking, he didn't want to take any chances, and the noise of the AC condenser would offer sufficient coverage.

"Okay," Madge began. "Explain."

Looking from one to the other, Donny said, "That event you had in the restroom resulted in us being here. The license plate netted us a name. The name led us to checking credit card lists, and, surprise, surprise, the young lady is a consummate credit card user. Her last charge was here in Maggie Valley. So, lucky you, here we are too. However, we're not actually going to be using the two of you. Sorry Madge. But this has the potential of getting ugly real fast. We have another operative here now and others coming in. That way we can maintain surveillance on Miss Hottie without having to be so sneaky. The more open we can be, the better the chance that at least one of us can actually make contact and, hopefully, be in a position to gain some real intelligence."

"Well, that makes sense, I guess," Madge said ruefully. "So, what? You're going to tag along where she goes? Won't she notice that?"

"Not if we aren't all tagging along, as you put it, at the same time. Because we can track her movements through her credit card use, we can constantly place different agents in her path. The number we tracked her cell phone call back to belongs to her cousin, so we hope she is unattached and that she will find one of our guys acceptably attractive."

"Are you two jumping into the contest?" Madge asked with obvious reservations.

"Don't know yet. We're both a little old, so we're sending in the younger guys first. The one that's here now is your buddy Greg. What do you think of his chances if he hits on her?"

Madge thought for a moment before saying, "Umm, that's iffy. Not having seen him in action, I don't know how cool he is with the girls. I'm not dead yet, and he didn't ring any of my bells. But then he's a bit skinny for my tastes. Cut his hair, put some meat on his bones, and get the earrings out of his ears and 'iffy' changes to 'maybe.' Also, I didn't see her with a guy, so there's no way of knowing what her type is." She stopped to think, then added, "Here's a thought. If she picked that vanity plate for herself, her ego is pretty wrapped up in her looks and sex appeal. If that's the case, she's probably going to go for the hunk type as far as looks go. But she'll be more attracted to the hunks that don't know they're hunks. Like Paul here. He's a hunk but doesn't know it, so he's not wrapped up in himself. Therefore, he's able to feed my ego without me always having to feed his."

Madge looked at the three men in her living room and found them looking at her like she had three heads.

"What?" she asked. "Did you have trouble following that line of thought?"

Troy blinked a couple of times, shook his head as if to clear the cobwebs, then responded quickly with, "No. No, the line of thought's fine. Just not one we've spent much time dwelling on. If we run this past Bev, she could run through our agent profiles and pick the most likely candidate. Could save us a lot of time in the long run. Madge, you are a gem!"

"I try," came the sage response.

Then Troy asked, "May I use your satphone?"

"Of course," Paul answered. "I'll get it." Then, looking at Madge, he asked, "Do you need anything from the store for tonight, or do you need to do anything to get ready for tonight?"

"Ummm—well, no. I think we have everything, except maybe enough ice cream. I need to get the baked beans on if they're going to be anything other than straight out of the can, and I need to pull the burgers and dogs from the freezer. Have buns for both. Catsup, mustard, relish, and onions—good. Lettuce and tomatoes—good. Mac salad—well—maybe I'll make a little more there. Yep—need to get cracking," Madge said in her get-the-job-done-no-nonsense way.

Then, turning to Troy and Donny, she added, "You two make yourselves comfortable but don't get out of my sight. Paul's going to run to the camp store for another pint of ice cream, and he can do that all by himself."

Chuckling, Donny said, "It's good to know we're hanging with the Madge we know and love."

CHAPTER 55

That evening, after supper, when Annie asked why Donny called Madge 'aunt' and didn't refer to Paul as 'uncle,' Madge had a coughing fit and Paul carefully cleared his throat. Unfazed, Donny simply stated the truth. "In the United States, the term 'aunt' is often used as a term of respect and endearment, even when the person is not an actual relation. I often introduce Madge as my 'aunt,' which simplifies explanations."

"Is 'uncle' not used the same way?" Annie asked.

"It could be. But in Paul's case it just didn't seem to fit. So he's just plain Paul," Donny answered with a twinkle in his eye.

"How did you happen to meet and become such close friends?" she pressed.

Troy jumped in with, "We were introduced through a mutual friend. We clicked right away, and then last year we ended up traveling together. Donny and I had some free time, rented a truck camper and joined Madge and Paul on a mini tour of the Southwest. That time together cemented our relationship."

"How interesting. Are you on vacation now?" Annie asked politely.

"Not really. We're what's known—in the DC area—as beltway bandits. We work as independent consultants and are between assignments. We keep in touch with the Franklins and thought it would be fun to be on the road, hanging out with them again. So here we are!"

That seemed to satisfy Annie's concern regarding the relationship between Madge and Paul and the two young men. Madge quickly moved the conversation to the plans Annie and Gerard had for the rest of their time in the US and then breathed a sigh of relief when Annie asked Troy and Donny about their own travels in the West. It seemed they had both been to Alaska, but at different times, and each offered a variety of interesting stories regarding their visits there.

Even though they didn't have far to go, Annie and Gerard wanted to turn in early. They excused themselves shortly after nine and arranged to see Madge and Paul in the morning before they left.

Speaking directly to Gerard, Paul said, "You've become an expert at hooking and unhooking the RV, but if you need any help, don't hesitate to let me know."

Smiling in understanding, Gerard simply nodded his ascent while quietly saying "Thank you" in English. That made everyone laugh and applaud as appropriate good nights were said all around.

Once Annie and Gerard left, Paul refreshed everyone's beverages before settling back in his chair. They had moved the chairs out from under the awning and were enjoying the star-filled night sky.

"Not quite a New Mexico sky but not bad," Paul said. After a pause he continued with, "You boys gonna fill us in on just how this is going to work? You say you are not going to use us, which is fine, but I have a feeling there's more to this than you are letting on."

"Yeah, there is—sort of," Donny said. "We have a lot of unknowns and, like before, we're playing it by ear. We don't like the sound of that phone call you heard, Madge. But we don't have enough information to actually follow up on anything."

Madge jumped in with, "But you said you traced it back to a cousin. Can't you check him out—somehow?"

"How," Troy asked, "without infringing on his rights? We've run his credit cards, and he hasn't bought anything suspicious or potentially dangerous on credit. We have no way of knowing what he's purchased with cash. We have eyes on him, and, as of now, that's all we can do."

"What about that fellow Marco told us about, the one he saw on Harker's Island and again in Stanley?" Madge asked.

"There again, not enough to go on. We don't even have a decent description," Troy said.

185

Sighing, Madge offered thoughtfully, "Can you think of any way I can justify asking Marco if he could describe the guy to a sketch artist?"

No one spoke for several minutes. Then, turning to Troy, Donny said, "You know, that's not a bad idea. Madge told him she was going to report the information to a friend who might know someone who might know someone, etcetera. So, it would be plausible if one of our people was to approach Marco asking him to work with a sketch artist. Can't hurt to run this one up the old flagpole and see who salutes. That satphone of yours still charged up?"

"Yep, come in and I'll get it for you," Paul said.

That left Madge and Troy sitting alone by the slowly dying fire when Troy looked at Madge and asked, "What's on your mind? I can hear the wheels turning."

Smiling, Madge said, "You have some really big issues to deal with. But they're not the only issues out there right now. Have you been keeping track of the hikers who have gone missing in the last few weeks from the drive and the parkway?"

"Keeping track? No. But I'm aware of it. Besides the fact that you care about people in general, what's your interest in this?"

"Well, it all started when some college girls found a human skull up in Shenandoah. Then the next day a hiker went missing. When we were at the Retreat, Ben and I researched the stats on missing hikers. Over the past ten years it's averaged two per year, nationwide. Now here we are and we have three from a relatively small area in a little over two weeks. I have a very bad feeling about this. Something's just not right."

"Are you suggesting those disappearances and our problems are connected?"

"Don't know. How do you feel about coincidences?" she asked.

CHAPTER 56

Madge and Paul rose early the next morning. Dressing quickly, Madge whipped up a batch of apricot-ginger scones and Paul brewed a full pot of coffee. When the scones came out of the oven, Paul filled two to-go cups and poured the remaining coffee into a thermos. Madge wrapped the warm scones in a tea towel, put them in a basket, and placed paper plates and napkins on top. They decided the night before to have breakfast outside by the river. The picnic table closest to the river also happened to be in front of Annie and Gerard's rig. The Franklins didn't want to interfere with the packing-up process, but they hoped to entice their friends into joining them by the river, at least for a last cup of coffee. If they didn't want to take the time to nibble on the scones, Madge figured she'd just send the scones along with them to Cherokee. They sat facing the RV with their backs to the water.

Dew clung tenaciously to the grass and wisps of light mist swirled here and there over the water rushing along the rocky river bed. Birds chirped loudly as they scurried about foraging for their early morning meal. An occasional breeze whispered by without even a hint of coolness, which reminded them it was July, not May or September.

Sighing, Madge finally said, "Annie and Gerard are going to have a wonderful adventure, and I'm trying not to be sad about missing out on it. They've been such fun to be with. I think I'd be less sad about not going on with them if we had something more concrete in our future. What are we supposed to do?" she said with growing frustration. "Wander around like lost puppies waiting for the next shoe to fall?"

"Hmm," Paul offered. "Drink some coffee and nibble on a scone." Then he quickly apologized, saying, "I'm sorry. That was unkind. I understand how you feel, and I don't know what we are supposed to do. Hopefully when we see the guys later this morning they'll have something more concrete to tell us. I know not having a definite direction will make you crazy, but I'll do all I can to keep you distracted," he said as he ran his hand up and down her back.

Instead of admonishing him as he expected, Madge snuggled closer, put her head on his shoulder and said, "Works for me."

"Well, then, let's grab the scones and head for home."

"Not now, Goofy. But you can distract me with a back rub any time you want."

"Good morning, you two," Annie sang out from the doorway of the RV. "Are you available for company?"

"We're just sitting here hoping you and Gerard would join us," Paul called back. "We have coffee. Just bring your cups."

Annie and Gerard smiled as they crossed the lawn and joined Madge and Paul. "We had coffee but did not make enough to put in to-go cups. We do not do that in Europe, so we forget that it is appropriate here in America."

"I don't know about appropriate but certainly traditional," Madge said warmly. As she lifted the napkins and paper plates off the basket, she added, "I baked scones. Kind of as a send-off gesture."

Reaching across the table for Madge's hand, Annie said, "You are a special friend. We will miss you."

"Let's not talk about that," Madge said. "Let's talk about the fun we've had, the fun you are going to have, and the fun we will have the next time we are together."

"And we can only hope that will be soon. Perhaps what you need to take care of will resolve quickly and you can join us out West," Annie suggested.

"We can only hope," Paul said with conviction. "I'd love to follow Gerard up the Al Can Highway. Make sure you watch out for those frost heaves. Go too fast over them and you'll get airborne."

When the laughter died down, Madge asked, "Are you ready to pull out?"

"Yes, we are," Annie said. "Everything is unhooked. Gerard has retracted the jacks, and we have checked all the lights as well as the air pressure in the tires. Everything in the RV is stowed for travel. I suppose the only thing left to do is thank you again for all you have done for us and to say . . . no. We will not say goodbye. We will say until we meet again."

The Franklins walked their friends back to their RV, watched as they settled in their seats, and waved as they drove away.

Paul draped his arm over his wife's shoulders and asked, "Well, Little One, you ready to meet with your boys?"

Smiling ruefully, Madge replied, "Yeah, I guess so. But right now I'm not feeling very upbeat."

"I noticed. What do you think we should do about that?"

"Go for a run!" came the instant and enthusiastic answer. "Do you know how long it's been since we've been for a run?"

"Ten days? Or more," Paul replied. "And you're right. A run will be just what the old doc ordered. I'll call the boys and see if they want to run with us or if they want to get together when we get back."

Feeling rejuvenated already, they made short work of changing into their running clothes and, after engaging in some serious stretching, were off for at least three miles. They planned to run into town and meet the boys at one of the pancake houses. They knew they could hitch a ride home with Troy if the run into town was enough. After a ten-day hiatus, they weren't sure what their bodies could stand.

Three miles turned out to have no negative effect on either Madge or Paul and, when they arrived at the pancake house, neither was even breathing hard. "Wow, why have we not been running?" Madge asked rhetorically. "We cannot neglect this—ever again. I actually feel alive for the first time since our last run!"

"Whatever it takes to put that smile back on your face. You're right. We need to do this every day," Paul said. Looking in the window, he asked, "Do you see the guys anywhere?"

"No," Madge answered. "Since the Hummer's in the parking lot, they must be here somewhere."

Stepping inside, they saw Donny and Troy in the far back booth. They were sitting side by side with their backs to the wall. When they saw the Franklins, they motioned to them with a brief wave, then returned to the business of attacking the stacks of pancakes sitting in front of them.

As she slid into the booth, Madge asked, "Fortifying for the winter?"

"Nope. Just never passing up an opportunity to fill up the corners. Feel free to think of us as your friendly Hobbits," Troy said between bites.

"Hobbits! Right!" Madge laughed. "You're eating more like Orcs!"

"Madge, it's not like you to be mean," Donny said. "You must be hungry." Forking a good helping of syrup-drenched pancake, he added, "Here, have a bite."

Laughing, Madge pushed Donny's arm away and said, "No thanks. You're dripping! I could use some coffee, dry toast, and a side order of patty sausage, though."

Motioning to a server, Troy placed Madge's order as well as a short stack and coffee for Paul.

"Okay," Paul said, "do we have a plan yet, or, as Madge here so aptly put it, are we going to wander around like lost puppies?"

"No lost puppies," Donny answered. "And we're working out a plan that allows for flexibility. A sketch artist will be here tomorrow to meet with Marco. Greg is going to see if he can strike up a conversation with Hottie, and we are going to hang loose until we have something more concrete to work with. Charles would like us to stay in contact, so, because cell service is so challenging in the mountains, wherever we go we take the satphone with us."

"And," Troy said, "your concern about the missing hikers does seem much too coincidental. If there really is a movement to create chaos and disruption, there has to be a funding issue involved. So, Madge, you may be onto something."

"Well, thank you. And the something I'd like someone to look into is an outfit called The Appalachian Trail Appreciation Team. And, yes, in case anyone asks, I have a license plate number," Madge announced with squared shoulders and a look of satisfaction on her face.

CHAPTER 57

Tuesday evening, Amy, the sketch artist, joined Madge and her boys for dinner at a small local eatery. When asked about her results with Marco, Amy said she probably could have done the sketch over the phone. What she ended up with was a totally generic, average-looking male of undetermined age.

She said, "Marco only saw him twice. Each time he was wearing a motorcycle helmet, dark glasses, a leather jacket, and gloves. As best Marco could remember, he was somewhere between five ten and six one. He's white. He could be late twenties to early forties. He was clean shaven the first time Marco saw him and had a three-day growth the next time. His only distinguishing features— that we know about—are a small dark mole at the base of his nose on the left and a prominent cleft in his chin. Weight somewhere around one eighty." She paused, looked around at the group, and added, "Like I said, garden-variety average Joe."

"I get that," Donny said, "but what about the bike? Or the clothes themselves. Anything?"

"Marco didn't see the bike, and there was nothing distinctive or unusual about the clothes. Biker black leather. Even the boots were the same as Marco wears. "Hey," Amy said, "I did my best, and so did Marco. He seemed genuinely concerned and totally willing to help."

"So where are we now?" Troy asked.

"Well," Amy replied, "I've faxed the sketches I made to— the proper people. I understand they will be sending them out to all local law enforcement agencies on the East Coast under the guise of him being 'a person of interest in a federal investigation.' For whatever that's worth." She paused, then asked, "Has anybody heard how Greg's making out with Hottie?" When everyone laughed, she added, "No pun intended."

"No word yet. I'm pretty sure he'll move slowly and carefully. He's good. And he knows we don't want to scare her off," Donny said. "But if he doesn't succeed in getting her interested, we have other options standing by."

"Any word on the Appalachian Trail Appreciation Team?" Madge asked.

"Yep," Troy said. "Aside from having a web page, there's no record of them. Their web page is basically noncommittal. It says they were formed nine years ago, have teams that rotate up and down the drive and the parkway and, if you feel you might need their help, to call the number listed. When we called, we got a taped message that said to leave a number and someone would return the call. The number traced to a burner phone, which we think is probably changed regularly."

"Did you leave a message?" Madge asked.

"I believe we did, Mata Hari," Donny said with a grin. "After all, this is not our first rodeo."

"Okay, Mr. Smarty," Madge said as she made a face at Donny, "who's gonna get the call?"

"That's not something that was shared with me. I imagine it will be one of our female operatives. But it could be a deskbound staffer trained to handle such stuff. Need to know basis and all that. And I don't have the need to know. Now, if they return the call and plans are made for a meet, then Troy and I will probably be involved. Just have to wait and see."

"Well, you know how I feel about waiting," Madge said with disgust.

That brought a laugh from all of the men, which made the sketch artist look confused. Paul explained. "Madge is a doer. She's a problem solver with a right-now attitude. Her having to wait for the action to begin is not usually pleasant to be around. She's a pacer and a fidgeter. We find keeping her occupied during the wait challenging, to say the least."

"Hello. You see me? I'm sitting right here and there's nothing wrong with my hearing. Neither am I pacing nor fidgeting," Madge said as she raised her chin and pursed her lips.

"She's right," Donny observed as he looked around at the group. "But the waiting has just begun. Let's see how she's doing this time tomorrow."

Raising her eyes to the ceiling, Madge simply sat and endured the hoots, jokes, and laughter that followed.

When the levity died down, Paul asked, "Speaking of tomorrow, it is the Fourth of July. Anybody made plans?"

Amy said she was braving the traffic and heading home. No one asked where home was, and she didn't say. Troy and Donny said they figured they would hang with Madge and Paul and thought they would all catch the fireworks in one of the nearby towns.

When the group realized they were the only ones left in the restaurant, they quickly paid their bill and apologized for any inconvenience they may have caused. The owner assured them they had not overstayed their welcome, thanked them for coming, and said she hoped to see them again. Paul invited the boys over to the RV for a nightcap, and was surprised when they didn't accept. Everyone thanked Amy, wished her safe travels, said good night, and went their separate ways.

CHAPTER 58

The next morning Madge awakened to the ringing of her phone. It showed the time as six twenty and the caller to be Donny. *Why on earth is that boy calling me at the butt crack of dawn?* she wondered as she slid her finger across the phone.

"Why are you awake? Better yet—why are you waking me up? This had better be good!"

"It is," Donny said. "We're buying breakfast, Subway sandwiches to go for lunch, and treating you two to supper. All you have to do is get up, get dressed, and meet us at Harry's Diner. Thirty minutes?"

"Ah, I guess so. Why the rush?"

"Tell you later. See you in thirty. Bye." And the connection disappeared.

Madge groaned as she snuggled back under the covers, stretched, then elbowed Paul. "I heard," came his groggy response to her punch. "What's up?"

"We're being treated to all our meals today. That is if we can get to Harry's Diner in thirty minutes," she said.

"Do we want to be treated?" Paul asked as he rolled over and reached for his wife.

Madge thought for only a brief moment before saying, "Sure. Free food is always good." Now fully awake, she added, "Let's roll," as she hopped out of bed before Paul could get his hands on her.

"You're slicker than an eel," Paul teased as he rounded the foot of the bed and tried to head her off.

Ducking under his arm, Madge giggled as she closed her bathroom door and said, "Hold that thought, Lover Boy. There's always tonight."

Less than thirty minutes later they entered Harry's and found the boys—again in a back booth—studying the menu. Four steaming cups of coffee sat on the table along with four sets of silverware wrapped tightly in napkins. Two additional menus lay on the unoccupied side of the table.

Madge slid in and said, "Thanks" as she took a sip of her coffee. "You guys are the greatest. But why are we here?"

"Because it's morning. It's time to eat breakfast, and Harry does a bang-up job on your favorite. Sausage gravy," Troy answered without looking up from his menu.

Madge looked long and hard at both men, then asked, "Does Harry stop serving breakfast at seven, or eight, or even nine?"

"Nope. He serves breakfast all day, but he only serves sausage gravy till he runs out, and that happens pretty quickly," Troy said.

Then Donny added, "We didn't want you to miss out."

"How thoughtful," Madge said sarcastically. "Guess there's no reason for me to look at the menu since I know what I'm having. Or have you already ordered for me?"

Laughing, both men looked at her and shook their heads in the negative. "No, just giving you a hard time," Troy said. "But we do have a cool plan for the day."

Before they could discuss the cool plan for the day, the waitress came to see if they were ready to order. She looked to be in her mid-twenties, had no rings on her fingers, had the face and figure of a Victoria's Secret model, and began unashamedly flirting with Donny and Troy.

After she walked away with their orders, Madge said with a smirk, "Well, now, if Greg is unable to score, no question who should take his place. But I guess you two would have to flip a coin."

"How come that never happens to me?" Paul asked.

"Because I'm here to protect you," Madge replied. "Women know better than to mess with my man," she added protectively.

Trying to look pathetic, Donny asked, "What about us, Mom? You just going to throw us to the wolves?"

Shaking her head in exasperation, Madge said, "You have my number. Probably on speed dial. Use it if you need it."

"All right," Paul said. "Let's get to the cool plan."

Troy didn't hesitate. "I've been checking around and found information on some gravel roads that might get us away from the crowds. If we take the parkway over to the Oconaluftee Visitor Center we can pick up Big Cove Road, which will take us to the Heintooga Ridge and Balsam Mountain Roads, which will take us back to the parkway and then back to Maggie Valley."

"I know that road," Madge said. "That would be fun, and we can even get in a couple of hikes. The Mingo Falls trail runs off Big Cove Road. Dang, Troy, you're more than just a big gorgeous hunk!" she said with a grin. "However, that drive won't take all day, so we'll probably get back in time to chill before supper. We can even have happy hour at our place."

Troy elbowed Donny and said in a theatrical whisper, "She thinks I'm gorgeous!"

"Good grief!" Madge said. "You're both gorgeous! As I'm sure our waitress will certify. Now, changing the subject, just in case you didn't bring an ice chest, we threw ours in the Jeep. We have water but we'll need to pick up ice."

Before the conversation could proceed, a server—not their waitress—came over with their breakfast. Little more was said as they all dug into the generous portions of biscuits and sausage gravy for Troy and Madge, and pancakes, sausage and eggs for Donny and Paul. Once their plates were cleaned, their coffee cups emptied, and the bill paid, they transferred the satphone and ice chest from the Jeep to the Hummer and were on their way to pick up subs and ice.

***

The number of cars on the parkway surprised everyone, but by the time they turned off onto Big Cove Road traffic thinned and remained light even after they turned onto the road to the Mingo Trail Campground, where the trail began. Busy, but not crazy busy, Troy found a spot for the Hummer. Madge had not told the boys the trail amounted to climbing about 150 steps to get to a small viewing platform at the base of the 120-foot falls.

They were not early enough to avoid the crowds, but they made quick work of snapping a few pictures before returning down the stairs.

"Whew," Madge said between swallows of water, "so much for getting away from the crowds."

"It'll get better. I just know it will," Troy said hopefully as he closed the driver's door and started the engine. And it did. Once they got on the gravel road, they proceeded slowly while enjoying the beauty of the forest and the sense of solitude it offered. They passed only a few cars and stopped at a wide spot in the road to have lunch. Sitting peacefully, enjoying their chips and subs, the ringing of the satphone startled them out of their reverie.

The ringing continued as Paul fumbled with the case and finally extracted the phone. "Hello?" he said questioningly. He heard an unfamiliar, no-nonsense female voice ask to speak with either Troy or Donny. "Sure, just a minute," he said and passed the phone to Donny, who was sitting beside him in the back.

"Banks, here." He listened for quite a while then said, "We're probably two hours out of Maggie Valley but are heading back now. We'll call as soon as we get into town." Then he handed the phone back to Paul.

Sitting back in his seat, breathing deeply and looking out the window, he said, "There's been an incident. It's going on as we speak. A truck plowed into an exhibit building being used for a quilt show, and, at roughly the same time, the local rescue squad/fire department experienced what they think was a gas explosion. No word on dead or injured. Right now, just total chaos. They want us standing by ASAP."

"Where'd it happen?" Troy asked.

"Tiny little berg outside of Christiansburg, Virginia. It's early in the day. Celebrations all over the place. There's real concern this may be the beginning or, if we're lucky, just a trial run."

Madge began wrapping up her unfinished sub and handed it to Paul to put back in the ice chest. No one spoke as Troy started the engine, pulled onto the road and sprayed gravel as he accelerated.

CHAPTER 59

Troy dropped Madge and Paul at the restaurant, where they picked up the Jeep. Then everyone gathered at the RV. They hoped to get more information from the TV news. At this point, without further direction, Troy and Donny remained in a holding pattern. Watching the news in stunned silence, they learned the situation deteriorated even further when several large trees inexplicably fell over the main road between Shelby and Christiansburg. Helicopter coverage showed emergency vehicles and TV news crews lined up on the road waiting for volunteers with chainsaws to clear a path into town. The only news coming out of Shelby came via cell phones from witnesses on the ground. However, the local TV station began announcing the cancellation of evening fireworks events in the surrounding area.

"So far our list of cancellations is short. We expect that, as we learn more about the tragedy in Shelby, additional communities may choose safety over potential sorrow or some may cancel celebrations out of respect for the residents of Shelby. Our information remains sketchy, but, as of now, no injuries have been reported in association with the explosion at the Shelby Fire and Rescue station house. Information on the number of casualties at the quilt show remains mixed. The local residents, on the scene with cell phones, have confirmed three dead and at least twenty injured but the extent of those injuries is unknown. As you can see from our News 4 helicopter, we are still unable to get news crews to the scene. We will update you on the tragic events in Shelby as soon as information is available. We now return you to our regularly scheduled program."

"Lovely," Madge said as she began to pace back and forth in the kitchen, "just lovely! And here we sit like birds on a wire doing absolutely nothing!"

199

Troy started to say something when Paul shook his head no. After so many years, Paul knew when confronted with an emergency Madge was either not involved in, or unable to control, she needed to vent. It didn't usually take long and, once she vented her frustration, she would be ready and able to focus on solutions. Pacing seemed to be her answer to kicking the cat, punching holes in the walls, or throwing things. After a few minutes, the pacing and verbal rantings began to slow. Then Madge stopped, placed her hands on the kitchen counter, and began to take slow, deep breaths. During all of this, the three men sat quietly watching some inane talk show. Finally, taking a last very deep breath, Madge returned to her place on the sofa and, looking directly at Donny and Troy, quietly asked, "Okay, what now?"

The men looked at each other before Troy answered, saying, "Unfortunately, we wait. Even with all the assets we have working on this, this one got by us. We need to reevaluate, restructure, and regroup. Sadly, that takes time. But our people are truly good at what they do—"

"Uh-huh," Madge interjected in disgust.

Troy looked long and hard at her before continuing. "Our people are truly good at what they do when it comes to shifting tactics and redeploying assets."

"Sorry," Madge muttered glumly.

"It's okay," Troy said gently. "I understand how you feel, and you're not alone. Donny and I've just been at this a long time and have had to learn how to manage the frustration so that it doesn't sap our strength or confuse our thinking. You know we're impressed with how well you and Paul adapt. That's why you're still part of the team."

Looking contrite, Madge simply said, "I love you guys."

"We know," Donny said. Then he continued, "Waiting is the hardest part. But I promise you, we will get a call before the day is over with new orders. We have ample manpower and unrestricted resources. Still, this one did get by us. Personally, I think that's because whoever's running this show has, as Charles put it, reverted to World War Two spy tactics instead of using social media. We came up short because we didn't adapt fast enough. We thought we had more time. We were looking at them not acting until fall festivals. New tactics mean more boots on the ground. Like Greg." He paused a moment, looked over at Troy, then said, "Why don't you give Greg a call? See if he's made any progress."

"Won't hurt," Troy said as he pulled out his cell phone and speed-dialed Greg's number. "Hey man, just rolled into town. How's life? . . . Really? That good. Any time for having a cold one with an old friend? . . . Sure. I can find it. What time? . . . How's the barbeque there? . . . Great. See you at six."

As he hung up, Troy said, "Evidently he's made contact. I'm meeting them both at six. No reason the three of you can't have supper out tonight. That is unless Madge is just dying to cook."

"Oh funny," Madge said with a grin and a shake of her head.

"Barbeque sounds awesome," Paul said as Breaking News flashed on the TV.

The picture showed emergency vehicles and news trucks streaming into Shelby through a break in the downed tree obstruction. The voice of a disembodied announcer said, "Thanks to the dedicated work of local volunteers, the road is now open. Our team of reporters will be on the scene shortly. Once they are set up, we will interrupt our regularly scheduled program to bring you the latest information—live from the scene."

"Aside from Greg at least making contact with Hottie, what do we know and, if you two were in charge, how would we proceed?" Madge asked.

"What you are really asking is, how involved will Paul and I be, right?" Donny asked with a grin.

Looking chagrined, Madge said, "Dang! You know me way too well!"

"As one of your trainers, that's what I get the big bucks for. But to answer your question, if it were up to me—and it isn't—I'd send you and Paul straight back to the parkway looking for that Appalachian Trail Assistance whatever. My gut tells me that, even if they're not involved in what happened today, they're up to no good and need to be investigated. And that, my dear, is something at which you and Paul excel."

Once again, the TV flashed Breaking News and the announcer said, "Our reporter Andrea Marshall is live in Shelby, Virginia. Andrea, what can you tell us?"

The camera focused on a young woman standing amid a confusion of people and assorted vehicles. In the background could be heard a babble of voices as well as the wailing of sirens.

"Well, Cal, because of the delay in access to the scene by first responders, there is fear the death toll may rise. Some of the seriously injured have now been triaged as critical. Arrangements are being made to have them airlifted to trauma centers as far away as Roanoke. Even though the fire trucks and ambulances were destroyed in the firehouse explosion, the EMTs who normally respond to the station responded directly to the quilt show. One of them told me that because they each carry extensive first-aid equipment in their personal vehicles, they were able to render reasonably acceptable assistance to the injured."

"Andrea, what do you know about the driver of that truck?"

"Cal, that's really odd. No one was in the truck. The authorities don't know if the driver jumped out and mixed with the crowd, or if he or she was hurt and mixed with the injured. I'm sure that will be thoroughly investigated as will the cause of those trees coming down on the highway and the explosion that destroyed the firehouse. That's all I have for now. Back to you in the studio, Cal."

"Thank you, Andrea. On the phone with us now is retired FBI Agent Dennis Delaney. Dennis, for many years you were closely involved with the anti-terrorist division of the FBI. Can you give us any idea of how this could happen and how the investigation into this event is going to proceed?"

"Those are two difficult questions, Cal. To answer the first one: It looks as though this was, more than likely, the act of a local person or persons. I understand the quilt show was being held in an exhibit hall owned by the fire department. Probably the person responsible for this horror has a personal beef with the town's fire and rescue service. Someone who let some injustice—real or imagined—boil and fester. Fortunately, people who harbor grudges like that are few because anticipating actions like this is virtually impossible. As far as the second question goes: I'm confident the authorities will be looking closely at any friction that has recently occurred within the fire or rescue service in Shelby."

"Then, Dennis, you don't see this as a terrorist event?"

"Well, Cal, it most certainly is a terrorist event. However, that term usually applies to some variety of outside influence. This has all the earmarks of a local Hatfield and McCoy type of retaliation."

"Dennis Delaney, formerly of the FBI. Thank you for your time, Dennis." Looking directly into the camera, the announcer said, "We will continue to bring you updates from the scene as they come in. Until then, we return now to our regularly scheduled program."

The four friends sat stunned. Finally, Madge said with total exasperation, "Well, now that that mystery is solved, guess they won't need us. Might as well go to dinner."

CHAPTER 60

When the satphone rang the next morning, Madge and Paul were still trying to process the events of the day before. Now that the dust had settled, the local broadcast stations agreed, at least on the basic information: five dead, three critical, ten still hospitalized, and eleven treated for minor injuries and released. A gas leak caused the firehouse explosion, but how that happened was still undetermined. The truck that ran into the exhibit building had been stolen that morning. The downed trees had been sawed. The authorities did not know when or by whom.

What they didn't agree on was the motive. One station stuck firmly to the theory offered by Dennis Delaney. Another station's counter-terrorism expert believed we had an Oklahoma City type bomber on our hands. Yet another thought a group of radicals were playing copycat games and testing the water, with more frequent and more serious incidents to come.

By the time Madge answered the phone, she felt that if she couldn't jump in and get involved, she'd be so frustrated she'd need to play ostrich—just stick her head in the sand and pretend nothing had happened.

"Madge here," she answered on the third ring.

"Madge, you do not sound too good," Charles said with unaccustomed concern.

"I'm fine, Charles," Madge said stoically. "Well, as fine as any of us can be, considering."

"That is why I am calling," he said. "We think this was a test run by the people we talked with you about. Because there has been nothing concerning this on social media—in that no one is taking credit—we are more convinced than ever that they are communicating through newspaper and magazine want ads and personals. Probably using drop boxes and chalk marks. All of the old-school spy tactics. Because of this, we need to get our people inserted into their operation as quickly as possible. Troy will work that end. What we need from you and Paul, if you are willing, is to make contact with that trail assistance outfit. I believe you are onto something there. An operation as potentially big as this needs funding. Unfortunately, human trafficking is highly profitable, and we feel there could be a connection. If it is not connected and they are legitimate, we can, at least, rule them out. Now, understand, I am not willing to send the two of you off on this alone. I am assigning Donny to travel with you. He will be on his motorcycle and either staying in a tent or using motels, whichever is appropriate at the time. I believe you are familiar with the Aunt Madge cover. You will be using that, if needed." Pausing, Charles waited for some response. "Madge? Are you still there?" he finally asked.

"I'm not sure," came the uncertain reply. "That's just what Donny said he would have us do if he were making the decisions." Then taking a cleansing breath, she said, "Wow. Of course, we accept. In fact, we can head out today. Any ideas about how we should go about looking for this outfit?"

Charles chuckled. "Yes, Madge. I have a very good idea. They responded to our phone message and will be at Newfound Gap tomorrow to pick up two hikers. The hikers want to go to Waynesville because the woman's sister works there as a nurse. The woman has gotten too sick to keep hiking and her boyfriend is staying with her until she is able to continue. Donny will be there on his motorcycle. He will attempt to attach a magnetic tracker on their vehicle. He will follow, observe, and let you and Paul know which way to head."

"Ah—okay. We'll try to make contact, but I've talked to that gal. I doubt we'll get too buddy-buddy."

"I understand," Charles said. "I am sure whatever approach you take will be appropriate. Just be careful. And do not forget to include Donny in your plans. I want an update each morning and any other time you have information. Thank you, Madge. If you do not have any questions, I will let you go."

"No questions, Charles. And thank you for putting us to work. Bye."

Hanging up, Madge realized she was smiling. She knew she wasn't in a position to deal with the people wanting to blow up the world. However, she was certain this 'appreciation' outfit was something she and Paul were perfectly capable of handling. Especially if Donny was going to be there as their backup. Just like before.

"Hey, Paul," she called from the bedroom, "time to saddle up." She put the satphone away then returned to the kitchen. Paul still sat at the table picking little coffee cake crumbs off his plate.

"I heard," Paul said as he licked a finger sticky with icing. "I wonder if Donny put this bug in Charles' ear or if Charles came up with it on his own."

Madge looked quizzically at her husband. "Does it matter?" she asked. "And do you have a problem with it?"

Paul looked up and said matter-of-factly. "No. No it doesn't matter." Looking back down at his plate, he continued, after loading another finger with sticky crumbs. "And, no, I don't have a problem with it." Licking his finger, he added, "Even though I'm the first one of us to think the people in the panel truck didn't fit the mold as campers, I'm not as convinced as you are that there's anything wrong with the appreciation outfit. Soooo, part of me feels like we're being shipped off on a wild goose chase to make sure we stay out of the way and out of trouble."

Madge shook her head and chuckled. "Cool. I'd feel the same way if Donny wasn't being sent along to babysit." Then, cocking her head to one side, she said, "Who are you? And what have you done with my husband? That observation you just made is very unPaul like. It's more like something I'd feel but probably wouldn't say."

Smiling, Paul said, "Guess I've been around you so long some of your little quirks are rubbing off. You're right, though. With Donny being sent along it must be a legit op." He paused, looked at his empty plate, and said, "Now that we are once again working stiffs, I believe I need to fortify myself for the challenges ahead."

"Oh good," Madge said as she put another slice of coffee cake on Paul's plate. "Welcome back, handsome. I missed you."

CHAPTER 61

Later that morning, Troy and Donny stopped by the RV to bring Madge and Paul up to speed. Troy saw his objective of finding and infiltrating whatever organization might exist as an interesting challenge. He explained that due to the event in Shelby, many teams, from a wide variety of agencies, had begun working up and down the East Coast. He also said that things had changed within the intelligence community. Egos within the alphabet soup of intelligence agencies had finally given way to concern for the greater good. Information sharing had, at last, become commonplace and effective. Moreover, in this case, a small contingent of representatives from each involved agency had been set up for coordinating and directing the operation. And, yes, Charles was part of that contingent. They, Madge and Paul, would continue to call into what they knew as the Brookville Travel Service with their daily check-in.

"I suppose everyone is looking for that biker Marco told us about," Madge said.

"Yeah, unless he's crawled under a rock somewhere, he'll show up on somebody's radar. We've all been instructed to watch for him and, if you should see him, do not approach! Call it in. Understood?"

Looking a bit hurt, Madge said, "Of course. What else would we possibly do?"

"Make sure you don't forget it."

Donny grinned and said, "Not to worry. I'll be with them. I'll keep them out of trouble."

Looking thoughtful, Paul spoke up, asking, "Did we tell you about seeing a white panel truck that looks like the one being used by the Appalachian Trail thing? It was in the RV park next door."

"Don't think you mentioned it," Troy said. "Why don't we mosey over that way and see if it's still there?"

"Not a bad idea," Madge said. "At least it'll give us something to do for the next five minutes."

No one spoke as the group walked along the riverbank toward the fence separating the two RV parks. Madge hoped they could pull a couple of chairs up to the swing and spend some time observing the activities next door. However, several elementary-aged children were playing at the water's edge while their moms visited from the porch swing. Since sitting and watching seemed impractical, Madge suggested they walk over. They could always use the excuse of visiting Marco. That is if they needed an excuse. Besides, the walk would do them all good.

They walked single file along the shoulder of the highway, and, as they turned into the entrance of the adjoining RV park, a lone biker turned in ahead of them. He turned right at the first street and stopped at the third campsite on the left. He removed his helmet and gloves, placed his gloves inside his helmet, hung his helmet on a handle bar, then knocked on the door of the large fifth wheel. He knocked twice—lightly—then opened the door and disappeared inside.

"I've seen that bike before," said Paul. "And that fifth wheel. They were at Fancy Gap."

"How can you be so sure they're the same ones?" asked Donny. "There are a lot of bikes and fifth wheels out there."

"Yep, there are," Paul said matter-of-factly, "but not that many with matching decals. The fifth wheel and the bike each sport a heart and dagger decal as well as a twisted star decal. If you wait long enough, I'll bet the farm that a big old Dodge Ram pickup's gonna back right up to that thar fifth wheel and it's gonna have the same two decals somewhere on it. Betcha," he finished with a grin.

"Amazing," Troy said. "Do you remember everything about all the bikes, RVs, trailers, fifth wheels and trucks that you see?"

"No, of course not. Just the ones that seem unusual. I had trouble sleeping one night while we were at Fancy Gap, so I went for a middle-of-the night walk around the campground. We had a full moon and there were no clouds so it was almost like daylight. I saw the decals on the truck first and thought them a little strange. Then I noticed they were also on the fifth wheel, so I looked for them on the bike. And there they were."

The guys just shook their heads as they continued to stroll around the campground. One or the other of them would comment now and then on this or that RV or camping setup until, as they turned a corner, Madge put out her arms and said, "Stop." Up ahead, at the far end of the row on their right, sat a dilapidated white panel truck.

CHAPTER 62

The next evening, Madge and Paul drove to Donny and Troy's motel to be included in a debriefing of the day's events. Donny, Troy, Andrea—the hiker, and Walter—her boyfriend, were already there. Donny looked comfortable by the window in the corner lounge chair. Troy looked official, sitting in the padded desk chair. Andrea and Walter appeared at home sitting on the queen bed closest to Donny. Madge and Paul camped out on the other queen bed, but not before Madge carefully rearranged the pillows so that she could sit with her back against the headboard. Finally settling into the already crowded room, Madge observed, "It's good to see you're being careful with my tax dollars, but, under the circumstances, I would have been willing to spring for a suite."

That served as a good icebreaker by making everyone laugh. Introductions were made and Troy called the meeting to order.

"Madge, Paul, to bring you up to speed, Donny arrived at Newfound Gap early and had time to talk with Andrea and Walter before their rescuers arrived. Arrangements had been made for our sick hiker to be waiting close to the women's restroom, which gave Donny a plausible reason for being in the area. Once the rescuers made contact, Donny ambled off and attached a magnetic tracking device to the panel truck. Since we knew they were going to the hospital, I drove there in the Hummer and waited to collect our brave warriors after they were dropped off. Donny picked up the ping outside of Lake Junaluska and, as you know, followed our little panel truck right back to where she was yesterday. Andrea, you can take over from here."

"Sure, Troy," Andrea said with a nod. "Sharon and her son Chad arrived on time. They seemed appropriately concerned for my welfare but did not go out of their way to be friendly. The inside of that panel truck is a long way from comfortable. The back of it is set up with two folding cots that are attached to the side of the truck. By folding, I mean the kind that are metal and can be folded up against the wall. So there's no place to sit except on one of those cots. They explained that the hikers they pick up are usually exhausted and have foot or ankle problems and are glad to be able to stretch out rather than having to sit up. Between each cot and the driver and passenger seats are what look like small Army surplus cabinets. Each with four drawers. They offered us water or juice from an ice chest that was behind one of the cots. Behind the other cot was another metal cabinet. That one is as deep as the cot is wide. I asked what was in the cabinets, and Sharon said the small ones contained first aid supplies and the taller one held bedding, blankets, pillows, etcetera."

She stopped and looked at Walter before saying, "Your turn."

"Okay," he said. "I tried to make light conversation with Chad, but I'm not sure he's playing with a full deck. He may just be shy, but he'd look at his mom before answering even the simplest questions. I put her somewhere in her fifties and Chad maybe in his mid-thirties. But, the really odd thing was that neither of them oozed compassion, and Sharon—well—that woman has the coldest eyes I've ever seen. Something about her makes me say I wouldn't want to be on the receiving end of her temper."

Madge and Paul remained silent so long that Donny finally asked, "Did you two fall asleep with your eyes open?"

"No, why?" Paul asked.

"Because I've never heard Madge stay quiet so long."

Giving Donny the evil eye, Madge said, "I'm digesting. That was a lot to process, and, seeing that we are the civilians here, I'd rather not make a complete fool of myself in front of people who don't know and love me. But, since you asked: What now?"

"Well," Troy said, "Walter and Andrea get to go home—or wherever—and we hang in and keep our eyes on Sharon and Chad. Do you know if Marco and his group might be off tonight?"

"I don't know," Madge said. "I could give him a call. Why? You into music?"

Chuckling, Troy answered, "No, but if he's home, we could offer to bring the beer and go sit outside at his place for a while."

"Dang," Madge said as she pulled her cell phone from her back pocket. Punching in Marco's number, she grinned at Troy and said, "Now I know why you get the big bucks!"

CHAPTER 63

Marco's group happened to be off that evening and Marco was delighted to have company that was furnishing the beer. He said he'd have the fire going, but the friends would have to park in the overflow section because he had a full complement of bikes at his site. After some discussion, they decided going in the Jeep would be the least noticeable option. They didn't think anyone would be interested in them, but they didn't want to unduly call attention to themselves by arriving in the Hummer.

Interestingly, Marco's campsite was just across and two sites down from the panel truck. That gave the group a perfect view of any and all action. As they settled into camp chairs around a low fire, they glanced over at the panel truck and wondered how Sharon and Chad managed to camp in that small space with no kitchen or bathroom. They'd positioned themselves so that Donny and Paul had the direct line of sight, while Madge and Troy were in a better position to look through to the other road.

Marco introduced his friends Jake and Sam. Both men apologized for not sticking around but said they had dates and each got on his bike and headed out. Paul gave Marco a long, hard look and asked, "What are we keeping you from?"

"Getting to bed on time if you stick around too long," came the honest reply. Then smiling, as though he understood the metamessage behind the question, he added, "I have a special lady waiting for me back home, so I don't play the field like my friends do. I think Paul Newman said it best, about his wife, Joanne Woodward: 'Why go out for hamburgers when I have steak at home?' I think you get what I mean."

Laughing, Madge said, "That's great, Marco. Yes, of course we get what you mean. I hope she knows what a lucky girl she is."

"We're both lucky. We've been together since kindergarten. Really. She'd travel with me except she's doing a summer internship with a law firm back home. She finishes law school next year and hopes to hire on with this firm."

"So," Madge began, "I'm starting to think maybe you don't spend all year riding around on a motorcycle searching for gigs."

Marco laughed and said, "You're right, but I try to downplay that I teach music at our local community college. This is an itch I need to scratch before Holly and I settle down and procreate."

"Amazing," Paul said. "You just never know about people. I never would have guessed."

"Uh-huh. And I'll bet you never would have guessed who's hanging out in that big old fifth wheel we were looking at earlier today," Troy said as he gestured through the trees. "Marco, why don't you haul out your guitar and strum a few bars for us. Wouldn't hurt for us to look like we belong."

"Okay, I can do that," Marco said as he opened his guitar case, "but if you know it, you'll have to sing along."

Donny dropped his head and began fiddling with the fire as Sharon and Chad walked past and entered the panel truck. In no time at all, Paul said softly, "They're coming back." This time Donny found something behind him extremely interesting until he heard Paul say, "Okay." By then Marco had gotten tuned up and was softly and gently strumming an Appalachian favorite, "Oh Shenandoah."

As he strummed, he looked around at his guests and observed quietly, "We're quite a collection, aren't we? Just as there is with me, I would wager there's more to you then meets the eye. I'd also wager that I shouldn't ask—so I won't. But if I can be of any assistance, in any way, just ask."

"You already have been," Troy said. "More than you may ever know. And that's just as well. We have some concerns about the folks in that panel truck, and now we also have some concerns about the folks in that fifth wheel. If you happen to see them, we'd be grateful for a description."

"Not a problem. Happy to help. But, if you can, tell me if I'm right about one thing," he asked looking at Donny with a sneaky little grin. "She's not really your aunt, is she?"

Donny thought for only a moment before he replied with a smile and a slap on Marco's back, "And it wasn't Professor Plum in the library with the rope either."

CHAPTER 64

At three miles from the campground, breakfasting at Harry's worked perfectly for Madge and Paul. They could run in, eat with the boys, and catch a ride back to the RV. On this morning, they arrived before the boys, and, as they entered the restaurant, Madge's cell phone buzzed. "I hope the boys aren't cancelling out on us," she said, but then frowned when she glanced at the caller ID.

"Morning, Marco. What's up?"

"Hi Madge. Troy said to call if I could give you a description of anyone in the fifth wheel. I thought I needed a bit of a walk this morning, and the guy who rides the bike was out messing with it as I went by. I stopped to talk to him about his bike, and Madge, this is hard to believe, but he's the guy. The one you're looking for. The one I told you about—with the mole and the cleft chin." He paused, waiting for a response. Finally he said, "Madge, are you there? Did you hear me?"

"Ah, yeah, Marco. I'm here, and I think I heard you say the motorcycle guy in the fifth wheel is the guy we're looking for?"

"Right."

"Ah, okay. I'll call you right back!" she said as she looked around frantically for the boys.

Paul was already opening the door as Madge speed dialed Troy's number. However, on the first ring, they saw the Hummer turning into the parking lot so Madge disconnected the call.

Troy and Donny jumped out of the Hummer full of their usual good humor, but as soon as they saw Madge and Paul, their demeanor changed. Donny was the first to ask, "What's wrong?"

Waves of controlled energy, excitement, and concern vibrated off the couple. Madge looked at Paul, who said, "Marco called.

He talked to the biker in the fifth wheel. He's the guy we're looking for."

Troy blinked and said, "You're kidding, right?"

"No—not kidding," Madge said. "I just talked to Marco and said we would call him right back."

She ran through the recent-calls setting, punched the number, and handed the phone to Troy.

Marco answered on the first ring. Troy walked to a deserted section of the parking lot and began talking quietly. In less than two minutes, he returned to the group and announced, "Well, that puts a whole new wrinkle in the mix."

He handed the phone back to Madge and, as he pulled out his own cell phone, said, "Marco's gonna keep an eye on things there and call you if our biker friend suits up and heads out. I need to make some calls, but there's no reason not to eat. You guys go on in, get seats, order us some coffee. We'll be right there."

The coffee arrived as the boys joined Madge and Paul at their booth in the back of the restaurant. "You folks ready to order?" asked the waitress, who was definitely not the Victoria's Secret model.

"Actually, yes," Donny said. "Pancake special for the two of us, half order of biscuits and sausage gravy for the lady, and a short stack with two over-easy on top for our friend."

"You got it," she said as she hustled off.

Madge sat twitching in her seat as she waited for the waitress to get out of earshot so Troy could fill them in on what was happening. Finally, not being able to contain herself any longer, she glared at Troy and said, "You're enjoying yourself, aren't you?"

"Um—you could say that," Troy said with a chuckle. "But I am afraid to drag this out much longer. You're starting to look dangerous, and I like being on your good side better."

"So talk!" Madge hissed.

Putting on his serious face, Troy said, "Change in plans. We now have three sets of suspects to watch. Which, ordinarily, would be a challenge. Fortunately, we are not in this by ourselves. In fact, we are so well covered we may end up tripping over each other." He stopped, shook his head, then continued. "Anyway, Madge, before you ask—yes—we already have assets on the biker. Well, we will have in another ten minutes. Marco talked to him—the biker—and he isn't planning to go out before lunch. More than enough time for us to get our people in position. Two of our people will hang out with Marco, which lets him off the hook. That puts the biker out of our area of concern. We need to concentrate on the fifth wheel and the panel truck. Which, unfortunately Madge, means we are once again playing the waiting game. Welcome to our world."

Madge lifted her arms shoulder high, made claws of her fingers and uttered a frustrated, "Arrgh!"

CHAPTER 65

Shortly after lunch, the biker, known as Karl, climbed on his bike and rode into Waynesville. He went directly to Terry's Tavern. Nodding to the few people shooting pool, he walked to the bar, ordered coffee to go, then used the men's room. Before leaving the men's room, he took out a felt-tipped permanent marker and drew a picture of a small twisted star just to the right of the doorknob. Going back to the bar, he paid for his coffee, took a few sips, then walked back outside to a picnic table sitting under a large oak tree. He sat down, slowly drank some of his coffee while looking around, then tossed his cup in the trash can, got on his bike, and rode off.

As he made the left turn into traffic, two bikers pulled out of the Dairy Queen across the street and fell into line three cars behind him.

From Waynesville, he rode to Brevard. There he stopped at The Roost. This time he ordered a beer, which he drank as he sat at a window table watching the world go by. When he finished his beer, he again used the men's room and, again, left a picture of a small twisted star by the right side of the men's room doorknob.

This time, when he turned right onto the road, he had to wait while a little silver pickup pulled out in front of him from the hardware store next door. The driver poked along to the traffic light and, when the light turned green, Karl zipped around him. However, by then it was rush hour, and any number of cars and trucks fell in between Karl and the pickup before Karl reached highway speed on the open road. He did notice the pickup far behind him but thought nothing of it. Especially when it drove on past as Karl parked his bike at Molly's in Silva.

By now it was the dinner hour and Karl made himself comfortable at a back corner table. He ordered the special—fried chicken, mashed potatoes and gravy, with green beans, rolls and butter. He ate slowly and took no notice of the young couple who came in and sat at the table in the opposite corner of the restaurant. When he finished his meal, he took out a pen and appeared to doodle on a napkin as he waited for his bill. When the waiter brought the bill, he also cleared away the empty dishes, collected the empty half-and-half cups, balled up the doodled-on napkin, and went on about his business.

Karl walked to the register, paid his bill—in cash—and left. The sun was just thinking about setting as he climbed on his bike and headed back to Maggie Valley. Karl hadn't gone more than two miles when the man who waited on him told the restaurant owner he thought he had the stomach flu and needed to go home. He said he'd already called the kid who often helped out in a pinch, and the kid would be in within the hour. Of course, the owner didn't want his people working when they were sick. Especially if they could spread intestinal and gastric problems. So the waiter left with the owner's blessing, got in his truck, and drove out in the same direction as Karl.

He drove fast, blasted past the Honda Civic that was going just above the speed limit and was soon right behind Karl's motorcycle.

Once back in Maggie Valley, Karl turned on a side road, drove down a narrow lane, and turned into a development of small vacation homes called park models. He drove to the end of one of the streets and parked his bike alongside of a tired-looking 1994 Ford Ranger. He removed his helmet and gloves, placed the gloves in the helmet, hung the helmet on the left handlebar of the bike, walked up to the door and knocked. Before the door opened a truck drove past, made a U-turn and parked on the street in front of the house next door. The waiter from the restaurant got out and met Karl on the doorstep as the door opened and the girl known as Hottie ushered them inside.

Karl acknowledged the two other men already there with a nod. No one spoke. Each of the five people in the room took a beer bottle from the bucket on the coffee table, popped the cap, raised the bottles in the air, clinked the bottles together and, together, shouted a resounding "YES!"

***

Two women sat at a folding table set up in the bedroom of the house next door. They wore headphones. One sat tapping keys on a laptop while the other messed with dials on a recording device. Both were in their mid-thirties. Both were dressed in REI-style outdoor wear. Both wore sturdy hiking boots. While both appeared physically fit, the one at the computer was visibly smaller than her partner. The one at the computer removed her headphones and donned a pair of horn-rimmed glasses. As she rose, her companion moved to the computer and nodded.

The smaller woman exited the building and walked next door. She knocked several times and, when Hottie answered, said, "I'm so sorry to bother you. I'm Joyce and my friend Claire and I have the park model next door. Is there any chance we could borrow a couple of eggs? I promise we'll replace them tomorrow."

Although she hesitated momentarily, Hottie finally smiled and said, "Sure, come on in."

Joyce kept her left hand in her pocket as she entered the living room and graced the men sitting there with a stunning smile. At the same time, Claire carefully saved the photos coming into the computer from the tiny camera in Joyce's horn-rimmed glasses.

Handing Joyce four eggs in a throw-away plastic tub, Hottie said, "No need to replace them. I'm probably leaving tomorrow and won't need them anyway." She added, "Enjoy," as she opened the door and ushered her neighbor back out into the night.

CHAPTER 66

After attending the Sunday morning worship service at the RV park, Madge and Paul met the boys for brunch. Back in their booth at Harry's, Troy felt he could share—at least in a general sort of way—some new information.

Between bites of syrup-laden pancake he said, "We got lucky. Good ole Greg scored—big time. Got to spend a night or two with Hottie. Seems the rental she's in will need an exterminator when she checks out."

Madge's face lit up with a huge smile as she immediately picked up on the inference. "Do tell," she said. "I'll just bet that place is filled with dirt."

"From what I hear, there'll be some heavy cleaning going on," Donny offered. "It's possible that we may even be asked to help out. Never can tell about stuff like that."

Paul dabbed a dribble of syrup off the corner of his mouth with his napkin and said, "I have a great idea. Why don't we finish up here, then I'll drive us over to Lake Junaluska. We can walk around the lake and work off some of these calories."

"Not a bad thought," said Troy. "But we could take the Hummer if you want."

"Nope. I'll drive," Paul said decisively. "Since you seem so chatty today, that'll free you up to talk without distractions."

Chuckling, Troy nodded in agreement. Having settled where they could talk freely, breakfast proceeded normally. When everyone finished eating, they each ordered coffee to go, paid their bill and loaded into the Jeep.

Once on the road, Madge said, "Okay, you know you are killing me. Fess up. Please!"

Sitting in the back seat, Troy and Donny looked at each other and shrugged their shoulders. Donny asked Troy, "Do you know what she's talking about?"

"Haven't the foggiest," he answered. "Hey, Paul, do you know what's eating your wife?"

Paul laughed and glanced in the rearview mirror before saying, "I have a pretty good idea. And I think it'll be barbequed Troy and Donny for dinner if you don't cut the crap and get to the point pretty quick."

Both Troy and Donny found that extremely amusing, but Donny said, "Madge, honey, we have a whole bunch of information, and, I promise, we'll tell all just as soon as we get somewhere where we can see each other and not have to worry about being overheard. So, Paul, what's this about Lake Junaluska?"

"It's a Methodist retreat center. Long history. Lots of buildings around a lake. Just thought we might be able to find a quiet spot. If you'd rather, we can always go back to the RV or to your motel."

"No," Troy said. "Let's at least take a look at the lake. What we have to say is sensitive stuff, and I don't want to take any chances. At this point we don't know who's involved. Could be someone working or staying at the motel or the RV park or someone just out for a walk."

Paul told them, "It's about a mile or a little more around the lake, and while there are big, beautiful trees around the buildings, there are no trees close to the lake. There's at least one picnic table that would give us three-sixty-degree visibility. Even though there will probably be a good number of walkers, runners, dog walkers, etcetera, we'll be able to see well in advance of anyone getting close enough to hear what we're talking about. Madge, you'll be fine till then, right, babe?"

"Of course," she said. "It's true I'm anxious and excited, but I can actually behave like a professional grown-up—when I have to," she added with a little giggle.

As Paul drove slowly toward the parking area, they saw a sleek black Lincoln backing out of a parking space. Paul grinned at Madge and easily worked the Jeep into the newly empty spot.

"Hey, Paul," Troy said, "This is okay. Really a pretty spot. Does it matter which way we walk?"

"Nope," Paul answered. "Path goes all the way around the lake, and, if I remember correctly, there are spots where we can sit and talk. So, clockwise, counter-clockwise, doesn't matter."

Madge said, "Look at that rose garden! Let's start over there."

That got the foursome walking clockwise around the egg-shaped lake. Manicured lawns edged the concrete sidewalk on their left, while, on their right, the lake water lapped gently against wooden bulkheads. Swans and ducks paddled around the far end of the lake where a little wooden bridge crossed the water at a narrow point.

No more than halfway around the lake they found a picnic table sitting on a small graveled spot between the sidewalk and the lake. With two sitting facing the lake and two sitting facing the sidewalk, it created the perfect spot for talking.

Once settled, Troy began by saying, "I think you got the idea that Greg placed several bugs in Hottie's rental. One of the other agencies we're working with rented the house next door and placed two female agents there. We didn't know if that would net us anything, but, since the Shelby incident, everyone is taking this threat seriously and pulling out all the stops. We had our people covering the biker who was all over the place yesterday. We still don't know how he's doing it, but he connected with three people who met him last night at Hottie's. One of the agents from next door went over to borrow some eggs and was able to photograph all of the men. That's huge, but not as huge as the information we learned from listening in on their meeting."

He stopped to be sure Madge and Paul were following. When they said nothing, Donny picked up the story:

"What we know was learned from the celebration the group had over the success of the Shelby operation. They spent a considerable amount of time rehashing that event and pointing out how well their system worked. And, yes, that was a test run. Their current plan calls for operations in September and October, which gives us some time."

Donny stopped here, expecting some comments or questions, but when none were forthcoming he continued. "It appears that the biker is the chief organizer. From what we heard, it sounds like he goes from town to town and recruits one person, who will then recruit three other people. We think he has the East Coast broken down into small sections like here, where he is meeting with only three leaders, as he calls them. It's almost like a pyramid scheme. Biker boy only connects with the people he recruits as leaders. The people he recruits are not the actual doers who execute the plans. As in Shelby, one person blew the firehouse, another jacked and drove the truck, and another cut the trees. None of them knew each other. Their only contact had been with a leader who told them exactly what to do and when to do it."

This time, when he paused for breath, Madge said, "Okay. That makes a certain amount of sense, but how's the Appalachian Trail Rescue involved?"

"That's where it gets interesting and where we come in," Troy answered. "Money. You know, follow the money. Our friends in the panel truck and fifth wheel are in the ugly business of human trafficking, which, by the way, appears to be financing this little operation. Donny and I spent a considerable amount of time last night on the phone with Charles and some other folks, and here's what's going to happen. Other agencies are getting involved in infiltrating and tracking and cutting off the head of this particular monster. We have no idea how far-reaching this is, how many layers are involved, or even if this is purely domestic. So we are no longer concerned with solving the mystery of who and how. Our focus is to stop this Appalachian group from continuing to engage in human trafficking. Your assignment stays the same. You will manage to be at the same campgrounds as they are as often as possible, and you will attempt to make contact. We aren't worried about losing track of them since all three vehicles now have magnetic trackers attached. Donny and I will be following along on bikes. Much of the details will have to be worked out on the fly, and Madge, that's where you shine, so don't look so concerned."

"I have to look concerned," Madge said with furrowed brow. "I have ten thousand questions and I don't even know which one to ask first. This is a lot to absorb and digest, and human trafficking makes me sick to my stomach. I'd like to get my hands on that Sharon person," she said through clenched teeth. Then more quietly she looked at Troy and asked, "Why are you not going to use your Hummer?"

"It's a little conspicuous. Don't you think? Low profile and all that rot. Besides, it's easier for Donny and me to work as a team when we're using the same type of transport. So, Aunt Madge and Uncle Paul, we want to thank you for letting us tag along while you scout out all those cool places for the Brookville Travel Service to recommend to their clients."

CHAPTER 67

By the time Madge and Paul returned to the RV they both felt exhausted. Their journey down the Skyline Drive and Blue Ridge Parkway with Annie and Gerard had been fun, and the occasional brushes with spook stuff added just enough excitement to keep life interesting. However, all of that felt more academic than actual. Even watching the events in Shelby unfold on TV felt more theatrical than real. Perhaps they had become emotionally immune. Every time they turned on the TV they were inundated with some human-caused tragedy or natural disaster. A person could internalize only so much suffering. Of course, they were horrified. Of course, they were saddened. Of course, they would contribute funds to the Red Cross or Doctors Without Borders or UMCOR. But none of that actually impacted their life. They could say a prayer, write their check and go off to bed with a clear conscious. So why did this suddenly become so real? They both felt like they'd had the wind knocked out of them. This wasn't some TV drama or far-away disaster. Some awful, sick, perverted people were right here in Madge and Paul's own backyard, and it had fallen in their lap to stop part of the insanity.

Collapsing into their chairs, they sat silently staring at nothing. As the sun sank behind the mountains and the RV began to grow dark, Paul finally sighed deeply and asked softly, "You gonna be okay?"

"Yeah. Eventually," Madge replied. "I'll pull it together and so will you. But knowing what I know now, I don't know if I can pull off any kind of nicey-nice act with Sharon. It was one thing on our last Brookville Travel adventure to hang out and become friends with Frank. I knew from the get-go he was a good guy. But this! I know she's lower than slime! Being two-faced isn't really in my DNA. And, contrary to popular opinion, I'm a terrible actress."

"Whatever. You're beginning to sound like you're coming around."

"Yeah, talking about it helped. Helped enough for me to realize I'm hungry. How about you?"

"I could eat," he said noncommittally. "What'd you have in mind?"

"Hmmm." Madge thought for a minute. "That's tough. I don't want to cook, and I don't want to go to a restaurant, and I don't want to go for take-out. Room service would be good. Guess that's not an option, though. So, what's your tummy interested in?"

"Pizza?" he said. "Bet someone around here would deliver."

"Oh, for crying out loud! Just call the boys and see what they're doing!" Madge said as she stomped off to the bathroom. Returning to the living room, she continued, "We need to get out of this funk, and hanging out here by ourselves won't do it. We need to have some fun. Wonder if there's anywhere around here where we could go shoot or if there's a gym where we could get in a good workout?"

"Welcome back," Paul said with a grin as he hung up the phone. "It's barbecue, not pizza. The boys will meet us at The Pig Pen in twenty minutes."

Madge and Paul found the boys camped out on the last picnic table on the porch. Seating in The Pig Pen consisted of wooden picnic tables lined up perpendicular along the outside edge of a screened-in porch that cantilevered over a babbling brook. On each table, rolls of paper towels rested in wooden vertical holders. Colored squeeze bottles of barbeque sauce— red for hot, yellow for mustard-based, and clear for sweet—sat lined up in little wooden boxes. Two plastic pitchers sat in front of the boys. One filled with sweet iced tea—for Paul— and one filled with frosty beer for the boys. They were never sure which way Madge would swing.

"Hallelujah!" Madge crowed. "Beer! You guys are the best!"

The boys high-fived each other and Madge looked questioningly at Paul and then at them.

"What was that all about?" she asked.

"Just glad to know we got it right," Troy said. "Sit. Drink. Enjoy. You both look better than you did earlier. We were a bit concerned about you when we parted."

"Yeah, well, you hit us with some pretty heavy stuff. Took a while to process," Madge said. "We'll be fine but needed to get out tonight. Thanks for meeting us."

"No prob. I know you don't want to talk about our problem. But we do have some good news to share," Donny said. "Between now and when this thing is over, we will have a swarm of other friends in and out of every campground. We won't be alone. And neither will you. So, don't worry. This one's not gonna get away."

At that they raised three beers and an iced tea glass in a toast.

CHAPTER 68

On their run the next morning, Donny surprised Madge and Paul by riding past them on his bike and swinging in front of them, then stopping.

"Time to turn around and head back," he said. "Need to get packed up. Sharon's heading out."

"But," Madge stammered, "that doesn't mean the fifth wheel's going anywhere."

"Well, actually it does. We've kind of eavesdropped a bit on them too, and they're both headed to a commercial campground outside of Cosby, Tennessee. We've already reserved sites for you two and for us, so there's no huge hurry, but it would be good to not dawdle."

"I can't believe you said dawdle," Paul stated in shocked disbelief. "Nobody but Madge says dawdle."

"Guess it rubbed off," Donny said with a grin as he spun his bike around and rode off.

Two hours later, Paul hitched the Jeep to the RV and he and Madge drove over the mountain to Merrywood RV Park outside of Cosby. Small, by most standards, Merrywood lived up to its name in that it was heavily wooded. In fact, so heavily wooded each campsite was shielded from the others by large bushes as well as big trees.

"Well, this is about useless," Madge grumbled as she set the camp chairs up around the fire ring. "How are we supposed to keep track of anything with all this shrubbery?"

"My, aren't you just Little Miss Cheery Sunshine?" quipped Paul. "Guess we'll have to fall back on Plan B. If I remember correctly, we have details that will have to be worked out on the fly, and that's something you're supposed to be especially good at. So, what's Plan B?"

"Cute. You really think you're cute. Tell you what, as soon as Plan B falls out of the sky and lands on my head, you'll be the first person I tell. How's that?"

"Just trying to jerk your chain," he said with a grin. "You know you're my best and only girl," he added as he came up behind her, slipping one arm around her waist and the other over her shoulders.

"No, you don't, big guy. You can't sweet talk yourself out of this one. Hey, look who's moving in across the street."

As Paul looked over the top of Madge's head, he watched a Dodge truck skillfully back a large fifth wheel into the site directly across from them. Amazingly there were no trees or bushes to block the view from their fire ring to the one across the street. And the door to the fifth wheel could be plainly seen as well.

"Plan B just arrived," Madge said with a grin as she elbowed Paul in the ribs.

"Break it up, you two," came a voice from the other side of the bushes on their left. "Can't really cut through here, so I'll walk around. If, of course, I won't be interrupting anything important," Troy said as he rounded the front of the bushes and walked past the front of the RV.

"Hey, where'd you come from? We didn't hear your bike," Paul said.

"That's because I got in about an hour ago. Got the tent set up. Donny's doing a recon of the area and should be back before dinner. Seems odd that the fifth wheel's here but no panel truck. She's parked on a side road off Route 32. Just sitting there, as far as we know. Have you seen anybody across the way?"

"Just the guy that backed the fifth wheel in," Madge answered. "Didn't get a real good look at him, but he looks like a big one. Broad shoulders. Shaved head. Not my type."

"If Sharon and the guy with her are sleeping in the fifth wheel, they won't even need to get a campsite. You can have two vehicles on a site, and there's plenty of room over there for the panel truck to fit nicely right beside the fifth wheel." Paul paused, looked thoughtful then continued. "Isn't that a toy hauler?"

"Uh-huh, it is," Troy said. "Why?"

"Oh, I don't know. Just because this isn't really toy hauler country, and I didn't see any sign of them using any sort of four-wheeler or dirt bike the whole time we were in Maggie Valley. Just seems odd. But considering—I don't know. Just seems odd."

"Well, if you come up with anything let me know. Now, Auntie Madge, what's for dinner?"

"Grasshoppers, bats' wings, and ants' eyebrows, nephew dear," Madge replied as she headed into the RV. "But I'll be right back with some chips, salsa, and cold stuff to help wash them down."

Settling into the camp chairs, Troy and Paul chatted about this and that while watching the man across the way go about connecting his water and electric and hooking up his sewer. They waited and waited and waited, and still he didn't come back around and go in the door. Finally, looking at each other, Troy asked, "What would you think about going over and making sure he's okay?"

"To be honest, not a whole hell of a lot. But it would be one way to make contact. Which one of us should go? Are you trying to stay unnoticed? Should we go together? I don't really want to go by myself. Maybe we should just send Madge," Paul said tongue in cheek.

"No, Madge is a bad idea. That guy wouldn't stand a chance. I don't think she's ready to play nicey-nice just yet. Since I'm sure he's seen us sitting here, we should just stroll over together."

When Madge came out of the RV with the munchies and drinks, she saw two empty chairs. Looking around, she was horrified to see Troy and Paul's backsides as the two men walked past the Dodge and knocked on the door of the fifth wheel.

Her heart sank when she heard Troy calling, "Hey neighbor. Everything all right over here?" and saw the driver of the truck come around the back of the fifth wheel and, scowling, walk toward Troy and Paul.

CHAPTER 69

"**H**ey, man, we didn't mean to intrude, but we saw you back in, hook up, and then nothing. We wanted to make sure everything was okay," Troy said as he extended his hand for a shake.

The man eyed his visitors before nodding and saying, "That's neighborly of you, but I was just working on some stuff in the back."

"Hey," Paul said, "this is a toy hauler, right? My wife and I've talked about trading for one. How do you like it?"

"It's good," the man said suspiciously. "Nice of you to come over, but I need to get some stuff done before my family gets in."

"Oh, sorry," Troy said. "Don't let us keep you. If you need any help, just give us a holler. We don't have any plans."

The man nodded again, turned, and walked back behind the fifth wheel.

"Quiet type," Paul observed as he and Troy settled back into their camp chairs.

"You two out of your minds?" Madge hissed between clenched teeth. "That is not a nice person!"

"We're supposed to make contact, remember?" Paul admonished.

"No, I'm supposed to make contact, remember?" came the clipped response.

Troy put his hand to his face to hide the smile he couldn't repress. He knew this side of Madge and loved to watch her in action.

With wide-eyed innocence, Paul pointed to Troy and said, "It was his idea. I suggested sending you, but he nixed it."

Turning her gaze on Troy, Madge smiled sweetly and asked, "Really? And why would you do that?"

"I was afraid you'd hurt him," Troy replied flatly.

Madge and Troy locked eyes. They held the stare as Madge's lips slowly curled into a little smile then into a full-blown grin.

"You're a hoot," she finally said while shaking her head. "So, Mister Hootie Owl, what was that all about?"

They heard Donny arrive as Troy finished filling Madge in on the events across the street. At about the same time, the panel truck arrived and backed in beside the fifth wheel. They watched as Sharon and the driver got out and went into the fifth wheel by the side door.

"Well, looks like all the chicks are home," Madge said. Then looking at Troy she added with a grin, "Sounds like you'll get to tell your tale again in a minute. I'll go get him a cold one. Do you need another?"

"Need? No. Want? Yes. Please and thank you," he said sweetly.

"Well, when you put it that way . . ." Madge answered as she disappeared into the RV.

Returning with two cold Dos Equis, Madge greeted Donny with a hug, saying, "I'm so glad you two delinquents agreed to hang with us for a while."

"We are too," he said with a laugh, "but, if you'll forgive me, I'm starved. What's for supper?"

"Build a fire and we'll grill some dogs. I'll put on some baked beans, and we can fill up on raw veggies till the coals get just right for dog roasting. How's that sound?"

"Like a plan." Then, trying to sound hurt, he asked, "Anybody want to hear about my day?"

The other three looked at each other and burst out laughing.

"Of course we want to hear about your day," Paul said sympathetically. "You have our undivided attention."

Donny sat facing the fire pit with his back to the road. Before beginning, he looked over his shoulder at the site across the street, then said softly, "I rode all over trying to keep an eye on that panel truck. But that fool woman turned down a side road off of Route 32, then parked in a wide spot where the Appalachian Trail crosses the road. The only thing I could do was park my bike and pretend to go for a hike. Unfortunately, I wasn't sure which way to hike, so I hiked south looking for a spot where I could sneak into the woods and watch the back of the truck. No luck there. So I hiked north and found a spot where I could watch the front of the truck without being noticed. But I couldn't see the back. I heard them open the back doors, and it sounded like they set up chairs, then—nothing. Nothing for hours except some brief distant conversation with a couple of groups of hikers. Two hiking south and one hiking north. Next thing I know, I hear some muted voices, they pack up whatever they've taken out, they close up the back doors, get in the truck, and drive away. My tracker shows she's at the grocery, so I hang out close by, and, when she pulls out of there, I take the chance of getting in front of her and coming on in. Looks like it may have been a quiet day. Was for me at least." He drained his beer and held it up, suggesting he'd like another one.

"May have been a quiet day," Madge said as she got up to get his beer, "but seems to have been a thirsty one."

"In case you missed that part of the training, Mata Hari, surveillance is thirsty work," Donny said with conviction as Troy echoed a hearty 'hear, hear.'

When Madge got back, Troy was telling Donny about the visit he and Paul had with the driver of the fifth wheel. "Not the warm, fuzzy type, to say the least. Too bad we don't have ears on over there like we did in Maggie Valley," he said.

"Yeah, why don't we?" Madge asked.

"Because the unit that has that capability is following the biker dude. Hopefully it will be able to catch up with us before the week is out," Troy told her.

"Makes it a little harder to know whether or not to settle in," Madge said. "But, you know, I have a funny feeling about today. For her to just sit in the woods all day makes no sense unless she hoped to find a hiker to grab." Looking at Donny, she continued, "Too bad you couldn't see the back of the truck. Guess that's where the action takes place. If they grabbed someone, you'd think there'd have been more noise, and I wouldn't think they'd just leave them in the truck. Makes me really uncomfortable to think there's even the remotest possibility that there's a kidnapped hiker over there somewhere. Wish I could see inside the back of the toy hauler."

"Why," Donny asked. "What are you thinking?"

"Oh, just how I would do it if I were in the business. Andrea and Walter said the truck had two metal cots bolted to the walls. Seems it would be easy enough to restrain someone there. However, I wouldn't think that would be a good place to hold anyone for any period of time." She paused as if to think through something, then continued. "A toy hauler, on the other hand, would be pretty ideal. We've seen them with their own little bathrooms and mini kitchens, TVs and even queen beds that drop down from the ceiling, all in the toy-hauler section of the RV. If, instead of using the queen bed, you bolted—say, two metal cots—one above the other—to either side of the walls, well, then you'd have yourself a nice, cozy little B&B. Just a thought."

The three men stared at her for a long time before Paul said, "I think I'm married to a sick puppy. Where did that come from?"

"Actually, it's pretty basic. When you're trying to catch a sick puppy, you have to think like a sick puppy," Madge said with great authority. "When this gig is over, I'll see about having my brain decontaminated."

CHAPTER 70

The next morning, Troy got up early to build a fire. That served as a good excuse to keep an eye on the site across the street. He watched as the panel truck drove out so early in the morning that spots of heavy mist still clung to low places in the area. With the GPS tracker still attached to the undercarriage of the truck, he had no concern about being able to locate it. Nevertheless, he shook Donny out and said he, Troy, would do truck surveillance that day. He quickly climbed into his biking gear and was on the road. Donny planned to stick with the Dodge and the fifth wheel, which might give him a lazy day in camp.

That was not to be. Shortly after he and the Franklins finished breakfast, the big Dodge started up and pulled out of the campsite with the fifth wheel in tow. Instead of following on his bike, Donny thought it would be better if they took the Jeep. Because they could only track, without knowing ahead of time where the vehicles were going, Donny took Madge with him and asked Paul to stay behind with the RV. That way, if the fifth wheel went to another campground, Paul got the lucky job of packing up Troy and Donny's tent as well as his own campsite. Otherwise, they might all be back there later that day.

As it turned out, Donny and Madge trailed the fifth wheel to a rest stop off Interstate 26 in North Carolina. There the fifth wheel pulled into the section for large trucks, RVs, and towed vehicles. Madge drove to the other area and parked in the section for cars only. Donny unpacked his camera with the long-range lens and a tripod. Madge reached into a tote bag in the back seat and pulled out a gray wig, a floppy sun hat, an oversized shirt, a pair of oversized sunglasses—the kind that can be worn over regular glasses—and a cane.

238

"What are you doing?" Donny asked with a look of total wonder on his face.

"Going undercover. What does it look like?"

"Like you're going to a costume party, maybe. What, this time I get Grandma Moses instead of Kitty Boyle?"

Madge laughed at the memory of their little undercover escapade in Tucson on their last adventure together.

"Yep, gotta keep the bad guys guessing," she said as she cackled like an old hag.

"That's not half bad. Really changes your look. Especially when you hobble," he added, laughing.

"Gotta look the part," Madge said emphatically. "Also, we need to eat," she said as she picked up a Walmart bag stuffed with peanut butter crackers, apples and bananas, and two packages of cookies. "You can take bird and flower pics while I stretch my legs."

They walked in the direction of the picnic tables, which happened to also be in the direction of the truck and RV parking area. They carefully selected the table with the best line of sight to the fifth wheel and promptly set up business.

Donny pulled out his cell phone and made a call. Obviously, Madge could only hear his side of the conversation, which consisted of telling someone where they were and what they were doing. While he was engaged in listening to the person on the other end, they saw a blue Toyota eight-passenger van drive in and stop next to the Dodge.

Donny said, "Gotta go. Call ya right back," and immediately began snapping pictures.

Both drivers got out, stood between the two vehicles, talked briefly, then entered the fifth wheel.

At that point, Madge picked up her cane and began hobbling in the direction of the suspects. She was about to cross the roadway when the driver of the van came out of the fifth wheel and opened the sliding door on the driver's side of the vehicle. He reached in and fiddled with something, then stood up, looked around, and moved to the steps of the fifth wheel. The door opened and the driver of the fifth wheel appeared in the door, supporting a young woman under her arms. The van driver reached up and took her weight and both men loaded her into the van.

By now, Madge had crossed the roadway and was at the back end of the fifth wheel hobbling toward the two men. "Hey there," she croaked. "Do you need some help with that poor little thing? I been a nurse for sixty years, and she don't look good."

The men looked at each other and the driver of the van said, "Thank you, ma'am, I'm taking her to the hospital."

The other man spoke up then, saying, "She's my sister. We've been camping with the family in the Smokies and June here got real sick. We're lucky that Joe lives so close and was willing to pick her up and get her to medical attention. She has some health issues, but we thought they were under control or we wouldn't have tried to do this trip."

Madge didn't push the issue or try to get a good look at the girl. She just said, "Well, if you're used to her problems I guess you know best. Just looked like you might need some help. I won't hold you up. Best you get that child to a doctor, though. Bless you now." And she hobbled off back across the roadway to the picnic table, where Donny sat holding his cell phone.

"You've got to have them stop that van," Madge said. "Don't look over there, but that's a kidnapped hiker. She looks heavily drugged, and if you can't stop that van she'll disappear forever."

"Did you hear?" he asked into the phone. He then gave a full description of the vehicle, including license number, and said he would text pictures.

Hanging up, he said, "Not to worry. This one's a done deal. We have a chopper up now and many, many units standing by. They will let us know as soon as they've pulled the van over and gotten the girl out. That was good work—as usual. Right now, our job is to stay with the fifth wheel and see where he heads."

CHAPTER 71

Madge and Donny continued to take photos and munch on crackers for as long as they thought made sense. Then they packed up and took turns using the facilities. Madge gave the Jeep's keys to Donny and used her time in the ladies' room to transform from hobbled old woman back to sleek, toned, energetic Madge.

As they sat in the Jeep waiting for the fifth wheel to move, Donny's cell phone buzzed. He answered with a simple "Banks" and began to nod. He listened for several minutes before saying "Thanks" and, when he'd disconnected, turned to Madge.

"Well, lady, she's safe. Some of our people pulled the van over and removed the hiker. The van and the driver—whose name is Stan— have been driven to an undisclosed location. The hiker has also been taken to one of our locations, where she will be nursed back to health and debriefed."

"Ah, that's great. What we'd hoped for, and I'm really relieved about the girl. But, Donny, this is the United States. You can't just make people disappear. Not even really bad people."

"That's true. But we also function on a need-to-know basis, and, truth is, you don't have the need to know. Accept that the girl is safe and that the driver will receive proper due process. Also, don't be surprised if the driver decides to change sides and work with us. If I were handling him, I'd suggest that he contact this papa person with some good excuse for being late with his delivery and assure papa that he would be coming at a later date with an even bigger catch. But that's just how I'd handle it. Besides, we still have to take down Sharon, her driver, the driver of the fifth wheel, and, if possible, the biker dude who hangs with them. So let's focus. Okay?"

"Okay," came the reluctant reply. "Look," she said, pointing to the fifth wheel. "He's pulling out. Should I fall in now or just wait and let the GPS do the tracking?"

"You can hang back for a few minutes. No point in taking any chance of spooking him. Although this is actually a good choice for a surveillance vehicle. There are a lot of red Jeep Cherokees on the road."

They sat for three minutes before pulling into the northbound lane of Interstate 26. Once they reached cruising speed, Madge asked, "Since we seem to be going away from Cosby, don't you think we should tell Paul to get packed up? It'll take him some time, considering he has both sites to deal with."

Donny thought for a minute, then punched Paul's number. After giving him a brief update, Donny suggested Paul might want to begin the packing-up process.

"Already done, my friend," came the happy answer. "I heard from Troy, who heard from somebody, that the powers that be feel she's headed for somewhere in the Erwin area. Seems teams of two or three have already been placed in every campground within a ten-mile radius of Erwin. Wherever she lands, we'll have significant backup. So I'm ready to head out at a moment's notice. And I hope it comes in time for me to get to wherever I'm going before dark. Hate parking this thing in the dark."

"Good grief, you sound like Madge," Donny said with a laugh. "Let's take a leap of faith. Let's say we'll be in the Erwin area, so you can just head that way. Shouldn't be too bad a drive. It's interstate almost all the way, and by the time you get close Sharon should have landed. Besides, Madge and I are on the fifth wheel and we'll be able to let you know. So, good buddy, head on out."

"Copy that," came the reply and both men disconnected.

Sure enough, shortly after crossing from North Carolina into Tennessee, the fifth wheel left the interstate. It traveled down a county road for several miles before turning left onto an unmarked, local road. Madge let the Dodge get completely out of sight before she, too, turned onto the unmarked road. There was a small sign at the corner telling people an RV park was three miles down the road. Madge and Donny shrugged and Madge said, "Paul's not going to like this road. The road's narrow, and the trees reach and try to grab RVs. That makes him grumpy. Just so you know. Anybody have a backup plan if this place doesn't have room for a big RV?"

Donny replied, "Like we said, we'll be playing a good bit of this by ear."

"In other words, no," Madge offered.

"Yep, but—"

"I know. I know. That's where I shine," Madge replied sulkily. Then more brightly, "Hold on. There it is."

Ahead on the right, a huge sign spanned the wide driveway into the Traveler's Rest RV Resort. Madge turned in slowly and followed the well-paved, curving road through a charming oak forest. Almost a mile later, the forest gave way to a series of grassy, rolling meadows. Dotted here and there were lovely small log cabins. The road continued around a curve and down a small hill until, on the right, it widened into an area with signs indicating campers should park there to register.

"Well, who would have thought?" Madge said as she parked the Jeep. "Let's go see if we can register. I'll go see while you give Paul directions. I'll let you take the heat for this one," she added with an evil little grin.

When she came back, she said, "That was easy. Seems this place has been newly renovated by new owners, who haven't gotten their new signs out. Umm—that's a lot of new. Anyway, they're not very crowded because they did a lot of expansion and most of the folks here are regulars who've been coming here for hundreds of years. They hope word of mouth will fill the place by fall or certainly by this time next year. I asked about the fifth wheel. They registered for three nights. I also asked not to be too close to them because we'd camped close to them before and we found them to be loud. She said she'd put us in a different loop so that wouldn't be a problem. I thought it would be best if we could keep that low profile we've talked about. By the way, did you get hold of Paul?"

"Uh-huh," Donny grunted. "And you're right. First thing he asked about was the width of the road and the trees. Sometimes you're scary."

Laughing, Madge said, "No, just married. You planning on registering or waiting for Troy to do that? Actually, why don't you go in and see if you can get a site on Loop C. Maybe you could even get one close to the fifth wheel. Easier to hang out with friends that way. Right?"

"I knew we kept you around as more than just the comic relief," Donny said with a grin. "Will do. Now, what site are you in? Need to let Paul know."

"Site A-7," Madge said. "But we may want to tell him to stop and get a map. I have a feeling he'll do better if he has one. This seems to be set up as a series of one-way loops in something of a cloverleaf pattern. We are in Loop A, and the fifth wheel is in Loop C, so they shouldn't see us at all."

After Donny registered, they drove slowly toward the camping area. Signs reading Speed Limit 13-1/2 mph were posted every hundred yards. They passed out of the meadow and into the trees. Here the roads had been widened and graded to accommodate the largest of RVs.

They saw the sign directing Loop A residents to turn left at the next corner. Site A-7 was almost at the curve where the one-way road looped back toward the main road. Madge pulled the Jeep off to the side and parked. She and Donny got out and walked into the campsite, which, by campground standards, was huge. The pad for the RV was almost a hundred feet long and backed up to a thick stand of laurel.

"This is terrific," Madge said. "Too bad we have to work. This would be a great place to just chill."

"Well, how about not chilling," Donny said. "If you park the Jeep, we have time to walk over to Loop C and check out my campsite. Along with the location of my neighbors."

"Not a prob," Madge said agreeably as she set about pulling the Jeep onto the parking pad. Once parked, she got two bottles of water out of the back and announced with a wicked little grin, "I have a better idea. Let's run!"

CHAPTER 72

By dusk that evening, all the players were assembled in their assorted campsites. Madge and Paul's RV backed up to Loop C, and a skinny, little man-made trail from Site A-6 allowed access to Site C-14. Both sites were empty. Donny and Troy snagged Site C-6 next to the fifth wheel in Site C-5. Unbeknownst to Madge and Paul, the two women in Site C-1, as well as the three men in Site B-4, were all agents from various cooperating agencies. All were in tents. Each of the women arrived in her own large, black SUV. Two of the men also arrived in large, black SUVs, while the other one came in on a motorcycle. The motorcycle belonged to Donny. Because he left his in Cosby, Charles had arranged for it to be delivered.

Meals had the potential to become something of an issue until Madge announced she would feed Donny and Troy in shifts. Paul also fixed up a Styrofoam ice chest for the boys and included a decent supply of necessary items. Under cover of darkness, Madge and Paul cut through to Loop C and joined the boys around a low campfire.

When Madge noticed Donny's motorcycle sitting beside Troy's, she furrowed her brow, shook her head several times, and asked Donny, "Did I miss a day or something? I would have sworn you came in with me in the Jeep but—that is your bike. Right?"

"Yeah, so?" Donny replied with wide-eyed innocence.

"Okay. Let's go over this," she said firmly. "Troy rode his bike in here. Paul drove our RV in here, and you and I drove in here in the Jeep. There's no question but that that is your bike. So, someone want to tell me how it got teleported over here? I know there's a lot of government stuff that's top, top, top secret. But this is ridiculous!"

Because Paul knew the story, he joined the boys in looking back and forth at each other and shrugging their shoulders.

Madge hooked her fingers together, rested her chin on her clenched fist, and said, "So, it's going to be that way, is it? Well, boys, guess someone forgot to tell you that there are three people you piss off at your peril. One is the boss's secretary. One is the head custodian. The other is the lunch lady. Feel free to think of me as a combination of all three." She paused before continuing.

"Now that you've had some time to think about it, has anyone reconsidered answering the question?"

"Let me make a quick call," Troy said as he stepped into the woods and mumbled into his phone.

Within a couple of minutes, a beautiful Honda Goldwing cruised into Loop C and drove directly into Site C-6. Two men got off the bike and were introduced as Ernie and Sam.

"You boys know anything about that green Harley over there?" Troy asked.

"Only that it's one fine ride," Sam said. "Might just have to get me one now that I know how good it really is."

"Okay, okay, okay. I get it," Madge said. "Need to know and all that rot."

Everyone laughed and Donny suggested Sam and Ernie join them around the fire. Paul distributed cold beverages all around and asked if he and Madge should head home so the four of them could talk.

"Of course not," Sam said. "You and Madge are as much a part of this operation as any of the rest of us. I have to confess, this little charade was deliberately conceived and well-thought-out. You can thank Charles when you see him," he added with a chuckle.

"Seems like you children should have more important tasks to think about than how to play practical jokes on innocent, unsuspecting females," Madge snipped, with her lips pursed and her nose in the air.

Sam and Ernie both raised their eyebrows and said, "Now we understand what Charles meant. Please accept our apologies for allowing ourselves to get sucked into such an underhanded ploy."

Madge grinned and said, "Apology accepted. Just don't let it happen again."

"Now that's out of the way, let's get down to business," Donny said. "What have we learned from the driver of the Toyota?"

Ernie spoke up. "The people in the fifth wheel and the motorcycle dude are all related. The woman, Sharon, and her son Chad handle the pickups, as he put it. Sharon is the sister of the other two men, who happen to be twins. The fifth wheel driver is Rolph, and the biker is Karl. They hold the women in the fifth wheel and, depending on the situation, transfer them to the van either at a campground, overlook, wide spot in the road, or, as they did this time, at a rest stop, where they are paid by the van driver—Stan. Stan then delivers the women to a man known only as Papa, and that delivery takes place at different locations all up and down the East Coast. Stan doesn't know what the money is used for or what happens to the women after they are delivered to Papa."

Madge listened carefully to what Ernie was saying, then asked rather sarcastically, "Was Stan just begging to share this with whomever happened to be around?"

Sam responded flatly by saying, "He understood it was in his best interest to be completely forthcoming. Now it's up to us to see that Papa goes out of business."

Looking uncomfortable, Madge asked, "I don't really want to know, do I?"

"Probably not," Ernie said. "Charles led us to believe you'd been trained and had it together. But you need to decide right now if this is getting too sticky for you."

All through this exchange, Troy, Donny, and Paul remained silent.

Madge looked hard at both Ernie and Sam and said very quietly, "The only sticky part for me is the possibility that one of you will try to stop me from doing serious damage to one or more of Papa's little foursome."

Troy and Donny just smiled as they exchanged long, hard looks with Sam and Ernie.

CHAPTER 73

Early the next morning, the two women in site C-1 jogged around Loop C wearing spandex exercise shorts and matching spandex sports bras. They stopped briefly across from site C-5 to stretch, do a couple of jumping jacks, and then broke into a comfortable run. Twenty minutes later they returned to Loop C, jogged once around the loop, then began walking the loop with hands raised over their heads in cool-down mode.

Rolph had been outside the first time they went past, and by the time they got back both he and Karl were sitting at the picnic table drinking coffee. By their third time around the loop, Sharon had joined her brothers at the picnic table. As the women strolled by at a slow pace, Sharon called to them.

"You gals are impressive!" she said. "I wish I hadn't stopped doing that. Just think what great shape I'd be in now if I'd kept it up."

The women stopped, smiled, then laughed softly. "It's not always easy or convenient, but with our jobs we really don't have a choice."

"If you have time, come join us," Sharon said. "If you drink coffee, I can offer you a fresh pot."

The women looked at each other for a moment, shrugged their shoulders, then the taller of the two said, "Sure. For the next two weeks, all we have is time."

"Great," Sharon said. "How do you take your coffee?"

"Black for both of us," the tall one said. "By the way, I'm Joyce, and this is my friend Emily."

"It's nice to meet you. I'm Sharon, and these are my baby twin brothers, Rolph and Karl," she said with a chuckle. "Visit with the children, and I'll be right back with your coffee."

Emily laughed and said as she smiled coyly at the two men across the table from her, "She likes to joke around, doesn't she?"

Rolph said, "Yeah, she's a real card. Actually, she's pretty much a pain in the ass. She's fifteen years older than we are. In truth, she pretty much raised us, so we let her think she can still push us around like she did when we were kids." He said that with a surprisingly disarming smile. Then he asked, "So why two weeks of time and the need to run?"

"Well," Joyce said, "we're on summer break from law school classes, which we are paying for by working as club dancers. Not strippers—exactly. But close. I know. That's not proper work for proper girls, but it pays the bills, and we really want to be lawyers."

Emily chimed in with, "We came up here to just hike and chill for two weeks, but we can't afford to let ourselves get out of condition. Cardio and flexibility are the two biggies in dancing."

Sharon returned with the coffee, sat down, and asked, "So why here of all places?"

"Several reasons," Joyce said. "One, I used to come here with my family when I was a kid. It's really changed since the new owners took over, but I like the changes. Secondly, the access to the Appalachian Trail is great. We don't want to get carried away, but we'd like to do a couple of overnights in each direction, with rest time here in between."

"Now that you know all about us, what's your story?" Emily asked.

"We're here pretty much for the same reason," Sharon answered. "Except that we haven't been here as kids. We actually run a rescue service for hikers and try to locate close to a trailhead."

"A rescue service! How cool is that?" Joyce said. "Are there really that many hikers that need rescuing?"

"Depends," Karl said. "Just yesterday we picked up a young woman who'd become sick while hiking with her family. We were able to take her to a rest stop, where a family friend picked her up and took her to get medical help. A couple of days before that, we were down in Maggie Valley, North Carolina, and got a call to assist a couple. The woman came down with something nasty and wanted to get to a nearby hospital where her sister worked as a nurse. So, it just depends. We get sprained ankles and a lot of blistered feet. Sharon, here, is a certified EMT and frequently can just give first aid. We have bed space in the fifth wheel, and sometimes we'll let folks rest there for a couple of days, then send them back on their way."

"It always feels good to give people a hand when they're having problems," Rolph said with that disarming smile of his.

"That's great. I've never heard of your service, so I think you should advertise more. Have you been doing this long?" Emily asked.

"This is our tenth year," Sharon answered with a satisfied look. "Ten great years."

Later that day, Sharon walked past the girls' site and noticed them sitting in lounge chairs reading.

"Hi," she called. "I'm glad I caught you. We were wondering if you would like to come over after supper and visit around the fire."

Joyce and Emily looked at each other and nodded.

"Sure," Emily said, "but we won't stay long. We want to get an early start in the morning. We plan to do our first overnight on the trail tomorrow. So, if you don't mind an early evening, that would be fine."

"No, no," Sharon said. "Whatever works for you. We just usually build a low fire and sit out and listen to the night sounds. If you feel like joining us—for whatever time you can—we'll be pleased for your company."

"That's nice of you," Joyce said. "Keeping it open-ended is always good. If we don't crash early we may come over for a bit. Thanks."

CHAPTER 74

The girls continued to read for a while, then Joyce stretched and said, "I feel the need for a walk. Care to join me?"

"Sure. A walk sounds great," Emily answered as she stretched and rose from her lounge chair.

They put their books inside the tent, picked up their water bottles, and casually walked down the one-way loop toward the main road into the campground. From there they turned right and walked down to Loop B. Turning left, they walked the Loop B circle counter-clockwise until they reached Site B-4. There they were hailed by three men holding up beer bottles and encouraging the women to join them.

Smiling and shrugging, Joyce and Emily walked in and sat at the picnic table. At that point, one of the men walked to one of the SUVs, lifted the hood and began messing around with the engine. He only worked from the passenger side, though, since that gave him a full view of the entrance to Loop B.

"Well, we're in," Emily said. "Invited over tonight to sit by the fire. Chances are we'll be spending the night. How long do you think this will take? By the way, we're Emily and Joyce."

"Good to meet you," Sam said. "We're Sam and Ernie, and that's Watson over by the SUV. To answer your question: with two of you, we think they'll want to make the exchange tomorrow," Ernie said. "At least that's what we're hoping for. We've got your back, and the plan is solid, but no one will blame you if you change your minds."

"We're not changing our minds," Emily said emphatically. "This effort won't put much of a dent in human trafficking, overall, but if we can save just one person from such a heinous fate it will be worth it. And if we can totally shut down this operation we'll consider it a huge success."

251

"Okay. But do you have any concerns that we can help with?" Sam asked.

"Just one," Joyce said. "I'm not interested in being sexually assaulted. Those twins look as though they'd think nothing of manhandling a woman. If I'm drugged I won't be able to protect myself. That's my only concern."

Ernie said, "According to Stan the van driver, Papa wants the merchandise in perfect condition, and all of the men involved have been told hands off. There will be five of us doing round-the-clock surveillance on the site over there. The three of us here, and Donny and Troy over on Loop A. If we hear so much as a hint of distress out of either of you, all five of us will be on that place like white on rice. Unfortunately, you're right about being drugged, though."

"How's this going to shake out?" Emily asked.

"Without too much encouragement, Stan agreed to cooperate. He will take the call from Sharon and insist on making the pickup here at the campground. We've installed a tracking device on the van as well as a mic. Our people will hear everything that is said. We'll know ahead of time where Stan is to meet with Papa to make the transfer, and, not only will we be following behind, we will have people at the meet location as well."

Emily and Joyce looked at each other, then at Sam and Ernie. "Okay," Emily said. "We're good. And we'd probably best get back now. It's a little weird, but nice, having so many different agencies working together. We don't even know who you're with, but, if we don't see you again, thanks in advance for watching our backs. Stay safe."

CHAPTER 75

The next morning a blue Toyota van pulled up in front of the Dodge and fifth wheel toy hauler in Site C-5. Stan, the driver, got out and knocked on the door of the RV. Sharon came out, talked briefly with the driver, then pulled her panel truck into the road. Stan backed the van into the spot the panel truck vacated, and Sharon went back inside the RV. Stan walked to the side of the van and opened the sliding door behind the driver's seat. Then he waited.

Shortly, Rolph came out from behind the toy hauler supporting a woman who could barely walk. He and the driver helped her into the van. The driver fiddled with something in the van, then stepped back as Karl came out with another woman. Once she was placed securely in the van, the driver withdrew an envelope from his back pocket and handed it to Sharon, who had come back outside. She thumbed through the contents, smiled in satisfaction, and said, "Tell Papa I'll get him more."

The driver closed the van door, started the engine, and drove off. As he exited the access road to Loop C, two large black SUVs drove slowly out behind him.

At the same time, Donny climbed down from a tree directly behind the fifth wheel, his camera stowed carefully in his backpack. He picked his way through the woods to Madge and Paul's site on Loop A, where he and Troy had parked their motorcycles. He had recorded everything. The evening around the fire. The drinks. The women collapsing and being carried into the toy hauler section of the fifth wheel. The night passing without incident, and the exchange of the women from the fifth wheel to the van in the morning.

Once the van left the site, Rolph rolled a motorcycle out of the back of the toy hauler and parked it beside Karl's bike.

Karl and Sharon came out of the RV and Karl said, "That was very profitable. Rolph and I are going to have some fun going on a recruitment campaign. We'll see you this evening."

"Don't expect to eat here," Sharon told them. "Chad and I plan to troll for more packages. Those two were a gift. I don't expect to have it that easy again, and once they're reported missing collecting will get extra hard. I figure we have two weeks at best before the word gets out. So, we're fishing for as large a catch as possible and may have to go farther away than we like. Could be quite late before we get back."

"Good luck," Rolph said as he donned his helmet, started his bike, and joined his twin, who was already out of sight.

Sharon thought nothing of the two motorcycles she heard leaving the campground from Loop A.

"Chad," she called. "How soon will you be ready?"

"I want to finish my show."

Sharon gritted her teeth and said as she reentered the RV, "Okay, honey, but Mommy wants to get on the road as soon as possible. We need to go fishing again. Remember, yesterday's catch has already gone away."

Over on Loop A, Madge and Paul sat on the picnic table in Site A-6 trying to devise a plan to affect Troy's parting shot as he and Donny rode after Karl and Rolph. "Even though we have a tracker on that panel truck, don't let it go anywhere."

"Maybe I should see if I can borrow a cup of sugar," Madge suggested sarcastically.

"Somehow I don't think that'll do it," Paul replied. "Short of out-and-out vehicle sabotage, I really don't see a viable plan."

"What kind of threat do you think Chad will be?" Madge asked.

"Probably depends on Mom. I think he's basically a gentle giant. I'm not sure he has any kind of a grasp of right and wrong beyond what Momma says to do. He's a momma's boy through and through, but I'll wager if Momma's not around to give him directions, he'll have trouble functioning. Chances are he'll respond to whatever authority figure is around at the time."

"Yeah, I almost feel sorry for him," Madge said. "You know, being so oblivious while living in a family full of sicko sociopaths or whatever. I'm still having trouble dealing with the reality of all of this."

"Well, see if you can put it together while we amble over to Loop C. Even though I don't know what we can do once we're there, we certainly can't control the situation from here," Paul said.

"Right. But I can't see going over there empty-handed," Madge said with that tone she used when she was ready for action. "You head through the path, and I'll be right behind you."

Looking askance at his wife, Paul climbed down off the picnic table and slowly, very slowly began to traverse the little man-made path between the two loops. He stood at the Loop-C end of the path waiting, and Madge arrived carrying a medium-sized tote bag.

"What's in the bag," he asked.

"This and that," she said.

"Oh, good. Secret agents should never leave home without their bag of this and that," he said sarcastically.

"Okay, wise guy. You'll thank me before the day is over."

CHAPTER 76

As they walked across the circle toward Site C-5, Sharon and Chad came out of the RV. Chad stood looking mystified. The panel truck wasn't where he'd left it.

He sounded bewildered when he asked, "Momma, where's the truck?"

"In the road on the other side of the Dodge. Remember, Momma had to move it so Stan could pick up the package."

Madge and Paul increased their pace and got to the panel truck just before Chad.

"Hi," Madge said in her cheeriest voice. "You're just the folks we hoped to see."

"I'm sorry, but we don't really have time to visit right now. Maybe later this evening we could chat by the fire," Sharon said, more businesslike than friendly.

"Oh, do you have a rescue?" Madge asked.

"Rescue?" Sharon asked.

"You know. Aren't you the Appalachian Trail Rescue Service or something like that?" Madge asked.

"Yes, why?" Sharon asked.

"Well, that's what we wanted to talk to you about. We looked you up on the Internet and your web page isn't too informative. We think the service is a wonderful idea and wanted to talk to you about all kinds of things. Like how to give it more coverage and how to put more information about it on the web and about putting signs on the truck here."

"Thank you for your interest, but now isn't a good time for us. Later this evening perhaps," Sharon said again as she moved toward the passenger door.

Madge placed her back against the passenger door and reached into her tote bag. She came out with a can of bear spray in her hand. She held it up and said, "I'm concerned that since you go into the mountains, you could meet up with a black bear. This is great stuff, and I wanted to suggest that you carry some at all times—if you don't already."

Growing visibly angry, Sharon said, "You need to move away from my truck."

Madge passed the bear spray off to Paul and, reaching into her bag again, brought out a bundle of zip ties and a roll of duct tape, which she also handed to Paul. As she did this, Paul moved away from her and inserted himself between Sharon and Chad.

"What's going on here?" Sharon demanded. "Move! Get away from my truck, before I call the police."

"The police! Really? You're sure you want to talk to the cops? You want to tell them all about your little kidnapping scheme? About your involvement in human trafficking? About your involvement in planning and financing terrorist activities?"

Sharon straightened and changed expressions. She looked at Paul and said, "Sir, your wife is a troubled woman. I certainly hope she is receiving medical attention. Is it possible that she neglected to take her medication today? If you need help dealing with her issues, I am a certified EMT and can offer you some assistance. But if you feel you can handle her on your own, we really do need to be on our way."

"Wow, you're good," Paul said. "Right, Madge?"

Sharon's expression changed again as she realized what was happening, and she shouted, "Chad, get him!"

As Chad charged Paul, Sharon lunged at Madge. Madge sidestepped the lunge, and Chad got a face full of bear spray for his trouble. He ended up on the ground with his wrists and ankles zip tied.

The sound of motorcycles caused Sharon to scream, "My brothers are coming, and you two are dead people!"

Sharon lunged at Madge again just as Troy and Donny rode into the campsite. Again, Madge sidestepped the lunge but this time asked with a smile, "You want to play?"

"Hey," Donny called, "need any help over there?"

"Nope. This one's all mine."

Chad was on the ground pitching a fit, so Paul tore off a piece of duct tape and slapped it over Chad's mouth. Then the three other men made themselves comfortable.

Madge smiled at Sharon and said, "What's the matter? Not used to dealing with wide-awake women? Come on, show me what you got."

Sharon snarled, and this time when she lunged, Madge stepped to the left, grabbed Sharon's right arm, flipped her onto her stomach, and did a quick knee drop to her back as she twisted Sharon's right arm up past her shoulder blade. Madge grabbed a handful of Sharon's hair and pulled her head back. "How's it feel?" Madge hissed between clenched teeth. "Too bad you get to go to prison instead of being sold to some slave trader, like the trash that you are."

On the sidelines, Paul looked at Donny and Troy and said, "One of you needs to break this up before it gets out of hand."

When they both looked at him, he said, "Don't look at me. I don't get paid enough to get in there."

CHAPTER 77

Thirty-six hours later, nine people sat around a crackling campfire at the Traveler's Rest RV Resort. Troy volunteered for fire detail; Donny accepted the position of beverage manager; Madge and Paul agreed to provide ice as well as chips and dip; Ernie, Sam, and Watson came in with marshmallows; and Joyce and Emily attended as the guests of honor.

After much backslapping and friendly banter, the group eventually settled into a comfortable silence. They sat peacefully around the low-burning fire that occasionally spit out a small shower of sparks as a gas bubble in the wood burned off. A nearby owl hooted out a neighborly hello, which was answered by another 'who, who, hoot' from further away. A few leftover, mid-summer fireflies blinked to each other from the forest depths. Finally, Madge opened the discussion that everyone wanted to have but no one wanted to start.

"It's been quite a summer, hasn't it?" she said softly. "I guess, for you guys, it's just another day at the office, but for Paul and me, this has been, well, a lot to work through. We love being a part of this but are glad our time with it is limited. I don't know that we're cut out for doing this day in and day out. Emily and Joyce—especially what you did. Do you mind if I ask—do you spend a lot of time undercover?"

Smiling, Joyce answered, "A lot? Well, no. There are some agents who make a career of undercover work. We've done a little. Certainly, we're trained. But this was a case of being available at the right time. And the cause is dear to our hearts. Being part of taking out such a long-running and successful slave trade makes any sacrifices we had to make worthwhile. However, none were actually required. We had this incredible team backing us up, and the drugs Sharon spiked our drinks with didn't create any serious problems. I have to admit, though, I was coming out of the haze before the van pulled over, and I was beginning to wonder how long it would be before we got to the drop-off point."

Emily laughed and said, "You weren't the only one. I was trying to look like I was still under the influence. I'd been dumped in a position that wasn't a problem as long as I was out. But once I came to, OMG, I really wanted to move!"

"What we're trying to say is, thank you, to everyone," Joyce said.

"No thanks necessary, ma'am," Ernie drawled. "Glad to oblige."

Paul finally asked, "Didn't Stan roll over and agree to turn state's evidence?"

"Yep, but we'd been told to continue to play the game as though we didn't know that," Emily explained. "That way, when we got to where the exchange was to take place, it would be easier for Stan to play his part. He actually got 'arrested' at the same time as Papa."

"Do we know how or why this all started?" Paul asked.

"All we know," Sam offered, "is that about ten years ago, Sharon and Chad made their first strike. They kidnapped a female hiker up in Shenandoah National Park, and Chad killed her male companion. Sharon sold her to a wealthy local man who wanted to give her as a birthday present to his son, who was turning twenty-one. That made Papa aware of the money he could make in human trafficking. He's a sick puppy anyway. He's white supremacist all the way and anti damn near everything else. Somehow, he made contact with people outside the US and began taking orders for young, attractive, athletic women. Those contacts put the disruption idea in his head and offered some training classes in how to achieve the result."

"Yuck!" Madge said. "I need a shower."

Troy smiled. "Wouldn't it be nice if we could just shower off all the ugliness we deal with? At least we've chopped the head off this particular snake."

Madge looked over at Donny and asked, "You gonna stick to the walked-into-a-door story for how you got that black eye?"

Looking chagrined, Donny said, "Nah, it was compliments of Karl. My error. Need to sharpen my ducking skills."

"What happens now to those leaders that Karl organized? Aren't they still planning their fall mischief?" Madge asked.

"More than likely," Sam said. "Obviously we're hoping Karl will share names, places, and dates. It's not likely. But we can hope. We have discovered his code for calling meetings and the way he's used personals and ads in local papers. Lots of folks out there, Madge. Some even like you and Paul. Don't forget, we're continuing to press the message to John Q. Citizen: if you see something, say something. That's really our best defense."

"One more question, please," Madge said. "How does Hottie fit into all of this?"

"Oh, her," replied Sam. "She's a cousin of Karl, Rolph, and Sharon and has something of a groupie mentality. She's been doing short-term rentals in areas where Karl could meet with leaders. According to her, it was just for fun. Maybe she'll have as much fun in whatever federal women's prison she ends up in."

Glasses, bottles, and Solo cups raised in a salute to that.

After being quiet for a bit, Madge looked at Sam and said, "Wait. Go back to what you said about Sharon and Chad ten years ago."

"Oh, you mean about their first kidnapping where Chad killed a guy? Actually, getting that information made it possible for Park Service law enforcement to close a cold case."

Madge and Paul locked eyes and smiled. "That's great," Paul said as he held his wife's gaze. "I'm sure we'll hear all about it when we go back."

EPILOG

A week later, Madge and Paul returned to Shenandoah National Park and checked in at the little log cabin that served as the registration station for Big Meadows campground.

"Boy, are we glad to see you two!" Brian said as he reissued their keys and radio. "I know you didn't plan on being back here, but you know what this place is like between now and the end of October. You really are needed."

Chuckling, Paul said, "It's nice to be needed, but, more importantly, it's nice to feel useful. Hosting here always makes us feel like we are making a difference. It's our pleasure," he added with a flourish.

"Besides," Madge chimed in, "how could we say no to spending time with one of our favorite people?"

"Okay, okay," Brian said. "Enough of the saccharin! Any more and your teeth will rot! Go get changed. Your shift began twenty minutes ago," he added with a grin.

"Ah, what do you mean?" Madge asked. "I thought we weren't on duty till tomorrow."

"Technically, that's true. But we have some issues out there," he said as he indicated the campground, "that need to be resolved, and I don't feel I can leave this place unattended. Since the Commers are not only off today—but are running errands in town—the quicker you can get back here and offer coverage, the quicker I can take care of problems out there."

"Well, all right then," Paul said. "Come on, pretty lady, let's suit up!"

Once in uniform, Madge and Paul fell right back into their hosting role. They hadn't been gone that long, and the routine was so familiar they felt like they hadn't been gone at all, especially when Miranda and Pablo stopped by the office to say hello.

"Hey, it's great that you two are back," Pablo said. "It's been a pretty quiet time. No crazy parties. No bear attacks and no more missing hikers. Hey, speaking of which, did you hear? You know that skull the girls found and told you about, well that was a cold case and it's been solved!"

"Really?" Madge said. "That's cool. How'd that happen?"

"That's the interesting part of the story. Seems it's all very hush-hush."

"Really? Wow! Amazing. And after all those years," Madge said. "Goes to show you just never know."

Whatever issues Brian needed to take care of in the campground occupied a couple of hours. By the time he got back, the check-in sheet had been reduced by half, the board had been tidied, and the filing had been done. They had taken care of giving directions, answering questions about various flowers in bloom, explaining about the Junior Ranger Program and encouraging participation in as many other ranger programs as time permitted. They assured a couple that the nightly entertainment at the lodge was family friendly and reminded them to take a flashlight if they decided to walk.

"Thank you again," Brian said as he came back in. "Sorry that took so long, but I appreciate the coverage. As far as I'm concerned, you guys are done for the day. Any plans?"

"I'm going to the lodge to check e-mail," Paul answered. "Somehow I've managed to avoid doing that for too long and don't feel I can put if off any longer."

"I know what you mean," Brian said. "Doesn't take long for it to get out of hand. Have fun."

As they walked back to the RV, Madge asked, "Do you want me to go with you, or can you handle the e-mail thing by yourself?"

"I think I'll manage," he replied. "We're not really very nested, and I figured you'd want to finish that before too much more time went by."

"You know me pretty well," Madge said as she slipped her arm around her husband's waist and gave him a squeeze. "I'll have our house in perfect order by the time you get back."

When Paul returned, he found Madge comfortably swinging in her hammock strung between the two largest oak trees on their site. She had the inside of the RV in perfect order, the patio swept, a summer centerpiece in the middle of the cloth-covered picnic table, and the chairs and side tables arranged on the rug under the awning.

"Goodness, looks like you deserve that break you're taking," Paul teased as he put the computer on the picnic table and walked over to give the hammock a push.

"Um, that's nice," Madge cooed as she swung gently back and forth. "You're hired."

Paul smiled down at his wife while he continued gently pushing the hammock back and forth. "You certainly look comfortable," he said with a sigh. "I know this place is special to you, but I need to ask you a question." Pausing for effect, he looked up into the leaves and, while trying to control the desire to laugh, he said, "We got an e-mail from Kaye-Lynn. How'd you like to spend next summer back in Alaska?"

Printed in the USA
CPSIA information can be obtained
at www.ICGtesting.com
BVHW031713300823
668989BV00002B/6